DON'T TELL MEG

DON'T TELL MEG TRILOGY BOOK 1

PAUL J. TEAGUE

Don't Tell Meg Trilogy

Book 1 - Don't Tell Meg

Book 2 - The Murder Place

Book 3 - The Forgotten Children

Standalone Thrillers

Dead of Night

Burden of Guilt

One Fatal Error

Who To Trust

Writing sci-fi as Paul Teague

Sci-Fi Starter Book - Phase 6

The Secret Bunker Trilogy

Book 1 - Darkness Falls

Books 2 - The Four Quadrants

Books 3 - Regeneration

The Grid Trilogy

Book 1 - Fall of Justice

Book 2 - Quest for Vengeance

Book 3 - Catharsis

CHAPTER ONE

I waited until my fortieth birthday before I betrayed my wife. If I hadn't spent that night with Ellie, who knows how things might have turned out. As it was, five people lost their lives before the truth was finally forced out of us all.

I'd been sent on a weekend training course with work. Perfect timing. I was celebrating my special birthday on the Saturday. I tried my luck at wriggling out of it, but my boss Diane wouldn't budge. She'd been promoted to managing editor less than a year ago, and she had a new boss of her own to impress. Perhaps I should have tried for the senior position when it came up, but I had other things on my mind. I was more interested in Meg.

Meg and I had been married for seven years. We met when I was thirty-one and Meg twenty-nine. She was sexy, gorgeous, great fun and an addiction for me. However long we spent together, I always wanted more. It was only a matter of time until we got married. We lasted two years, then got hitched. It was the natural conclusion to the most intense, passionate and exciting time of my life. We were crazy in love. We didn't bother living together for years and years, there was no dithering about commitment, we both dived straight in, not even bothering to look for rocks.

But the hazards are always there, in any marriage. I gleaned that little nugget from Martin, our marriage counsellor.

The marriage was good for the first six years. It was better than good, it was great. Work was going well, Meg and I were happy, life was sweet. Then Meg decided she wanted a baby. It's not that I didn't want kids. I was neither here nor there with it. If we'd had a happy accident, I'd have been fine with that. But even though we'd taken risks in the past, Meg had never got pregnant. We'd never had any near misses or scares. That should have alerted both of us that there was trouble ahead. Meg started to actively seek that happy accident, but it didn't come. We moved from wonderful unrestrained hot sex to trying to make a baby. Some big ugly black boulders had just appeared right in front of us.

It was no surprise to me when Meg didn't get pregnant, I'd heard the story a hundred times before. As a radio journalist I talked to people who had encountered every human trial that you could imagine. Ordinary people with exceptional tales to tell, that's how we like it on the radio. I'd listened to the accounts of IVF treatments and fertility tests which seemed to go on for years. I knew about the poking, the prodding, the plastic containers and the indignity of it all. Sometimes it had a happy ending, many times it didn't.

I'd wound up in the middle of one of my own radio reports. Pete Bailey, age 40, firing blanks. Or perhaps it was Meg who had the problem. It didn't matter. It had driven a huge wedge through our relationship.

She seemed completely fixated on getting pregnant. I wasn't so bothered. I can't say it mattered much to me if I was sending out lazy ones. All the important bits were working just fine.

I'd had mixed reactions when I told people this. Some thought I was heartless and callous, that I'd get to old age and regret not having a family, but friends with children assured me that if they had their time again they'd think very hard about having kids. We were a hot couple, and they warned me that it would all be over once the babies came along.

It was Meg I worried about. I loved her, I could see what she was going through, I didn't want to hurt her.

Meg and I had discussed doing something special for my birthday, but we'd had to put it on hold. In truth, I wasn't too disappointed about being away that weekend. People who work in broadcasting are great fun. They're on TV and radio for a living, they're used to being larger than life. Get a few beers in them, and it doesn't take too long before you're in the middle of a party.

I knew that if Meg and I went out, however much we tried, eventually it would come back to the IVF. And the counselling. And that little shit Martin.

I wasn't plotting anything then. I didn't know how it was all going to turn out. If I had, I'd have settled for a quiet pizza at Alfonso's in town. I'd have been grateful for a bag of chips and a dodgy burger from a mobile van if I could have steered clear of everything that happened afterwards.

I did a good job of looking disappointed when I broke the news to Meg. She was lovely actually, it made me feel like a right piece of shit. 'We'll do something special when you get back,' she said. 'Maybe we can have a night in, get a takeaway ... watch a film in bed?'

I hesitated. Was Meg reaching out here? Did she sense how I was feeling? It had always been a bit of a joke before the IVF thing had started and made life such hard work. We'd never made it to the end of a film while we were watching in bed. She was doing exactly what I'd been craving for months. She was being sexy, planning a rendezvous between lovers, a good old-fashioned romantic evening and a night of hot, IVF-free sex.

But when I told her that I'd be away on the Friday and Saturday nights, I reckon that's when she started hatching her plan. If she'd left me to it, let me go away for a weekend of strategic boredom, punctuated by two evenings of laughs and booze, everything would have been okay.

I would have still messed up. But nobody would have got killed.

All I craved was a night in with Meg, like the old days. I couldn't wait to ditch all the other crap that had ripped apart the lovely marital bubble that we'd created for ourselves.

Part of that baggage was our counsellor, Martin Travis. It had been a long time since I'd taken such an immediate adverse reaction to someone. He annoyed me the minute I saw his stupid face grinning out of the leaflet that Meg was clutching in her hand.

'I really think that we should give it a try, Pete. We both know things have been hard work recently.'

She could say that again. Resentful IVF sex is what I called it. It was the least exciting form of interaction a man could possibly have with his wife. It's where thrills and arousal go to die. But I'd settle for that now, I'd do anything for more time with Meg. That's not going to happen, though, not after what happened.

'Can't we figure it out ourselves, Meggy? Why don't we try a date night or something like that? We don't need some kid telling us how to run our marriage. How old is he anyway?'

'He's twenty-nine, but he comes very highly recommended, he was a superstar in his counselling course.'

'Is he even married?'

'Pete, it doesn't matter, he knows what he's doing.'

Her hand scrunched the leaflet and I could see it was time to cool things down. She'd done her research, she wanted this hobbit boy to be our counsellor. He had that tousled hair that made it look as if he'd just got out of bed, but Martin's locks were artfully untidy. His beard probably took him hours to trim to perfection.

'Okay, he looks like he knows his stuff, I trust your judgment.' Meg smiled and squeezed my arm. The first physical contact we'd had that day. I felt the thrill of her touch shoot through my body. God, I loved that woman. Why couldn't things just go back to how they were?

She put the kettle on, and I sat at the table, flattening the creased leaflet so I could do my best to give it some serious attention. It had been printed on green paper and, to cut Martin some slack, the picture quality was so poor it had been a bit unfair of me to make such a hasty judgment. It was the idea of having to endure any counselling at all that riled me, and my irritation was focused on Martin and everything he represented.

As far as it went, the counselling looked fine, there were all sorts of reassurances about confidentiality and discretion.

I have to think about these things. I'm on the radio. That makes me gossip-worthy, a person of interest. I didn't want some marriage counsellor getting all excited about having a minor celebrity in his office and telling his dinner party pals how bad things had been in the bedroom – even in veiled terms.

Meg never thought of potential hazards like that. She worked in the probation service, she just had to worry about getting killed by clients— I can't believe I said that. Jeez, what a stupid thing to say. But it was true, Meg's biggest concern was some junkie taking a fancy to her, or running into one of her more unsavoury clients on a night out in town.

It was the slogan on the leaflet that finally made me buck up and do it for Meg's sake. Cracks in your relationship? it asked. Don't paper over them, let's fix them together! There were very definitely cracks in our relationship. We were barely speaking, hardly touching or kissing, and the conversation between us was tense and functional. Just like the sex, the schedule for which was largely determined by Dr Richard Kirk, IVF specialist. The irony of his first name wasn't wasted on me, but Meg didn't find it amusing. Doctor Dick. Dick doctor. We'd have laughed out loud at that in less troubled times.

Martin Travis had all the relevant qualifications, and a quick search on my phone informed me that it's quite usual for relationship counsellors not to be married themselves. It's the counselling they're qualified for, not the marriage bit.

I wanted it to succeed, I really did. I didn't want to have to endure the process but I desperately wanted me and Meg back on course. Essentially, I think, and I really believe this is true, we loved each other, in spite of everything. Meggy wanted things back as they were, she must have done. But we'd turned off along a particular road and there were no exits on the horizon. We were stuck on that course. There was no way off until the baby thing got resolved. We had to hope that we could keep everything going for a bit longer, until things changed for the better.

As things turned out, it didn't work out that way. I was to head for Newcastle to spend a weekend locked in a conference room in a bland budget hotel. The days would be spent in a creative explosion of blue-sky thinking, or whatever it was we were supposed to be doing. The evenings would be good – at the very least it was a chance to get away from home and think things through. A bit of space.

Of course, at that time I hadn't met Ellie. Meeting Ellie would change everything. For everybody.

We'd already seen Martin for four of our six sessions, and we had to squeeze in another visit before I headed off to Newcastle. I think it was that session with Martin which began the downwards spiral for me. It was what made Ellie such a deadly person to meet at that particular time.

It didn't start well. I was supposed to be there for midday but the news editor had made a mess of the schedule, and there was nobody to read the bulletin. So I texted Meg, grabbed the pile of scripts and did my duty with the 12 o'clock news.

I was only two minutes in when I began to curse my luck. I hadn't scanned the scripts, I'd grabbed them from the producer's desk, run into the studio, opened up the microphone and begun speaking.

'The midday news, I'm Peter Bailey.'

It was Peter on air, Pete to my friends and family. Peter was a hangover from the old days of broadcasting. I can still remember being admonished as a cub reporter for using Pete.

The Middle East always got me. While political leaders were more concerned with world peace and harmony, newsreaders have to panic about the next deadly foreign name that's lying in wait ready to trip us up in a news script.

I got caught good and proper: Abd al-Qadir Amirmoez ... I didn't stand a chance without some warning. I messed it up completely, got a round of applause from the bastards in the office when I left the news cubicle, and arrived at the marriage guidance offices twenty minutes late, bad-tempered and sweating profusely.

I could almost hear what Martin Travis was thinking as I walked into his office: a beautiful woman like you really wants to have a baby with this man?

He stroked his daft tuft of a beard as he stood up to welcome me a little too effusively. I think he hated me as much as I hated him. He and Meg had been laughing at a shared joke when I was shown into the room by the receptionist. Another reason to dislike him.

The mood changed as I sat down next to Meg. As an afterthought I leant over to kiss her. It was proprietorial more than anything, what an imbecile I was, but I didn't want that young git to think he was better than me. What did he know? These youngsters think they deserve a celebratory cake if they're still together at the end of a month, they don't know anything about the ebb and flow of a long-term relationship.

You could tell he wasn't married, any wife worth her salt would demand he shave off that beard for starters. He had a know-it-all demeanour, almost a sneer, whenever he spoke to me. When it came to Meg, his face lit up. They clearly liked each other and got on well.

I resented it. Martin seemed to offer her everything I couldn't. He comforted her, he made her laugh, helped her forget. He was young and good looking. He was so damn skinny too – how do these youngsters do it? My stomach had begun the inevitable process of rounding when I was about 35. He was personable, funny and charming. And I was none of those things. Certainly not at that time. Not to Meg anyway. And I was sharing the most intimate details of my relationship with him. I was giving him every scrap of information that he needed to woo my wife.

'When was the last time you and Meg made love?' he asked.

None of your business! is what I wanted to say. Instead, I gave Martin chapter and verse on how making love had been replaced by filling plastic cups for Dr Dick and specially scheduled sessions which were akin to intensive factory farming.

I saw the twinkle in his eye when I told him that. I knew what he was thinking, the little shit. Write what you want on your leaflet about impartial advice and non-judgmental listening, Martin Travis wanted to sleep with my wife and, in my eyes, he was probably about 70 percent on his way to doing so.

He knew what our problems were, and he knew precisely what to do to give Meg exactly what she wanted.

'I want Pete to make me laugh like he used to,' she would say. 'I want to feel his hunger and passion for me. I don't see it anymore.'

I knew what she meant, I desperately wanted it too. As I watched Martin's eyes dance around Meg's face, I doubted myself for a moment. Would things ever be the way they'd been before? It all seemed to be slipping away from us. I loved Meg so much, I wanted her so badly, but there seemed to be a gulf between us now and no way of bridging it.

Damn Martin Travis! He turned a bad mood – which would have passed soon enough – into a stewing, smouldering mash-up.

'You're being ridiculous,' Meg said afterwards. 'He's just good at his job. You say it yourself about people in the media. You chat people up for a living.'

'Yes,' I replied, 'but we use our superpowers for good, to put guests at their ease, it's to make sure they sound great on the radio. He just wants into your knickers.'

There it was. The suggestion of sex for lust's sake. Nothing to do with samples, plastic cups or microscopes. Meg always baulked when I brought it up in any way. It was as if I were forcing her to confront what we used to have. It had been good, we'd both liked it, surely she wanted that feeling back again?

Her face reddened, she averted her eyes, then brought them back to my face, realising what she'd done. Maybe she'd given too much away.

'He's a professional, Pete. He makes me laugh and he understands how I feel. Is that so bad?'

'Of course it's not,' I replied, grasping for the words to express what I meant. I should have told her that I was jealous of him. I could feel her slipping away from me and I felt powerless to stop it. I loved her more than anything or anybody on the planet, but I seemed to be so far away from her at that time. I desperately wanted to hold her, kiss her, make love to her like we did when we first met, so that we could feel that frisson of excitement and possibility in the air.

All I could do was to force out a non-committal grunt and head upstairs to pack my case. It wasn't how I wanted it to go, but that's how it happened. My contribution to the welfare of our relationship was a grunt.

What would Martin Travis have said?

'Perhaps you could articulate that more specifically, Peter. Try to say it without the anger.'

I couldn't believe that I was now hearing Martin Jarvis in my internal dialogue. But he probably had a point. I walked downstairs quietly and moved gently towards Meg who was standing by the window, deep in her own thoughts.

'I love you, Meggy. I'm sorry.'

She moved in closer and pulled me in tight. It was perfect. We stood like that for what seemed like ages, for a moment recapturing what we'd once had. Total silence, just holding each other. I'm so pleased I did that. I have Martin Travis to thank for letting me experience that closeness with my beautiful wife one last time.

Meg had a final gift to offer me, which I didn't discover until afterwards, but knowing that just made everything that happened even sadder.

Looking back on it, I don't know if it was anybody's fault in particular. We all had some blame in this, and nobody walked away unscathed. I knew that what I was going to do was wrong from the moment I first smiled at Ellie. Yet I told myself all along that it would be okay, I was in control, I could stop at any time. It was just a bit of fun. I loved Meg, I'd never do anything to hurt her.

I think it was probably too late even then. I wonder if we both realised it as we stood there hugging as if we were never going to hold each other again like that. Did we know it was over? How could we have known?

Meg must have already hatched her plan for the weekend, and I hadn't even met Ellie at that stage. How could we possibly have sensed what was waiting for us?

Something was in the air that day, that's for sure. Who knows what it was, but I felt it, and I'm convinced that Meg did. Beautiful Meg. I'm so sorry for what I put you through. If I could take it all back, I would in a heartbeat.

CHAPTER TWO

I was soon on my way to Newcastle, and a weekend of whatever it was Diane wanted us to discuss. I wasn't in the best frame of mind to spend time with other people. Martin had put me in a bad mood, but at least my moment with Meg had set me off on a more even keel. I was beginning to think that some special time with Meg on my birthday might have been the better option after all. She'd certainly made an effort to reach out to me before I left.

As I drove towards Newcastle, in the silence of my car I considered coming up with a mystery illness or a sudden migraine. Would Diane fall for it? I'd already made the fatal error of telling her that it was my fortieth, I should have kept quiet about that one.

I was committed to the weekend, even though my mind was half at home still. I was conflicted. Once upon a time, the prospect of a weekend alone with lovely Meg would have been glorious. Now our separation gave me a break from the same old conversations, the painful routines and the incessant marital introspection.

Martin Travis and Dr Richard Kirk had cast a long

shadow over our lives. I wanted them exorcised, but Meg saw both as a positive influence. We'd done fine without them for nine years, and I was certain as I weaved in and out of the lanes on the dual carriageway that we'd figure out a solution. Together.

My thoughts were interrupted by a call on my mobile phone. I hadn't quite managed to go hands free at that time, my car was a bit too old to have all the bits and pieces that it needed to link to Bluetooth. I glanced down at my phone on the passenger seat, screening for a call from Meg or anybody else who might be important. I glanced from phone to road and back again, making a feeble attempt to compensate for my distracted driving.

It was Jem, my friend from work. Probably nothing of importance, just catching up for a gossip. He'd want to know how the marriage guidance was going. Jem had recently split from his own wife. They'd done a bit of counselling, passing Go without collecting their £200, and heading straight for jail. Or court, as it was away from the Monopoly board. The split was new, sudden, unexpected and ugly. Jem was in a very dark place.

He wouldn't tell me what had happened. I pieced it together as best I could. Jem couldn't keep his eyes – or his hands – off the young reporters who flowed in and out of the office via a never-ending post-university conveyor belt. They were future starlets destined for TV and radio careers, straight out of media courses and wet behind the ears.

I'll admit that this was a constant source of temptation before I met Meg. These bright-eyed, beautiful young women would be eager for any bit of advice that could accelerate them up the greasy pole towards presenting shows and getting on TV. It didn't seem to bother them that

I was some ageing journalist stuck in the regional pool until retirement or redundancy beckoned. Or, more likely, a heart attack at my desk. They were so upfront about it too. I'm not sure what they thought I could do for them. I will admit, though, there were times when I tucked into the buffet, but when Meg came along I lost interest completely, they just seemed like young girls to me. But Jem could never resist, in spite of having a beautiful wife and five wonderful kids.

When I was a child at secondary school, we used to have an RE teacher who sold us posters for our bedroom walls. I had one that showed four cows, each one with its neck thrust through the fence of the next field eating its neighbour's grass. The caption was: The grass is always greener.

That's what Jem reminded me of. He had everything that Meg and I wanted – well, everything that Meg wanted and I wasn't fussed about it either way. Yet he couldn't help sticking his neck through the barbed wire and munching the grass in the next field. That poster was made for people like him. Within the next twenty-four hours it would take on a whole new relevance to me.

I assumed that Jem had been caught in the act by Sally, his wife. His wife of twenty years, I should add, and partner of who knows how long? They met at university, married young and started a family in their thirties. The kids were still young, they were all of school age, and it was very destructive for everybody.

Jem had indulged in indiscretions in the past, but they were always brief and both parties involved seemed to know the lie of the land. They appeared to be casual flings between an older producer who was married and a young journalist who thought that she could move on her career by sleeping with someone in a senior position.

I often wondered how long these women would have to work in the organisation to realise how low down the food chain we were. Still, it was a pretence that Jem was happy to maintain and, until he got caught, it didn't seem to harm anyone.

When the crash came for Jem, it was sudden and final. I had been surprised that Sally took it so far since it was only a casual office fling. All those years of marriage, the kids and the long journey they'd travelled together, and she just seemed to throw in the towel. I didn't know Sally well, she tended to stay away from our broadcasters' nights out. Media people can seem very confident and overbearing at times, and social occasions are not a good place for partners who prefer a quiet night in.

Meg always loved work nights out, she threw herself right into them.

'How exciting do you think a probation service night out gets?' she'd laugh. 'Imagine talking about no-hopers all night ... and that's just the staff!'

Meg always made me laugh. Correction, she used to make me laugh. We'd howl at some of the things the young idiots got caught with when they were shoplifting in local stores. What made them pinch that stuff? One got caught with three tubes of AnusSooth cream in his inside pocket, yet he'd got over a tenner on him at the time. And for the privilege he got to pay for his crimes with fifty hours of community service.

'Let's hope whatever they asked him to do involved lots of sitting, at least he'd got the cream for it!'

God, I'd laughed when she said that. It wasn't that funny, but when you're in love and feeling connected you'll laugh at anything and everything. When did the laughing stop? I can't even remember now.

So Jem was a fool. I loved the guy, I really did, but imagine throwing all that away? How do you recover your life after you mess it up like he did?

Sally was a real Rottweiler going for him like that, though. She wouldn't listen to any of his pleas for mediation, conciliation and all the other things that keep you away from the more costly services offered by the legal profession. She went straight for the kill. The couples counselling was brief and perfunctory from her point of view. She threw him out of the house for starters. Stopped him seeing the kids for a while. That was harsh.

Jem moved into one of those clichéd flats that estranged dads always end up in while the money is being sorted out. Filled with the terminally unemployed. I felt sorry for him, talk about being a poster boy for keeping it in your trousers.

I couldn't understand why Sally would be so extreme when it was just a stupid fling with some naive young reporter. It wasn't going anywhere, it was no threat to the marriage. I didn't condone it, of course I didn't. Jem needed to spend some time out in the cold, he had to understand that he'd been caught and that it must never happen again. But Sally wanted blood. She needed to see a dead body.

She got her decree nisi in the quickest time possible. Jem didn't fight it, she had him over a barrel with the kids. She took the house and left him to fend for himself. It served him right, I know that. But it was as if she wanted him gone, there didn't seem to be any sadness there. Just anger, hate and a desire for revenge. It was shocking, watching it on the sidelines.

I know she had loved Jem up to the point she found out what he was up to. How can love take a 180 degree turn like that, even though Jem had cheated on her? Sally wanted the relationship over, there was no going back.

He wouldn't divulge which of the trainees it was, he'd clam up whenever I pushed him on the matter. I'd get the occasional snippet from him such as 'This was different, Pete,' or 'It's too painful to talk about,' and he'd move the conversation onto other topics.

Knowing what I know now, I wish to God that I'd pushed him more. I could have helped Meg if I had.

I'd seen a real decline in the quality of hotel accommodation that we were allowed to use in recent years. When I was a cub reporter, you could get a great night-out in London all covered by expenses. You could even travel first class on the train. Human resources had put a stop to that a long time ago. That's why I was now standing outside the OverNight Inn bracing myself for what I might find inside. Diane had vowed to make better use of the radio station's budget, so she'd sorted out a block-booking deal. Actually, Jem had copped for that job, he'd made the bookings on Diane's behalf. Fifty pounds per person per night.

I walked into the hotel under a brightly coloured sign proudly boasting their 'Snug-at-Night Guarantee'. I checked my phone before I walked into reception – I could see there was a bit of a queue there. There was a voice message from Jem, just a quick one.

'Hi Pete, I've cried off travelling over tonight, I'll be there sometime tomorrow. Diane knows, got some Sally business to take care of. See you Saturday. Mine's a pint.'

He sounded tense and distracted. Crafty git. He'd played the marital crisis card with Diane. It outflanks a fortieth birthday every time. Good on him, he'd escape a day of 'brakes-off thinking'. That phrase made me want to scream. Diane must have picked it up from one of her self-development podcasts, everything had been 'brakes off' for the past week.

Nothing from Meg. I was a bit disappointed about that. I'd hoped that she would pick up on our moment before I left, maybe with a follow-up message or something like that. An indication that she gave a shit. The cupboard was bare. For an instant I toyed with sending her a text. Maybe I should set the example I wanted her to follow, perhaps she'd pick up on my lead? To my shame, I got distracted by a Facebook post instead: *Click here to see what this man can make with 100 pipe-cleaners. You won't BELIEVE picture number 3!*

If I had sent that text, it would have been one of the last messages that got through to Meg before everything began to unravel. But I'd completely forgotten about Meg by the time I'd scrolled through the slideshow of images on my phone. I had to agree, I didn't believe what I saw in picture 3, it was amazing. So when Jenny Cox welcomed me to the OverNight Inn in Newcastle's city centre, I was totally distracted.

'Welcome to the OverNight Inn, Newcastle City, we guarantee that you'll be snug at night the whole night through. How may I help you?'

Poor old Jenny. She'd worked through a line of nine guests before me and she'd had to run through her corporate patter every time. I liked her immediately. She was young and full of enthusiasm. If anybody could deliver those turgid corporate lines with any degree of commitment, it was Jenny. She had one of those eager bright faces that make you want to feel the same zest for life that you had yourself at that age. That positivity and sense of hope for the future.

She'd been reading a thick paperback book, which was resting face down on the counter.

'*Little Dorrit*, that's quite a read. Is it a long shift?' I asked her, smiling.

'Yes, I'm doing an Open University degree, can't afford to go to proper uni, so I work here and study whenever I'm working nights.'

'There's absolutely nothing wrong with that. You'll get a real degree, just like everybody else, and you're cannier than the rest because you won't have as much debt. Good on you, Jenny.'

She seemed genuinely touched by that. I suppose most people didn't particularly care what she was reading or even if she had any hopes and dreams.

'That's a really kind thing to say, thank you, Mr ...' Jenny checked back at her PC screen. 'Thank you, Mr Bailey.

'Enjoy your stay at the OverNight Inn, Newcastle City, if at any time you find that you're not snug at night the whole night through, I'll be here to help. I hope you enjoy your stay!'

'Thank you, Jenny,' I replied politely. 'You've been a great help. Which way is my room?'

'Through the door, turn right, then it's keep right all along the corridor to the end. I've given you one of the best rooms, it's away from the main doors and at the empty end of the car park.'

I began the fire-door-and-wheeled-suitcase dance that all hotel dwellers must endure. Push the fire door, place foot to hold it open, roll case through the door, step forward, release foot. Repeat four times. Jenny had certainly given me a quiet location, but it felt like an assault course getting my gear to the end of that long row of doors.

Eventually I got there. Room 123. The numbering made no sense to me whatsoever, but so long as I remembered it was right and right I'd be able to manage, even if I got a bit merry in the evenings.

I barely noticed it as I stepped up to my room, it didn't seem significant then. Why would it? I assumed that the cleaners were still working in the bedrooms of the late departures.

The door to the room next to mine was slightly open. It was hardly noticeable, there was no great gap. It just hadn't completely closed. Maybe somebody was crossing over to a friend or a family member in the room opposite, probably getting fed up with having to insert a key card every time. I'd had the same problem myself when travelling in groups. You can really learn to hate fire doors sometimes.

I ignored it, it was one of the thousands of negligible things that flash in and out of your mind every day. Navy blue carpet with purple dots along the corridor. Stickers on doors saying No Smoking Room, one torn at Room 114. Big scratch on the woodwork of the second fire door along my corridor. Door slightly open at the room next to mine.

The open door registered in my mind, then faded into the background, only to be replaced by some other insignificant piece of information moments later.

But it wasn't insignificant. Later he'd be in there. Waiting. Watching. Listening. Ready to start the events that would screw up our lives forever.

Physical attraction is such a weird thing.

For instance, Jenny on the reception desk was a lovely person: strikingly attractive, glowing, amiable. But I didn't fancy her. There was no reason why not, it was just that she wasn't my type.

Meg, however, was burned into my soul from the minute I saw her. I loved her before I even knew her, my attraction to her was so complete and absolute that I really did believe that it was unassailable. Until Ellie walked into the room.

I keep thinking back to my state of mind on that night, trying to look for some reason why it all played out like it did. Was it entirely my fault? I don't think so, but I do acknowledge my part in it. I didn't light the fire, but I did fan the flames.

Talking to Jenny had lifted my mood. I'd been torn when I left Meg, preoccupied with my thoughts in the car, then buoyed up by Jenny's welcome. I'd been hacked off by Martin – really hacked off – and, looking back, I think that was still eating away in the background.

I hadn't been totally honest with myself about that perfect moment I'd shared with Meg earlier in the day. Yes, I'd seen a tiny glimmer of hope, but only to have it withdrawn again when I'd messed it up and moved my hand towards her exposed midriff, sliding it up her untucked shirt. She'd pushed my hand away as if I was a dodgy stranger on a train.

'You'd better think about getting ready, Pete – don't want to keep Diane waiting.'

I think that's what Martin would call deflection. It was a block from Meg, I didn't need to wade through a counselling qualification to know that. She knew what I was doing, daring to suggest that we might, for once in a long time, forget the training course, the washing up, the shopping and the electricity bill and dive into bed together.

That's it, just there. That's how I was feeling when I met Ellie. Blocked. Frustrated. Spurned. By my wife. That's what made me do what I did. I know it's no excuse, I'm not trying to justify it. But I do need to explain it, or else everything that happened afterwards is too much to bear.

Meg loved me, I was certain of that, but for some reason she didn't want to be close to me. Yet I longed to be close to her. At that moment, I desperately wanted to make love to her. Not have sex. This was about love. I needed her. And she pushed me away.

My room at the OverNight Inn was what you'd expect. The carpets and curtains were in navy blue corporate colours, functional and clean. The bed was luxurious, better than the one we had at home. There was a desk and flat screen TV opposite the bed and a small chair tucked into the corner. The bathroom was impressive and had a large walk-in shower with a glass panel to keep the water in and a mirrored wall opposite. I've always had a thing about mirrored walls. I wouldn't have one at home, that's a bit tacky. But in a hotel? Sexy as anything! If Meg had been in there with me, we'd both have clocked that sex in the shower was something that would definitely happen that weekend.

Then I felt the loneliness. The old Meg would have seen that. The old Meg would have given me a suggestive smile and told me that she couldn't wait to get in there with me. But the Meg I'd left at home would have gone in to freshen up, locked the door, then emerged fully clothed. No chance of me catching her naked and maybe chancing my luck. The old Meg would have left the door open and called me in. It's not just the absence of the sex, it's what it means and how we got there. It's the blocking and pushing away that's involved that had made me feel so isolated. Lonely. I shouldn't have felt so lonely when I was with Meg.

I wasn't getting a very strong mobile signal in my room, that was annoying. Not that it mattered anyway, my battery was about to die. Meg knew where I was. If she needed me, she would call reception if there was no joy from my mobile. I put the phone on charge then muted the sound so it wouldn't disturb any other guests if it rang while I was out.

I took a shower, changed into jeans and a casual shirt and brushed my teeth. We'd arranged to meet in the pub adjacent to the OverNight Inn at 7 o' clock, deciding to forgo the bar in the building. I was running a little late. The hotel was quiet, I hadn't heard any voices that I recognised along the corridor so I guessed that we were evenly spread about the accommodation. I preferred it that way. It's a bit intense if you can't even step out to the vending machine without running into one of your colleagues.

I turned off all the lights except for the cool blue back-light behind the headboard. That was nice – sexy – the sort of lighting Meg and I would have gone for to set the mood. It was also just enough light to make my way back from the bar when drunk without having to turn on the main lights and dazzle myself out of my drunken state. I wasn't plan-ning anything at that stage. I was going to meet my colleagues, get some food down me fast, have a few drinks and a laugh, then get back to my room for some sleep.

I had a presentation to make the next day, not first thing but about 11 o'clock. I could let my hair down more on the

Saturday night, the day of my birthday. I had to stay sharp for Diane's sake.

I heard the loud laughter as I walked into the bar. That had to be the broadcasting bunch. It was, and our numbers were already strong. The various teams from around the country had homed in on each other and were already enjoying some boisterous company. One chap, who I didn't know but whose voice I'd heard on the radio, was telling a story about how one of his colleagues had been having an intimate conversation about a personal problem in one of the studios, and it had gone out on air. A five-minute description of a problematical prostate examination broadcast across the whole of London and it had taken the tech-ops five minutes to locate and terminate the open microphone.

There were huge guffaws around the table. God forbid if Introverts International were meeting in the same pub that night, they'd have run a mile. As the laughs subsided from the prostate story, and one of my own colleagues raised the stakes with a 'sex with a guest in the studio' anecdote, I got the people on the long couch to shuffle along and introduced myself. After a couple of minutes of chat and trying hard to remember the new names, I asked if anybody wanted a drink. They were all newly fuelled so it was a cheap round to start the evening, just a pint and some dinner for me. I stepped over to the bar and picked up a menu. Regular pub grub, exactly what I wanted.

I caught sight of a woman outside the bar talking on her mobile. She was having a heated row with somebody, a man I guessed, and she sounded exasperated. I caught the tail end of a 'Get lost, Dave!' before she terminated the call, then went into the toilets, presumably to compose herself.

She emerged a few minutes later visibly more relaxed. I was still waiting to get served, there didn't appear to be any staff around. At least not any who were actually awake.

She came up to the bar and looked about her.

'I'm starving, is there anybody serving?' she asked.

With a voice like that, if she wasn't a broadcaster already, we'd all be recruiting her before the evening was out. She was friendly, confident and assured. It immediately reminded me of my earlier conversation with Meg: broadcasters seduce people for a living – I'd said it many times, but I didn't mean in a predatory way. We make people feel at ease quickly, we get them talking, bring them out of their shell.

That's exactly what Ellie did with me. Whatever had happened on the phone had done something to her, she was in that bar to put it all behind her. I was the first person she saw. I introduced myself and she shook my hand, squeezing my arm with her free hand as she did so.

At first, I just thought she was being friendly. It's what broadcasters are like. But it soon became clear that it wasn't an interview she was after. In the state of mind I was in, she caught me at the wrong time, my defences were weak. If I'd have been a little bit stronger, we could have prevented the violent storm that was about to sweep through our lives and change things forever.

CHAPTER THREE

I met Meg while I was recording for the radio at the probation service offices. I'd made arrangements to speak to some 'bad lads', as we called them in the office. It was a report about a new community initiative to encourage ex-offenders to start their own online businesses. It was a good idea, as far as I could tell.

I've always hated having anything to do with ex-cons and people who are perpetually being recycled within the justice system. I want to be able to walk about town without running into them. Meg was always diving into shops to avoid somebody she'd been working with.

'That's Max Donovan, he was in two weeks ago for aggravated assault,' she'd say. Just the person you want to run into at the supermarket for a chitchat over the frozen foods counter. Meg enjoyed her work, it was engaging and absorbing for her, but it would have been nice if she'd worked in another town or city so it didn't intrude so much in our domestic lives.

Occasionally she'd get probationers who would latch onto her, mistaking professional interest for genuine concern. They'd make promises to her about how they were going to turn their lives around and swear blind they'd stop doing whatever they were doing. They'd see Meg as their road to Damascus, wanting to spend more time with her and seeking a social connection.

It was a hazard of the job. Meg was constantly having to define limits and restrictions at work. She'd stopped telling me about these incidents some time ago, it worried me and made me feel that she was vulnerable.

In my profession we seldom come face-to-face with the perpetrators. We get unique access to investigators, politicians, crime-scene investigators, lawyers and the like, but it was the posh side of crime. I'd got my shorthand as a rookie journalist, but I'd never used it since leaving university, it was only court reporters who got to see any direct bad-boy action. I was office based most of the time, reporting on what had happened rather than getting my own hands dirty.

I worried about Meg, though. We'd met because of an incident in her offices, so in a way I actually have her clients to thank for getting us together in the first place. Like a villainous version of Blind Date.

I was in an office at the probation service talking to three men about their community payback arrangements and how they were being given the chance to exchange removing graffiti from community centre walls for learning how to start up web-based businesses. All of a sudden a door slammed in the corridor outside followed by a loud scream.

It was a woman, furious at something or other. She was spouting a lexicon of every offensive word you could possibly think of. The probation officer who was sitting in on my interviews suddenly tensed and went into difficult-client mode.

Several members of staff were attempting to calm the woman down, but there was one person who caught my attention immediately. I can still remember it with precision. It was as if somebody had muted the commotion going on outside and blurred the movement of bodies rushing up and down the corridor. All I could see in HD clarity was Meg.

It's only ever happened once like that in my life – and that was with Meg. Meeting her must be what people refer to when they say they fell in love at first sight. She took my breath away. That's a cliché, I know, but that's how it felt.

'Are we doing this or what?'

My moment had been rudely interrupted by one of the interviewees. We'd all stopped what we were doing when the uproar began, but they were more used to this abrasive way of living than I was. For them, the rows, the shouting, the wild accusations were all part of their day-to-day lives.

'We'll just give it five minutes until the noise dies down,' I replied. 'Don't want all that racket on the recording.'

I looked back towards Meg. She'd seen me and was torn between looking at what I was doing and monitoring the progress of her angry client. She seemed shaken. I guessed that most days things didn't kick off like that.

I stood up and walked towards the open door.

'Are you okay?' I asked, genuinely concerned – she looked really rattled.

Meg was the most beautiful woman I'd ever seen. I don't mean in an Angelina Jolie or Penélope Cruz film star kind of way. Meg was a wonderful person, I picked up on it immediately, and her soul shone through to me. I've never believed all that nonsense about auras, but if anybody had one, it would be Meg.

Our eyes met, she felt it too, it was an immediate attraction. I'm no hunk. I'm in reasonable shape for my age, but I'm not the kind of guy women look at and then can't help themselves. I've had to work hard with women all my life. I get on well with them, in fact, I probably have more female friends than male. But I'm not good at converting liking to romance. With Meg, though, it was instant.

We laughed about it later. We were being watched by three minor criminals, four members of staff were calming an irate client just along the corridor, and Meg and I were standing there like starry-eyed teenagers.

The journalist in me tends to make me prone to cynicism, but in the privacy of our relationship I admitted to Meg that I'd loved her deeply from the moment I saw her. Everything was there – love, liking, lust, attraction, desire, wonder – and I didn't even know her name. She became a compulsion from the minute we met, a fever that burned fiercely, and one that I couldn't shake off.

The client had now calmed down. She was taken to a different room, and another member of staff rushed to the kitchen to get her a glass of water.

'I'll finish her off if you want,' said the colleague who'd been sitting in on my interviews. 'Let her cool off a bit.'

'Thanks,' Meg replied, grateful for a bit of time to recover herself. 'It wasn't aimed at me. They've stopped her benefits, she was sounding off about it, got a bit carried away.'

Her colleague nodded. It was an occupational hazard as I learnt later on. But it gave me an opportunity to get to know Meg much better.

I picked up my interview recording, suddenly self-conscious that I was being watched by this astonishing woman. I asked my questions, checked the audio and thanked the men who'd taken part. Meg showed them out of the building.

'Back in a moment,' she'd said. 'Fancy a coffee?'

'I'd love one, thanks,' I smiled.

It was very fast after that. Meg returned with the coffee. We swiftly moved from pleasantries to personal information. One minute she was explaining how the clients kicked off sometimes and that it didn't usually shake her, the next we were discussing where we lived.

'I recognise your voice don't I? You're Peter Bailey aren't you?'

'Pete,' I replied. 'Always Pete to my friends. Yes, if you listen to the local station you might have heard me.'

She smiled. God, I loved that smile. She had beautiful teeth, white and even.

We moved quickly to a first date. That night. I didn't even ask her if she was in a relationship. I wasn't at the time, and I assumed that because she was sending out such strong signals to me, she had to be a free agent too.

We almost devoured each other in that office. We went out for a meal together, barely finishing the first course before we rushed straight home to Meg's place, stopping to kiss passionately along the street as we went.

I'd experienced instant sexual attraction before, many a time, but this was something different. We had to possess each other, it was our destiny. That night had to happen, it was inevitable from the moment that we met. Meg felt it too – we discussed it many times afterwards. It had to happen, there was nothing we could do to stop it.

We burst into her room, tearing our clothes off and hurling them around the place to get them out of our way.

We fell onto her bed and made love, our lips pressed together as if we were going to consume each other.

It was urgent, frantic, passionate sex, a collision of two people who had to be together. We made love another four times that same night as if we would never have the chance to do it again, like lovers who were about to be torn apart. It was perfect, the most loving, sexy, passionate, connected experience I'd ever experienced with a woman.

Then Meg's boyfriend came home.

The connection with Ellie was instant too. It was nothing like my first meeting with Meg, it wasn't 'destiny' or anything like that.

It was completely different with Ellie. It was a sexual thing, there was never going to be a lifelong relationship there, there was no expectation of one on either side. We met, we liked each other, there was an immediate attraction and we had a lot in common. I liked her, but I'd never love her, and she'd never love me. We were both consenting adults, maybe not free agents, so it was fair enough. I knew it wasn't right, we both did, but at that moment in time, for both of us, it was exactly what we needed.

Sometimes you have to get some clarity. Relationships are tricky things. If you've been married to somebody for twenty years, you don't separate on a whim. It's slow burning, the thoughts creep in over time.

'Do I still love her? Is this what I want for my life? Have we gone stale?'

You don't end a relationship because you happen to think one of those thoughts in isolation. It's only when they add up over time and reach a critical mass that you might be spurred into action. You reach a tipping point.

In many ways, it's easier if somebody cheats or is violent, it forces the decision. Most relationships die slowly and painfully, they win temporary reprieves and postponements, but still limp slowly towards the abyss.

Meg and I were in that zone. There was lots of love there, I still believe that she loved me when it all happened, I really do. I loved her, I know I did, I was desperate to reclaim what had driven us on that first day that we met. I was certain that we had not burned out. When I thought back to how things had been, I longed to go back to how we were. I wanted the relationship to survive.

Why did I sleep with Ellie? We're only human, not that far removed from the animals, we apply all these social constraints and make things more important than they really are. It's not that it was unimportant, I was a cheating little shit, but in my mind it made no difference to me and Meg. So long as she never found out. In fact, the very act of betrayal made me resolve to work even harder to save our relationship. It took being unfaithful to my wife to understand how much I wanted her. I know that would never stand up in the high court of human relationships, but it was true.

I knew I'd have to try to live with my secret for the rest of our lives together. You have to keep a deception like that to yourself, it's a cancer that must fester within you and be taken to the grave. I should know – the pain of betrayal can destroy. If you reveal your horrible little secret, or if it's ever discovered, it's game over, the trust can never be restored. You only needed to look at what had happened to Jem to understand that one.

As Ellie and I lay in bed together, I knew that I could

never breathe a word about what I'd done, to Meg or anybody else. It was my secret, I understood the lesson, but it had to remain hidden from Meg. I was certain that Ellie would keep that pact, she had as much at stake as I did.

———————

As we stood at the bar waiting to place our orders, the chat flowed easily between us. Ellie worked in TV, she was quite a celebrity in Bristol, often asked to host business awards and local ceremonies. It was one step up the minor celebrity ladder from my position. I was WI meetings and school assemblies. Ellie was official events and posh dinners. My radio audience was measured in the hundreds of thousands, Ellie's broke the two million mark. She was famous enough to be recognised for all the right reasons when walking down the street.

'You look like that Ellie Turner off the TV!' they'd say. We both laughed at that one, but Ellie had got past being flattered by it and had moved on to the stage where it had become a bit tiresome.

I'd get, 'Blimey, you don't half sound like that Peter Bailey fella off the radio!' though it was easier for me to hide, only the diehard listeners who procured presenter photos knew what I looked like. I wasn't even a presenter, but because I appeared on air on a regular basis they got presenter postcards printed. The print run was only a thousand for me, they got five thousand of the proper presenters. See, a minor celebrity.

'It's actually a relief to be in Newcastle where nobody knows me,' Ellie had said, then, suggestively, 'Nobody knows what I'm getting up to this weekend.'

That one hung there for a moment. I studied her face

for a clue, but it was definitely an initial come-on, she didn't cover her tracks. She was putting out feelers. I felt a prickle of excitement the way I did when Meg showered immediately before bedtime. It was a promise of something to come. Ellie was testing the water.

Although broadcasting is an incestuous industry, I'd never met Ellie before, or even heard of her. She had changed her career. She'd started her working life as a nurse, hated it, and gone back to university to get a postgraduate qualification in TV and radio.

'I couldn't face wiping arses and scraping shit off my uniform for the rest of my life,' she laughed, then followed it up immediately with the hint of something more sinister. 'Only it didn't quite work out that way, there's still plenty of shit flying around in my life.'

I wasn't sure how to take that one. It was a bit of a mood dampener after her previous flirtation. She sensed it too and changed the tone fast.

'I always feel a bit naughty when I come on these training events. What goes on in Newcastle and all that!'

'I know what you mean,' I agreed. 'I always seem to end up in some sort of mischief at these things. It's the heady combination of an expenses tab, a night in the OverNight Inn and being away from home.'

'We never got weekends like this when I was a nurse, it's still fresh enough to be exciting to me. I know we have to sit through all the corporate crap on Saturday and Sunday, but there are worse people to be locked up with in prison.'

She was right. Being away all weekend, all expenses paid, albeit within strict HR-defined guidelines, was a bit of a First World problem. It was a break from routine, a chance to get away from the relentless grind of IVF and marriage guidance. My beer arrived and I took a long cool sip, marking the weekend's socialising officially open. Ellie had wine. She held up her glass and clinked it gently against my pint.

'To a weekend of fun and adventure,' she smiled.

I shudder now when I think back to Meg's boyfriend walking into her flat. It wasn't as if she was forbidden from having a boyfriend. But Christ, I'd nearly shit myself when he walked through the door. She hadn't mentioned that. She hadn't had time and I hadn't asked, of course. What a way to start a relationship.

We were lying naked in bed, crumpled sheets thrown onto the floor, clothes all over the place, dishevelled and totally guilty. The door to the flat banged shut. Meg jumped up in bed, I was stirred by her movement and all I heard was 'Oh shit!' muttered several times.

It was too late to try to cover up, besides he'd have seen what was going on the minute he walked into the living room. My boxers were hanging off one of the chairs in the dining area, there was no chance of talking our way out of it.

I wince to think of it, even now. Me sitting stark naked in bed while Daniel talked to Meg as if I wasn't even there. She was naked too, but had at least managed to find a T-shirt on the floor at her side of the bed, one of Daniel's with a Queen album cover on it. An excellent way to add insult to injury.

It didn't take long for me to learn what Meg probably should have mentioned the night before: Daniel worked nights, Meg worked days. But the relationship had run its course. Daniel's ego was hurt, but they both knew it was coming. It was Meg's flat, Daniel was a bit of a freeloader, so it was he who had to pack his bags and leave. He huffed and puffed, cursed and stomped, but he left surprisingly quickly. He didn't even acknowledge me until he was leaving the flat, all of his possessions thrown into two suitcases.

'Screw you!' was all he said, and he gave me the finger.

'And damn you too, Meg!' he shouted, throwing his keys across the room then melodramatically storming through the door and slamming it shut.

'Hell, sorry!' said Meg. 'I meant to tell you, I thought you'd be out of here before he came back. I'm so sorry, I know that's really slutty. I didn't think I'd be so tired this morning, I'm usually awake before seven.'

We looked at each other and I smiled at her cautiously, not sure which way the wind was blowing.

'It's been on the cards for a long time,' Meg began to explain. 'I should have ended it a long time ago. I ought to have told you, I know I should, but in my mind, we've been over for months. I should have put him out of his misery sooner.'

'Is that the end of it?' I asked. 'Will he make life difficult for you?'

'I doubt it,' she said, moving her hand to the bottom of her T-shirt. Daniel's T-shirt. She started to work it up over her shoulders. In spite of the gravity of the situation with Daniel, I'd noticed how tantalisingly high its hem sat on her legs. Every time she moved her hands, it would pull up slightly, just revealing a provocative glimpse of pubic hair. Holding my gaze, she let it drop to the floor. I'd barely had time the night before to take in just how stunning she was. She was absolutely beautiful, I felt myself hardening. She looked down at me and smiled.

'Let's see what we can do with that,' she said. I felt a

surge of excitement and guilt, fuelled by the adrenalin of the skirmish with Daniel. I was enjoying the most exciting sex of my life with this woman, who clearly felt the same passion for me as I felt for her.

It was only as we lay in bed afterwards, having both phoned into work sick, that it occurred to me. This woman who had created such a sudden and urgent need in me had just cheated on her partner.

Had she done this before? When the time came, if the circumstances were right, would Meg do the same to me?

After a while, Ellie and I guiltily decided that we'd better join the main group. We'd been chatting at the bar for quite a time. Back with the others, we were now separated, unable to continue our conversation.

They were a good bunch of people, it didn't take long until we were all gossiping away exchanging journalistic tales across the table as if we were old friends. That's the thing about corporate events, you all have a certain amount of common experience, and as long as you keep things work-based, the conversations are easy. There were five teams gathered for our weekend of brakes-off thinking, it was quite a shindig. Two of the teams were from TV, the rest from radio.

It was our task to come up with ways that we could supercharge our output to harness the force of social media and the web. The penny was beginning to drop with senior management that our days were numbered if we didn't learn some new tricks fast. Internet radios were being installed in cars, everybody had a smartphone glued to their ears; nobody would tolerate the intermittent signals from regional radio for much longer.

You could usually rely on the grey-hair brigade to keep the listening figures strong, but even the pensioners were adopting the new technology. Before long, Ethel from the old folks' home would be tuning into non-stop songs from the fifties on some 24/7 streaming station based in the USA. When that happened, there would be nobody left to hang onto every word of the mart prices and the local share price fluctuations. It was touch and go as to whether I'd make it to pension age before it all caved in on us. My pensionable age kept getting further off and the imminent demise of radio got closer and closer, the spectre of Netflix and Spotify casting their dark shadow over my future mortgage payments.

There was a touch of gallows humour about the whole occasion, among the staff that is, not the managers. I had a foot in both camps. I was low-level management, I was still allowed to drink with the troops and poke fun at our bosses. So long as your shift still entailed working on the shop floor, you remained one of the guys.

It was an uproarious alcohol-fuelled evening, cooking up spoof social media campaigns to revive our broadcasting fortunes. Ellie was really rude, she almost made me blush, but she'd look over at me every time something risqué emerged from her mouth, and I knew that she was marking us out for later. It was for my benefit as much as anybody else's, she was letting me know that she was no prude.

As the evening progressed and the numbers around the table began to dwindle, Ellie and I edged nearer and nearer until at long last we were sitting next to each other. Her leg brushed mine. She was wearing a short skirt. I imagined what it would be like to stroke her long, smooth, athletic legs and have them wrapped around me.

Immediately I felt guilty, thinking of Meg, and dismissed the thought from my mind. But Ellie kept moving her leg against mine, and each time she did so, I got a little jump of excitement.

There were only a few diehards left at the table, the time was rapidly approaching when I'd have to make my final call with Ellie. She'd started to touch my arm when we were speaking, we were so close that I could feel her breath on my face. It was an intoxicating closeness as if I only had to say the word and we would fall into each other's arms.

I thought about Meg and how we'd met. What I was feeling with Ellie at that moment was conjuring up that enticing cocktail of sexual promise and excitement. For a moment, Meg felt like the enemy. She was driving me to this. I was desperate for physical contact, for the warmth and closeness of my wife. Yet she denied me that, I was frustrated, lonely, in a corner. I wanted my wife, but she wouldn't let me get close to her.

I knew it was treacherous as I was doing it, there's no excuse for what happened. I even convinced myself that it would be therapeutic for us, that sleeping with Ellie would release some of the tension around the counselling and IVF, it would give me the impetus to keep trying to work things out.

My deception grew closer and more certain every time that Ellie's leg moved nearer to mine and with every touch of my arm. She had small, soft and really feminine hands, Meg's were much more functional, I'd never found a person's hands so sexy before. I imagined her holding me in those hands and taking me in her mouth. She looked at me and smiled. Ellie knew that she'd got me.

CHAPTER FOUR

I should have spotted the signs before I got in too deep. It's only in looking back that I can see the hazard lights flashing all around me in the lead up to those events. I was blind to them, and in the state of mind I was in I'm not sure I even cared.

Jem was the first red flag. We'd been friends for years, I'd known him before I met Meg. He'd started at the radio station a month or two before me; we'd both been recruited as radio producers so we had to work together closely.

I was grateful to Jem, he showed me the ropes at the new station and got me up to speed. He even saved my life on air a few times.

Mispronouncing a Middle Eastern politician's name or making a pig's ear of a Russian diplomat's official title is an occupational hazard for a radio presenter, but get a local place name wrong and you'll be lynched. Broadcasters can be right bastards too, they won't warn you.

There was the time that once again I hadn't read through my scripts before dashing into the studio for the news bulletin. The second item was an alleged assault in a local hotspot called Minge Street. Luckily the top story was an international incident, so it gave Jem ten seconds to leap into the studio while my microphone was closed and hiss 'min-gay'.

As the short audio clip came to an end and my eyes returned to my script, I opened my microphone, and my eyes fell on the dreaded words, Minge Street. Surely it wasn't as it looked? The penny dropped. Jem had given me warning, it was pronounced 'min-gay'. He'd spotted the hazard while scanning the news scripts on his PC. I owed him one for that.

So Jem became an office pal early on in my life at the radio station. We were similar in age and we'd both been to the same university to get our broadcasting qualifications, even though he'd been there two years earlier than me.

We didn't really socialise with wives and families, broadcasting is funny like that. We went out together when someone was leaving, for stag nights, birthday celebrations and so on, but spouses and partners tended to keep away most of the time. I guess it can be a bit intimidating to go on a night out with people who tell stories for a living.

I was aware of Sally, I knew about Jem's kids, I'd absorbed the basics of his life, but we weren't intimately acquainted. Looking back, I knew more about Jem's liaisons with the nubile reporters than I did about his relationship with his wife. I don't think he was unhappy with Sally, I suspect he was more unhappy with himself.

Jem had been destined for great things in broadcasting. He'd been the star of his year at university, securing a prestigious work placement in London and getting his voice on national radio before he was even clutching a qualification in his hand.

As a teenager, desperate to secure a place in the media,

he'd worked his way through the ranks of hospital radio. The senior volunteers, who all had names like Geoff or Bill, blocked his path to the hospital radio airwaves for four years before they gave him a slot reading out dedications on somebody else's show.

What a bunch of tossers. I'd heard Jem's demo, which he'd recorded in his bedroom at the age of fourteen; he was brilliant even then, had a real feel for the medium. Geoff, Bill and Frederick – or whatever they were called – were just a bunch of grumpy old gits intent on stopping a talented youngster from getting his hand on their coveted show slots.

They probably thought the world would fall apart if Geoff's Weekend Warblers or Bill's Bandstand Extra were replaced by anything vaguely interesting that Jem might have produced.

I knew this story well, Jem had shared it many a time. It was often how he started bonding with the sexy young reporters – there's nothing like a 'how I got into broadcasting' tale to loosen the elastic on even the securest pair of knickers.

Jem had really fought to get into radio. I'd just breezed in, though I had only a fraction of Jem's talent. I'd done a short stint on student radio at university, got caught by the bug – and the women – and stuck with it. I was gifted with a decent voice and the ability to work accurately at speed.

I really believe that Jem loved Sally, but he also blamed her for his stalled career. They'd met at university, married and procreated, and he missed out on 'the London thing'. He landed his first job in the north, got caught up young with houses and domestic life, and was then unable to make the move to London where all the best jobs were located. He'd missed his moment, and he knew it.

He would grumble to me about former reporters, who'd been attractive but fairly useless, moving through the ranks at a meteoric speed. When did you last see an ugly presenter? Never, is the answer to that question. In spite of diversity, quotas and equality, the day you see a fat and unattractive presenter on screen, I'll eat my recording equipment. That doesn't count Eamon Holmes, he's got a job already.

So for Jem, as a middle-aged bloke with a glorious radio voice and broadcasting instincts to die for, the world of radio was becoming dominated by trendy young things with posh names that were unpronounceable. And Jem was stuck on a regional radio station warning people like me of the hazards of a place called Minge Street and reporting on mid-weight crime stories with a peppering of escaped sheep news for added zest.

I understood his frustration, broadcasting is an ambitious world, it's hard to watch people leaping ahead of you onto national radio and TV programmes. It's difficult at times to keep jealousy at bay. If I pushed Jem he'd admit that he could never make the move to London, it was too late for him, they couldn't afford it, and the family was too far entrenched in local life.

I think his dalliances with younger female reporters were an expression of his frustration and perhaps a taste of the glamorous life he might have known. Instead, he became one of the broadcasting world's might-have-beens, only touching the robes of those destined for great things and never getting to wear them himself.

I didn't condone his sleeping with the reporters, but I wasn't going to condemn him for it either. He was a mate, he was great company, we laughed a lot and he pulled his weight in the office. It was up to him to deal with matters of conscience, not me.

When one of my colleagues handed me his phone saying that Jem wanted to speak to me, I was a little surprised.

'Why aren't you answering your phone, you wanker?' he asked.

My hand moved down to my back pocket.

'Shit, sorry, I left it in my room on charge. You'd think they could create a mobile phone battery that lasts for more than five minutes. Come back Nokia, we love you really!'

Normally, he'd have laughed at that, but he was very businesslike. Distracted even.

'Okay, look I can't make it to Newcastle, something has come up.'

Then, almost as an afterthought, 'It's Sally and the kids, it's a bloody mess.'

I knew better than to ask. Besides, I'd just caught Ellie's eye and she'd leant over to pick up her wine. I got a full view of her cleavage nestling below the third button on her white blouse. I was less interested in Jem's latest crap-fest and more motivated by Ellie's quite obvious attempts to turn me on. She'd succeeded. It wasn't difficult.

'Have you told Diane yet?' I asked, not even attempting to conceal from Ellie where my real attention was focused. She smiled at me, a lovely sparkle when she did so. God, she was sexy. I'd need to lay off the beer soon or I'd be an embarrassment in bed. I was certain we'd be spending the night together by then, and Jem was getting in the way.

'No, can you let her know, make it sound like I had no choice? No need to give her any details, just mention the family and the kids and she'll get the gist.'

'Will you be able to get here at all, or is it off for the

entire weekend?' I asked, tearing my eyes off Ellie's breasts for a moment to attend to my friend.

'Probably not. If I can, I will,' came Jem's reply, he seemed distracted again.

'Okay, see you whenever.' I signed off. The line went dead. Unusual that. Jem had a thing about saying goodbye. He'd always rant about how Americans on the TV just finish a call without a 'cheerio' or 'see you'. Yet there he was, just ending the call. If I hadn't been so excited by Ellie and the pink bra that was peeking over the top of her white blouse, I might have paid a little more attention to what was going on with Jem.

But Ellie had a surprise waiting for me before we finally tumbled into my room to seal my final betrayal of Meg.

Talk about nearly killing the mood. I made the foolish mistake of asking Ellie about her heated conversation in the corridor just before we'd met at the bar. What a dickhead!

She didn't want to tell me, and as soon as she started explaining, I realised that I really should have kept my big, stupid mouth shut. What an obstacle to place in the path of a sexual liaison which was, by that stage, almost a done deal.

Ignoring Ellie's quite obvious signals not to force the issue, I made her tell me about her possessive, prone-to-violence boyfriend called Dave. I was so pleased that I had asked. Ellie was quick to add that Dave had never been violent with her. He'd been threatening, but never violent. What a relief.

She'd been with Dave for a little under two years. She'd known that he had to be ditched after a month, but it had never happened. Her only consolation was that he was good looking and muscular, so although she knew she had to get out at some point, the wait wasn't all bad.

'It's only a feeling,' Ellie had tried to explain. 'He's never done anything to hurt me, not even physically threatened me in any way. It just feels like he might do, it's the way he talks sometimes and how he is with other people. He hates me looking at other men, he doesn't even like me talking to them. He knew what I do for a living, it's hardly a surprise that I get to talk to lots of blokes.'

A possessive, jealous boyfriend, perhaps prone to violence. Not the aphrodisiac I had in mind.

'Why don't you leave him?' I asked, wishing I'd kept my eyes firmly on Ellie's pink bra and my mouth firmly shut.

'I will, I really will. He's not that bad, honestly. I just know he's not the man I'll be spending the rest of my life with.'

I thought back to the episode with Daniel when I'd first met Meg. If I'd have known about Daniel before I slept with Meg, I'm not sure it would have made any difference. It helped that when he found out what we'd done, he wasn't violent. But Dave seemed to be a different prospect altogether, and I knew about him this time. Here was a real test of my moral fibre. I'd never knowingly cheated on anybody, yet here I was considering the double. Cheating on Meg and cheating on Dave. Prone-to-violence Dave.

Just like Meg, Ellie was planning on ending it. Meg and I had never looked back, it had given Daniel and her the push they needed. They'd run into each other a year or so later and Daniel had even admitted as much. He'd been furious at the time, but in the long term, it had worked out well. He had a new girlfriend, they were very happy, it had turned out for the best.

I couldn't believe that I was trying to reframe my

intended infidelity as a social service. It was only Ellie's assurance that the relationship was definitely over after their phone row that made me feel better about what we both intended to do.

It was a row over nothing, as most relationship rows are. That day Ellie had filmed a TV insert with a bunch of rugby players. She'd had a bit of fun with it, been creative with the report and flirted with the guys. We all have to do it, it goes with the job, we have to make people look and sound good and try to tell an interesting story in the process.

Dave had seen the report on the TV, well after Ellie had left for her weekend away in Newcastle, and he wasn't happy. Did she have to be so obvious about wanting to shag those guys? Her tongue had been hanging out, according to Dave – he didn't know how she'd managed to keep her drool off the camera. Ridiculous nonsense of course, but that's what Dave had seen when he saw the report.

'I'd decided it was over before I met you at the bar,' Ellie said, making me feel better about things. I told him it was over on the phone, but I'm going to have to go through the whole face-to-face, did-you-mean-what-you-said shit to put the final nail in the coffin. I told him to clear out his stuff, it's my house, I pay the mortgage, so it should all be nice and clean cut. I'll have to see him again, I guess, tell him to his face. He wasn't happy. I'm glad he had a go at me, it gave me the chance to end it at last.'

Then the conversation turned and with Dave nicely dispatched and the morality of the situation a little clearer, Ellie made her intentions known once again. Just in case I'd forgotten.

'Besides, I didn't want to shag those bloody rugby play-ers, they're not my type. I'm hoping that if you stop talking about Dave and his worrying paranoia for more than five minutes, it'll be me and you who are rolling in the sheets by the end of the evening.'

The noises coming from the room next door hadn't particularly bothered me. After all, Ellie and I were making noises of our own. We were in a hotel, the OverNight Inn no less, there were constantly people walking up and down the corridors. If we'd known what was going on in there, right through the wall from us, we'd have been horrified.

Needless to say, my attempts at completely sabotaging the evening with Ellie came to nothing in the end, and having seen off interruptions from Jem and Dave, we were back on course. Without actually saying anything, I think that we both accepted that we'd have to be the last people at the table if we were going to be able to sneak off without anybody else knowing. I certainly wasn't going to be brazen about my infidelity. I hadn't really thought it through, but I knew that if Meg never found out it would just be between me and Ellie. She was a grown woman, she could make up her own mind. So long as we were both consenting adults, it didn't need to go any further. She was on the TV, I assumed it was important to her to be discreet about things, not that I asked, but I felt as if she could be trusted.

We weren't going to see each other again, our paths wouldn't cross at work, this would be a one-time thing that would stay between us. Ellie was sure to work her way up the broadcasting food chain really fast, she'd be more anxious for me to keep my mouth shut than I was for her to do the same.

I thought it was safe, I'd been working through it all night in my head, in between being reeled in slowly but surely by touching legs, pink bras and flashes of cleavage. I was desperate to have sex with Ellie. It wasn't the same as it had been with Meg, nothing like it. This was good old-fashioned carnal lust. There would be no relationship there, no expectation of one on either side. I wanted to have sex with Ellie and conclude a great night of IVF-free flirtation and suggestiveness.

There was no emotional tab to pick up, no question of 'Do you think I'll get pregnant this time?' Just a bloody good shag with a woman who was incredibly sexy and great company. And who wanted to do the same thing with me.

I know it's the flimsiest justification ever, but sod it, I was ready for that night with Ellie, even though everything ended the way it did.

It was just before midnight when the last boring drunk finally went and left us to make our way to my room. Neither of us knew this guy, he was from another station. Fergus Ogilvy I think his name was. I guess he must have been an engineer, but he certainly wasn't reading our vibes very well: 'Time to head off to bed! Time to head off to bed!'

It took ages for him to go. He was getting excited about the next day's agenda.

'This is way overdue, I can't wait to share my ideas on our current social media strategy ...'

Ellie and I had exchanged a smile. Before he started to outline his fascinating ideas, the barman told us to drink up. We were being thrown out. Thank heavens for pubs that still close by midnight.

We made a fuss of gathering bags and making sure we'd got our belongings, taking enough time to allow Mr Bean to make his way out of the pub and give himself a good head start back to the hotel.

'I thought he'd never go!' Ellie laughed, touching my arm.

The electricity of sexual excitement surged through my body. This was it. Either I had to back out now or go through with it. Ellie had made it perfectly clear that she was up for this. My loosening moral code had got around her recent break-up with Dave, all I had to reconcile in my mind was what I was about to do to Meg.

If she never knew, it would never hurt her. I would have to keep the secret forever. Could I do that? I was not going to be one of those morons who confessed all, expecting my true love to forgive me. There's no coming back from a betrayal. Either you take it to the grave or your relationship perishes. Nobody can deal with betrayal, it poisons the soil and forever damages the crops.

There would be no telling Jem either. He might have been a mate, but I didn't trust anybody to keep their mouth shut, and certainly not him. As we made our way out of the pub and thanked the barman, who was locking the door behind us, I decided that I could keep the secret. I wasn't sure if Meg and I were going to last anyway if something didn't force the issue soon, so I resolved to stop arguing with myself and see it through to the bitter end. I would keep it to myself, absorb the guilt. Meg would never know.

Ellie put her arm around my waist and pulled me to the side of the pub's entrance, out of sight. Her lips touched mine, gently at first, tentatively, then more urgently. It was a long, deep, passionate kiss. Her tongue moved towards mine as she slipped her hand down towards my crotch. I was hard. She held me firmly as her kiss became more sexually charged.

'Come,' she said, taking my hand, 'let's go back to your room.'

'You sure you're okay with this?' I asked.

It was a long time since I'd slept with a woman other than Meg, I wanted to be absolutely certain that I hadn't misread the signals.

'I'm sure,' she replied, 'I want this, I want you.'

I was pleased that lovely Jenny wasn't on reception when we pushed our way through the doors. I liked her and didn't want her to see what I was doing. I'd have felt ashamed somehow, and if I could keep it between Ellie and me it would be easier to hide it from Meg. There was a notice on reception which read: *Please ring the bell for attention. Members of staff may be dealing with customers elsewhere in the building.*

'Let's not go to my room,' Ellie urged. 'There're lots of people from work on my floor, yours sounds more private.'

We made our way as quietly as we could along the long corridor, taking care not to let the fire doors bang. My room seemed miles away, Ellie's soft hands touching mine only fuelled my desperation to take her there and then.

The last thing I noticed as I fumbled for the key card outside my room was that the door next to mine was still slightly open, only now there was a dim light escaping through it. None of my business. Who cared? For all I knew, they were doing some maintenance in there.

Finally we were through the door.

'Do you have condoms?' I asked, risking a mood kill once again. I felt that I owed Meg that much.

'I'm safe, are you?' Ellie replied.

I'd been with Meg and no one else for almost a decade, I couldn't risk catching anything nasty. Ellie sensed my doubt.

'I'm on the pill and me and Dave haven't done it for ages.'

I always hated condoms. They're for teenagers. I took Ellie's word for it, I knew I was safe, there was no reason for her to take any risks.

'One moment,' she said, slipping into the bathroom. As she did so, she turned off the main lights so that all that was left for illumination was the sexy blue lamp that I'd observed earlier. She pushed the door of the bathroom so that I couldn't see inside, and I noticed a light come on through the gap under the door. Not the bathroom light, she'd put the torch on her phone on.

It reminded me about my own phone. I could see it flashing on the other side of the room. Had Meg called? Jem's frustrated messages would be there too. Would I have enough time to check them before Ellie came out?

Too late. For the phone and for me. Her phone torch was shining up towards the bathroom ceiling. Along with the blue light in the main room, it had the effect of creating a more romantic environment. She was standing there in just her underwear. It was matching underwear too. Christ, it had been so long since Meg had worn matching under-wear, it was one more sign to me that she'd given up thinking of sex as recreational or fun.

Now here was Ellie in a lacy set of pink undies with matching bra, looking like it was straight off the shelf of a lingerie store. She turned her back to me, indicating that I should unhook her bra. She stepped out of her undies, opened the shower door and invited me to join her. As the water began to run warm, she stepped underneath the spray wetting her hair so that it lay in strands across her breasts.

It was what I'd imagined doing with Meg. If the devil had been sent to tempt me, he couldn't have come up with a better trap. I started to undress, standing for a moment in my boxers, watching the water drip over Ellie's gorgeous body, then eased my underwear over my erection and joined her.

As I stepped towards Ellie, she cupped my balls, handling them gently, expertly. She caressed the shaft of my penis, moving up and down, teasing, a promise of what was to come. I took her breasts in my hands, nuzzling her nipples, gently sucking and circling them with my tongue. I was on fire. For an instant, in that light, I mistook her for Meg. But it was Ellie that I wanted at that moment, even though I imagined Meg's face before I betrayed her. I pictured her crying, asking me 'Why would you do this?'

It was too late. Ellie had pushed her lips against mine once again, one hand cradling my balls, the other clutching my buttock. I closed my eyes and returned her kisses, our tongues caressing, my right hand gently squeezing her nipple.

'Come,' she said, taking my hand with her own. Such a small, smooth, gentle hand. How can hands be so sexy?

Still wet from the shower, we fell onto the bed, pushing our bodies together in a frenzy of passion. I wanted it to last forever and I couldn't wait for it to happen. I moved my mouth from hers, down her neck, gently kissing the skin above her breasts. She closed her eyes, luxuriating in the feel of my touch. I kissed her beautiful soft breasts, moved down her stomach then began to take her in my mouth. Gently licking, gliding my tongue the way that Meg had always loved it. Ellie was partially shaved, I liked that, it turned me on even more.

I wanted to make sure that she came, there was no way I could hold on once I was inside her. She began to groan quietly. As her cries became more urgent, so my tongue worked faster until she came, clutching the sheets, moaning loudly.

It must have been this which covered up the noises in the room next door. I'm certain that I never heard them.

As her body relaxed, she turned herself over, pushed out her curvaceous arse and gently parted her legs. I entered her from behind, kissing her long smooth back and cupping her left breast in my hand. I came almost immediately, it was an explosion of joy, relief, passion – and escape from my life at home. At that moment I forgot all the shit that was going on elsewhere and for a few seconds, in that hotel room in Newcastle, I felt a freedom and elation that I hadn't experienced in a long time.

Ellie and I made love two more times that night. Neither was as urgent as the first time. As she slipped away from me the final time, sweating, hot and damp from our encounter, we both knew that it was over. We'd both done whatever we needed to do that night.

I'd needed to get something out of my system with Meg, and Ellie had shit to deal with after her break-up with Dave. We had both wanted it, but while we held each others' hands as we lay in bed, our thoughts returned to our separate lives and the partners we would now have to face.

Lying there, we both thought it was over. But it was only just beginning.

CHAPTER FIVE

I thought that psychic powers were a load of nonsense until I had a chance encounter with Steven Terry, clairvoyant to the stars.

It was a few months before the working weekend in Newcastle. I'd almost forgotten it, but Steven Terry's warning came back to haunt me. He couldn't have been more correct with his predictions than if he'd been able to travel into the future and see things for himself.

We were short of staff in the office, one of those bugs that does the rounds. One of the studio operations guys, Dennis, had come into the office when he clearly should have been at home with his head in a bucket. He was one of those people who struggle into work however ill they are, thinking that it's somehow like a knight's oath of allegiance to turn up at the office every day.

This is how the zombie apocalypse will begin. Some silly bugger like Dennis Williams will struggle into work, eyeball hanging onto his cheek, flesh decomposing on his body, and inform us all in his zombie voice that it's important to take work seriously and not throw sickies every time you're running a bit of a temperature.

So our numbers were severely depleted and I'd had to ditch my regular duties in the newsroom to cover for the complete lack of broadcast assistants who normally did the running about on the radio station.

On that particular day it meant having to meet Steven Terry, clairvoyant to the stars, and babysit him while he sat in our remote studio which linked him up to other radio stations in our network.

He was promoting his new book *Past & Present: My Life Seeing The Future* and was doing the rounds recording a series of interviews with radio presenters from around the country via our tiny studio.

I had no interest in the man whatsoever. I'm a newsman through and through. I want to know the truth, what's real and what's being concealed from view. I have no interest in ghosts, Tarot cards, the supernatural or fortune telling, other than if it's where it rightly belongs, and that's in fiction books or films.

I resented having to sit with Steven Terry, clairvoyant to the stars, when my more pressing issue was who was going to be presenting the next day's breakfast show. The regular presenter had had to make an emergency dash to the loo in the middle of that day's paper review and hadn't returned, leaving the next presenter to pick up ten minutes before her own show was due to begin.

As Steven Terry sat there wittering away about the gift he'd been born with, how he didn't realise he was different from anybody else until he was nine years old, and why he felt it was the purpose of his birth to share his gift with anybody who had a credit card or bank account, I tried to figure out which member of staff could be moved where to keep the radio station on air.

I was a bit rude to him in all honesty, quite obviously dismissive of his gift and impatient to be done with him and get back up to my desk in the office.

He had six interviews in all, each slot fifteen minutes in duration, so it had taken almost two hours out of my day. I texted Meg as he droned on in the background explaining how he saw things that others didn't. I wish you could see how to fill in this bloody rota, was all I could think. I was going to be back late that night, there was no way I was leaving the office on time. I switched my phone to silent, remembering that any vibrations or beeps would be heard on air. Meg texted me back saying that it was fine with her. She'd go out for food with a friend after she finished work, and she'd see me later in the evening.

At last Steven Terry finished his interview slots. I closed his microphone, turned off the power in the small studio and stood up to leave. He might have been good at seeing things, but he didn't notice that I wanted to get rid of him so that I could return to my real work.

He just sat there, looking at me. I sensed a clairvoyant moment coming on. I braced myself to dispatch his nonsense quickly, much as I did when the Jehovah's Witnesses called at the front door. I would deliver an assertive 'No thank you, you're probably a very nice person, but I'm not the slightest bit interested in what you're saying,' and see him on his way.

He caught me completely off guard.

'Meg is in danger, do you know that?'

I couldn't have been more surprised if he'd stood up and punched me.

'I beg your pardon?'

'Someone called Meg is very close to you, I sense danger in her life.'

My mind worked fast. How did he know about Meg? The fraud, he'd been watching me text her.

'Been watching me on my phone have you?' I smiled at him, waiting to see his face when he realised I'd rumbled his trick.

'I can see things very clearly for you, Peter, it's very rare that my precognition is so strong.'

I retained my cynical journalistic snarl, but he'd caught my interest. Why would he claim that Meg was in danger, even if he had caught a glimpse of her name on my phone?

'I take it you'll give me more information if I get out my credit card and make a payment for your consultancy services?' I asked, perhaps a little hostile bearing in mind he was a guest of the radio station.

'Peter, I don't want or need your money. I'm concerned about Meg. Is she in danger?'

'No, of course not!' I replied.

'I see three things very clearly,' he continued. 'It really is my gift in life to help people, Peter. I have to tell you this, even if you think I'm a complete charlatan.'

He was dead earnest, there was no smirk or showbiz gleam in his eye.

'I see very clearly that Meg is in danger. I can't tell how or why, but it comes from her unhappiness. She's very unhappy, Peter. Did you know?'

Of course I knew, it tormented me every time I saw her. But danger? From where? Her work could be a bit tumultuous at times, I'd seen it for myself the first time we met, but it wasn't dangerous, more hazardous or unpredictable.

'You both have a terrible journey ahead. You in particular, Peter. I see fear, worry, torment in your future. You will have to make a difficult decision, it will shape the rest of your life.'

Again I thought it through. He'd caught me on the hop, I hadn't expected this. My scepticism kicked in again. A difficult decision could refer to anything. The IVF treatment, for instance. Or I might have to trade my preferred summer holiday dates with somebody else in the office. It could be anything. I turned towards the door. I'd heard enough.

'Wait, Peter!' Steven grabbed my arm, it was urgent. You wouldn't normally do that with a stranger.

'Please listen, I know you think this is nonsense. I don't think I've ever seen it so clearly. Meg is in danger, you have a difficult decision ahead, you're going to have to let something very precious go. And there's a third thing.'

He didn't look as if he wanted to tell me the next prediction but he'd got my full attention now.

'You're going to hurt each other,' he began. 'There's a lot of love in your relationship, but in spite of that, you're going to hurt each other. I feel so much love in this relationship, it's very strong, but you will deeply wound each other nonetheless.'

I looked at him. What do you do when somebody tells you something like that?

'I'm sorry, Peter. One of my trials in life is deciding what I tell people. I see this so clearly, I have to tell you. I'm sorry I can't give you more detail, but you can change things, you can alter the future.'

'I appreciate you sharing it with me,' I replied, 'but I am very doubtful about this. I'm a journalist, I pick holes in stories for a living.'

He nodded.

'I know, I understand, but I hope this will help you,

Peter. Please let it guide you at least. Take care of Meg, please make sure she's okay.'

'I will,' I said, anxious to terminate our conversation and get back to my desk. He'd shaken me a little, but as I escorted him to the reception area to sign out and leave the building, all I could think to myself was, what a load of old bollocks!

'He's good that Steven Terry,' said Pam, the reception-ist. 'I went to one of his events once. He was completely accurate, got everything right about me and John.'

'I just don't believe it I'm afraid, Pam,' I replied. 'They know exactly which buttons to press and they never give any real detail.'

'He knew that John was poorly, even told us it was cancer. There's something about him, I think he's for real.'

I smiled at Pam. Her husband, John, had died two years ago. I didn't want to rain on her parade. If she believed there was some mystic quality to the man, I had no wish to take that away from her.

I shouldn't have been so dismissive. I forgot what Steven Terry had told me almost instantly, there was so much crap to deal with back in the office. But if I had listened more closely, if I'd been willing to hear what he was saying, I'd have known the truth sooner.

Meg had been with another man and eventually, as Steven had predicted, it would place her in mortal danger.

I was out stone cold. A combination of a few beers and three-times sex had knocked me out completely. At the age of thirty I might have been able to stay awake a little longer, but on the day of my fortieth birthday I was flagging by 1:15am, and Ellie and I had drifted off to sleep.

We were rudely awoken by the fire alarm.

'Pete, Pete, come on, we've got to leave the room.'

Slowly I came to my senses. Ellie, not Meg. We'd had sex. Three times. It was good. Great. I was naked. She was moving, trying to find her bra, without success. And there was this deafening sound. What a noise that thing made, there was no missing the alarm at the OverNight Inn. That was their snug-at-night guarantee up the Swanee for starters.

'What a bloody racket!' I said, desperately trying to force myself back into full consciousness. I saw Ellie pull on her lacy undies and felt a pang of indecision. The previous night's activities had been fun, would we stretch them to the Saturday night too? The last time we'd made love it had felt as though it was over, but now, seeing her only in her underwear, I was fired up again. She was hot, that was for sure.

The fire alarm carried on, it was making my ears hurt. I'd hoped that it would be a false alarm. Probably some arsehole smoking or vaping in their room.

'Ellie, wait, we need to take care how we leave the room. Don't want anybody from work spotting us.'

'You're not ashamed are you?'

She looked at me, accusatory at first, then couldn't help her smile.

'Not at all,' I smiled back. 'It's my fortieth birthday today, I can't think of a hotter way of seeing in a new decade.'

Except perhaps by having sex with my own wife? I didn't mention that one to Ellie. I think we were both trying to figure out if it was going to happen again. We were keeping our options open – like relationship cheats do.

Our clothes were all over the place. If ever there was a post-coital scene, this was it. Ellie had amazing post-sex hair. Nothing like the films where they seem to get their locks attended to by a stylist while they sleep. We both looked like we'd had sex three times after one too many drinks.

I could hear doors opening and slamming outside the room and the murmuring voices of other guests asking 'What's going on?' and 'Probably some bloody smoker couldn't hang on until the morning.'

Ellie and I quickly located and pulled on our clothes. I combed my hair with my fingers, allowing Ellie to untangle her long hair with my brush. I thought back to the sex, getting horny again at the thought of it. For a moment I was tempted to suggest that we stay back, make love again, ignore the alarm, and slip out when the flashing lights turned up outside. But Ellie seemed to want to go, so I didn't mention it. Maybe it was best, they'd probably come checking all the rooms before the firefighters got there. I didn't particularly want Jenny from reception to catch me in the middle of a sex act.

'I'll check the corridor first,' I suggested to Ellie. 'If it's clear, you go outside and head for the assembly point. I'll follow afterwards. It sounds like it's dying down a bit now.'

Ellie nodded and moved closer to me. She kissed me on the cheek.

'Happy birthday, Pete. I really enjoyed last night. It's just what I needed, you're a nice guy.'

She smiled at me.

Just what I needed, she'd said. She was right, it was what we both needed. There's no such thing as meaningless sex, it certainly means something in the heat of the moment. Sex with Ellie was hot, exciting, passionate, but it wasn't love, it wasn't what I had with Meg. What I'd *had* with Meg. Ellie had got it exactly right.

So we had to slip out discreetly. The secrecy and subterfuge began the moment we stepped out of that door. It had to remain our secret, no drunken revelations to friends or hushed conversations with best pals, this betrayal of our partners had to stay between us. Private, a one-time thing. The knowledge was only dangerous if somebody else found out. That was never going to happen as far as I was concerned. My working life didn't bring me into contact with Ellie or her social circle, so that wouldn't be a problem. Just don't tell Meg. Don't ever tell Meg. She didn't need to know.

'Okay, you're clear to go.'

Ellie slipped into the corridor, and straight out of the fire door, which was directly outside my room. Thanks to lovely Jenny for putting me right at the end of the long corridor. It made the walk of shame minimal, it would be dead easy to conceal the fact that Ellie had been in my room.

I gave it a few minutes. I could hear that somebody was making their way down the long corridor knocking on doors and making sure the rooms were clear.

'What's going on?' I asked as I emerged in mock-dazed confusion.

It wasn't Jenny, that was good, it was some guy I hadn't seen when I checked in.

'There's no fire,' he said. 'Not that we can see. But we have to evacuate to be on the safe side. Probably a guest having a crafty fag in their room.'

I pushed the bar of the fire door, then remembered my mobile phone. I'd probably missed loads of messages since I'd been in Newcastle, at least a fully charged mobile would give me something to do while shivering outside.

'Can I just grab my phone?' I asked as the man made his way along the doors.

'Not really,' he replied, 'but do it fast and nobody will know.'

I was in and out of my room in no time at all. When I re-emerged, the man was standing outside the room next to mine opening and shutting the door as if he was testing it. I could see his name badge, he was called Derek Walker.

'You heard anything out here tonight?' he asked.

'No, nothing, just the normal comings and goings. What's up?'

'This door was prevented from closing with a bit of cardboard. It opened when I knocked on it.'

'It was open earlier,' I offered. 'Didn't see anybody in there, though. It's all been quiet next door.'

'It's funny,' Derek continued. 'This room is unoccupied. It's a late arrivals room, one of the last to go. It must have been a cleaner.'

With that, he made sure the door was pulled firmly shut then indicated that it was time to leave. I pushed through the fire door and walked straight out into the pouring rain.

Discovering Meg's brief affair was the first time I'd given any real consideration to what Steven Terry had said. It all came flooding back to me as Martin Travis sat there in our first counselling session, stroking his beard and no doubt thinking that he might like a crack at my wife too.

Steven's words rang through my mind as Meg explained to a caring, considerate and sensitive Martin Travis how she'd had a sexual encounter with another man. She'd certainly hurt me alright, Steven was bang-on about that. I had to rush out of the consulting room and throw up. I just made it to the toilets in time. I'm not sure that the potpourri in Martin's office would have masked the smell of that.

I entered the room again, white and suddenly very weary. I'd seen my face as I left the toilet, I looked like I'd seen a ghost. What do you say after you've heard your wife reveal that piece of news?

'How does what Meg said make you feel?' asked Martin as I sank back into the sofa, further away from Meg this time.

'Sick, Martin, as you can see it makes me feel quite sick.'

'Uh huh, uh huh, understandably, Peter. Anything else?'

He insisted on calling me Peter. Meg called me Pete, I called me Pete, Martin called me Peter.

'Pretty darn angry actually!'

'Pete, calm down. I've said I'm sorry, I've apologised. I felt ... so damn lonely. You've been so remote since the IVF began, I feel like you're not there anymore. It only happened once. We were talking, it started with him just listening to me ... It meant nothing, it's over, it was just a terrible mistake. I don't even know why it happened ...'

I didn't understand at the time how those words would come back to me over the following weeks. *It meant nothing.* I didn't get it when Meg was saying them to me, but I wised up after I'd slept with Ellie. It certainly meant something while it was happening. But it really did mean nothing in terms of what we wanted for our relationship. We wanted it to work, Meg's infidelity would hurt us terribly, but it didn't have to finish us. Steven Terry didn't have to be right. Yet it meant everything to the wounded party. Me. It was the end of trust and naive abandon. How could anything ever be the same after Meg confessed that?

'Who was it with?' I asked. Did I even want to know? Probably not. I'm not a violent man, but at that moment I really wanted to get it out of my system. Hitting Martin would have been a start.

'It's often better not to find out the details,' Martin began. 'For many people that can be too hurtful.'

'You don't know him,' Meg chipped in. 'He's not from my work either, I won't see him again.'

'How do you feel about Meg now that you know this, Peter?' Martin asked.

I looked at her. I was trying very hard not to cry. I didn't mind Meg seeing me cry, but I didn't want Martin to see it.

'I feel like I can't express how much I love her, even though I also hate her right now. And I know it was my fault that she did it. I'm angry and hurt and jealous at whoever got to sleep with my wife. But I feel angry that we let it get to this. I want my wife back, I want our marriage back. I don't want it to end.'

Martin might describe that as a 'breakthrough moment'. I did begin to cry, and Meg put her arms around me and she started crying too. I wanted Martin to buzz off and leave us to it, but he sat there observing us as if we were two animals in the lab.

'That's good, that's really good,' he said after a few minutes. 'It's very encouraging that you can express it in this way. Many people resort to anger, even violence, Peter. It's good that you let it out this way.'

We emerged from our first session as if we'd just exited the most traumatic Jeremy Kyle show ever. My eyes and face were red, as were Meg's, there was no hiding the fact that we'd been for one heck of a ride.

Another couple was sitting in the waiting area. Martin's next victims, no doubt. They were young, very young, surely not of an age where they should need marriage counselling. There can't have been much time for anything to go wrong in their relationship.

'We went in there laughing our heads off,' I said to the bloke. 'You might want to ask for your money back before it's too late.'

He gave me an uncomfortable smile and took his companion's hand. He probably wondered what he'd let himself in for.

Meg and I headed for the toilets and made ourselves respectable once again. I felt drained and washed out. There was no way I was returning to work, I'd call Diane and tell her I'd need some time.

Meg couldn't have dropped a bigger bomb on me if she'd tried. But, that said, it wasn't entirely unexpected. I'd thought about it myself more than once since the IVF hell had begun. Was it unfaithful if it only happened in the mind? Probably not, but I knew exactly why Meg had done it. I hated that she had, but what did I expect? If it hadn't been her, it would have been me.

'Did you use protection?' I asked when she finally emerged from the ladies' toilets. She looked calmer, the redness had gone.

'There's no chance I'm going to end up as a dad to some other guy's kid am I?'

She looked taken aback as if she hadn't been prepared for that question.

'There's ... there's no chance of that, Pete ... no chance. There's no way it's going to interfere with the IVF. I want your child, Pete, nobody else's.'

I believed her completely. I wanted to scream at her, beat the shit out of the guy she'd slept with and smash up everything in the reception area of the marriage guidance building. But, more than anything, I knew that I wanted my wife back. It made me resolve to hang on in there, to try a little harder. Maybe Daniel had just got his revenge on me for sleeping with Meg while they were still together. Perhaps it was karma.

I tormented myself with images of Meg rolling in the sheets with some guy. What had he done with her? Had she taken him in her mouth? Had he kissed her gorgeous breasts and fingered her caressingly as she loved me to do? Some bastard had violated our territory, Meg had let him. But we'd both had sexual partners before, there was no sense torturing myself with who did what to whom. Meg had once done something very dirty with one of her exes, she'd let it slip once when we were talking filthy, but it was just something that I didn't fancy, it didn't turn me on. Relationships are sacred, they are what they are, they're different with everyone. It does nobody any good to hear what their wife got up to with some boyfriend from years back. I'd never told Meg what I'd done with Janet Fitch at university. God, that girl had some imagination. There were parts of my romantic life that I'd never even mentioned. You've lived a lot already when you meet somebody later in life, you're not always going to mention everything. Some things need to stay private. If I pushed Meg for the details, I'd turn into a bitter, twisted, broken wreck. I saw that with some clarity, in spite of my burning anger.

I was jealous of him too. Jealous that he'd somehow brought pleasure to my wife in a way that I was presently unable to. All I wanted was my hot, sexy, happy wife back again. I knew I'd have to work harder at it. What had happened was really crappy.

The IVF sex was even more problematic after that. I'd had difficulty getting hard, I kept thinking about what she'd done. Was Meg comparing me with him? Did I disappoint her? Was I giving her what she craved?

We both had separate follow-up sessions with Martin. Meg went first, she felt it was doing some good. She was relieved to have her secret out in the open. She hated herself, would never forgive herself, it was meaningless she assured me.

That word 'meaningless' again. When I thought of another man taking my wife in bed, it made me wild with resentment.

I didn't even fancy him, Pete. He caught me when I was weak. It was the closeness I wanted at first, someone to talk to. About you ... about us. I've said I'm sorry. You know I want us to work things out. Start a family.'

I did know that. She might not have fancied him, but she still slept with him. Martin had urged me not to push any further, I knew he was right, but every now and then I felt as if I wanted to know everything: what they did together, how long it lasted, if he did anything that I didn't do. It would eat me up if I didn't get a handle on it, I saw that.

Much as I'm reluctant to acknowledge it, my one-to-one with Martin did me a world of good. He let me get angry, I swore a lot and cursed whoever it was that Meg had slept with. Martin let me get on with it. I think I was saying all the things that I wanted to say to Meg, but I knew that it would destroy us if I did. I cried in Martin's office for the second time. Perhaps that was why I hated him so much. He made me vulnerable where my own wife was concerned. He made me admit how much I loved her.

'You know, Peter, Meg feels exactly the same about you. You really shouldn't let this slip through your fingers. If you can possibly forgive Meg, or at least move past it, you have the chance to save your relationship. Meg wants it. You want it. You've both told me individually in this room that's what you want. Now tell it to each other and make it happen.'

He was right. That highly groomed, stupidly bearded, unmarried marriage guidance counsellor was, unfortunately, completely correct. We had to move past it, we had to fight for our marriage.

I'd never loved anyone as much as Meg, I couldn't imagine ever finding someone that I loved as much as her. We were meant to be together, she knew it, I knew it. Even Martin knew it. We would have to fight even harder to save our relationship. I would keep working at the IVF, attend the counselling sessions, work with Meg to put her cheating behind us.

It wasn't an affair, there was no relationship, it was no worse than a one-night stand, a mistake, one born out of sadness, loneliness and frustration. It was more about us than it was the sex. However hard it was, I got that.

It was only when I stepped out of Martin's consulting room feeling much brighter and more positive than I had for many weeks that Steven Terry's warning came back to me.

You're going to hurt each other, he'd said. Well, Meg had already completed her part of the prediction. There was just me to follow. But I couldn't imagine anything else coming true, it was pure coincidence. Steven Terry must have been talking nonsense when he'd warned me that we would deeply wound each other.

I would never have hurt Meg. Never.

CHAPTER SIX

It was wet and cold in the car park. There must have been over a hundred people out there who'd been evacuated from the OverNight Inn. There was a hubbub of chatter as the guests and a handful of staff from the twilight shift made their way to the registration area.

It appeared that a senior manager had been summoned to take charge, so Derek and Jenny were lurking with the rest of us, waiting for the fire service to arrive.

I made my way towards Jenny, she was clearly visible because of her blue uniform.

'Is that the boss?' I asked.

'Yes, he's Bob Hays, he's the manager. He gets a call automatically if there's a problem at night. Poor bloke, it's the second time this week,'

'So why are we all standing out here in the cold?'

'It was a ground floor alarm going off – your floor actually – we don't know why yet. It's not fire, I'm sure of that. Derek doesn't think it's a fire either. It's so wet out here – I hope they get it sorted out quickly.'

'How long do you reckon it will take until we're back inside?'

'About half an hour usually, they have to go through the building, make sure it's clear.'

'Plenty of time to get *Little Dorrit* read then?' I suggested.

'With any luck it's what they used to start the fire!'

Jenny was fun. Away from the corporate nonsense and scripted welcomes hid a mischievous personality. I liked her.

Bob was calling for her to come over. I could see that he was not a particularly pleasant boss by the way he abruptly summoned her. She looked at me to indicate that she needed to go.

'Good luck with the boss,' I offered, 'he doesn't look like a happy bloke!'

She shook her head and made her way over to Bob.

With Jenny now in conversation with a concerned looking Bob, I moved through the crowd, seeking out familiar faces. Most people had their heads buried in phones, and I decided to join them. Mine was on full charge, it had been plugged in for several hours.

A couple of nights during the course of a month, I'd be on call. It went with the job. It was a bit of a pain, but most nights any calls were from bewildered listeners who'd lost their dog or who had a village fete that they wanted to get advertised on air. At two o' clock in the morning.

I wasn't on call that weekend, so it had given me the chance to be slacker with my phone checking. The screen illuminated and I checked my text messages. Jem really had been trying hard to get hold of me. There were almost ten messages there. I deleted them without reading, they were all sent before his call got through to me in the bar, there would be nothing new.

Once Jem's messages had gone, it left just two more. One from Meg, one from my mum. The message from my mum was one of her regular misfires. She was really making an effort to get to grips with the technology. I'd bought her a super simple phone with extra large buttons. All you could do on it was to phone or text. That was it – big buttons and very limited functionality. Mum had obviously been feeling adventurous that night. She'd texted me my own phone number. She must have got mixed up with dialling and texting. I resolved to go through it with her again next time I saw her. For my own sanity rather than hers.

The final text was from Meg. It had been sent late on Friday evening, several hours after I'd left for Newcastle.

Live your! Got a specially surprised for your northeast. Seems you're laterally! xxx

When it came to mobile phones, Meg shared a talent with my mum. It was like putting a dangerous weapon in the hands of a toddler. She couldn't get the hang of changing the suggested words in the predictive text on her phone. Every message from her was like a scene from The Imitation Game, I felt like Alan Turing trying to figure out what she was trying to say.

'*Live your!*' was easy, I'd seen that many times before. It was 'Love you!' Good news, it was a conciliatory text. I thought back to what I'd been doing a couple of hours earlier with Ellie. For the first time since cheating, I sensed the weight of the secret I was going to have to carry. Was I cut out for such deception? Meg had just said that she loved me, and I already felt like a despicable love rat.

I looked at the other words. What on earth was she trying to say? Got a special surprise? That looked likely. But what was the northeast bit? I'd have to key in the message as if I was about to send it myself and look at the matching words which came up, I was completely thrown by the northeast bit. I was in the northeast, in Newcastle. What was Meg trying to say?

I sensed someone moving towards me. It was Ellie. I put my phone in my pocket, I'd decipher Meg's message later. It seemed to be friendly, at least.

'Cold out here, isn't it?' she said, breaking the ice.

There was no need for things to be awkward. We were both adults, we'd both had sex before. Nobody knew we'd been together. As far as any of my colleagues were aware, we were just chatting after meeting in the bar earlier that night.

'It's not the quiet night in I'd expected. Do you think they have to pay out under their guarantee when something like this happens?'

'They'll lose a fortune if they do,' Ellie replied, then looked up as the flashing lights from a fire engine drew everybody's attention.

There was a ripple of 'At last!' comments, like a verbal Mexican wave. It was cold and wet out in the car park.

'Any news from your bloke?' I asked.

'Don't talk to me about Dave! I've had three missed calls and fourteen text messages from him. All ranting about what a slut I am. I mean, I guess I have been a bit of a slut, but only tonight. I'm not usually like that.'

She'd lowered her voice for the last two sentences, making sure nobody could hear. I was feeling bad about Meg's text, how she'd reached out while I was making plans to betray her. I didn't feel like playing the flirtation game with Ellie.

'Is this Dave guy likely to cause you any problems or is he just getting it out of his system?'

'Difficult to say,' said Ellie, watching the firefighters as they prepared to enter the building. They were liaising with Bob.

'He can be a real weirdo sometimes, he's so suspicious and jealous ...'

Ellie paused. She looked as if she'd just seen Fred West, Norman Bates and Sweeney Todd walking towards her.'

'Oh no, surely not here ...'

Her eyes searched desperately in the distance, she was trying to make out something – or somebody.

'What is it, Ellie? What's up?'

She'd changed completely from the playful woman of moments before. She was deadly serious. She was scared.

'Shit! Shit, shit, shit, shit!'

'Ellie, what's up? Tell me.'

She continued scanning the crowd, she was hunting for a face. We had only the light from the street lamps to work with, the flashes of the fire engine made things even harder to make out. She calmed down, visibly relaxing.

'It can't have been him, surely not here in Newcastle. There's no way he could know I was here.'

'Ellie, what's going on? What are you talking about?'

'It's not him I'm sure. They warned him off. He can't possibly be here.'

I could see that she was really rattled. She'd completely changed from the woman I'd met earlier.

'Who is it, Ellie? Is it Dave? Has he come down here?'

'No, it's not Dave,' she picked up, at last averting her eyes from the crowd of people and looking directly at me.

'It's not Dave. I thought it was a guy called Tony Miller.

I was sure I saw him in the crowd, but it can't be him. He was with a woman – it must be a hotel guest – there's no reason for him to be here.'

'Who is Tony Miller?' I asked, desperate to know what had shaken her.

'It's one of the perks of being on TV, Pete. It attracts the weirdos. Tony Miller is my stalker. He's not supposed to come anywhere near me. I haven't seen him for months now. But it messes you up having a stalker, Pete. I thought I saw him. For a moment I was certain he was in the crowd.'

Things were tough for a few days after I'd learnt about Meg's infidelity. They continued to be difficult, of course, but the rage inside me soon began to die down a little. The bottom line was that I knew exactly why she'd done it, it was the same reason that I was feeling so lost at that time. It didn't make it any easier to deal with, but it didn't feel like an act of spite. In some bizarre way, it had come out of a misguided attempt to put things right.

I tried to move on, not to dwell on things. My chat with Martin had been useful, more helpful than I would ever admit. That whole ugly episode had made me realise how much I wanted to fight for our marriage. I wanted it to work.

In spite of me stepping up to this latest relationship challenge, things immediately took a downturn in the bedroom. We had an IVF schedule to observe after all. But when it came to it, I couldn't get turned on. I just thought about what Meg had done and how that man – whoever he was – had made love to my wife. The very thought of it made everything sink, not just my heart. The increasing irony of having a doctor named Dick struck me once again. Only this time, I didn't find it funny.

So now in our next session with Martin he would get to hear about my erectile dysfunction. It was only a new thing, hopefully temporary, but it was yet another block to making things right with Meg. It was a lost opportunity, another night on which there was no chance of her conceiving.

How long would it take until things got back to normal? I thought about Meg's fling, who would have had no problems in the bedroom department. Would she go back to him? Did she fancy him? This infidelity was burning me up, I needed to move beyond it. If I didn't, the marriage would struggle even more. We'd drift even further apart.

When Meg announced that she was going out with a friend, my immediate reaction was to ask her 'Which friend?' I held back, I knew it wouldn't be helpful. I'd heard Meg in the counselling sessions, I really believed that she wanted our relationship to work, as I did. I had to trust her and move on. Besides, I wanted a bit of time to place a private online order.

Meg anticipated my concern and attempted to put my mind at ease.

'It's not him, Pete. Don't worry, it's over. It won't happen again. It was a mistake, I know it was. I can't ever put it right, but please trust me, I want this to work.'

I kissed her, she hugged me back, it felt okay. When Meg had left the house, I was straight onto my computer. I opened up the incognito link and started browsing. Bingo! You could buy erection pills online without having to see a doctor. Self-certification, I love the internet. It was a reputable site too, no dodgy stuff from a backstreet store. I'd seen the posters in the toilets in motorway service stations, but I hadn't needed it then. I needed a quick fix, I didn't

want it to be something that I had to share with Doctor Dick
or Martin. I ordered two packets of four for starters, I hoped
the problem would pass soon enough, but it would be useful
to have the cavalry on hand just in case.

I thought nothing more of that night until a casual
conversation in the office with Jem a couple of weeks later.
I'd received my small parcel of pills by that stage, taken a
few and then discovered to my joy that they were no longer
required. However, they were quite useful in terms of my
ability to make sure that Meg was left fully satisfied, so I
ordered a couple more packets for recreational purposes. I
thought they might come in handy, they were quite a nice
little extra in the bedroom.

Jem and I were chatting over some staff issue in the
kitchen. His mood was quite low. I can't really remember
how it came up, but my antennae were immediately alert.

'I saw Meg out in the town centre the other night, I
don't think she saw me though ...'

'Oh yes, who was she with, a man or woman?' I asked,
trying to conceal my immediate alarm.

'The guy from the counselling place. I'm sure it was
Meg, it looked like her. The guy has one of those stupid
beards, looks a bit of a twit to be honest with you. Martin
something, I forget his surname.'

Martin Travis. The bastard! She'd been seeing Martin
outside of our sessions. And she hadn't thought that it was
important to tell me.

'When was this, Jem? I'm just trying to work out who it
was,' I probed, my mind now racing.

'Last Wednesday maybe, it was in town, they were
eating Thai.'

I hate Thai food. Meg had been out on Tuesday. Eating
Thai food with Martin.

'You're not mistaking it for Tuesday are you? She was definitely out that night.'

'Now you mention it, yes, it was Tuesday. I was eating alone, couldn't face cooking in my bedsit.'

He seemed to want to know as much about the meeting as I did.

'If he had a silly beard, it'll be one of her colleagues from work.'

I lied. I didn't want to tell him about that bastard Martin. I'd confront Meg with it later.

'Thought I recognised him from somewhere, didn't get a proper look. Seemed like a complete prat!' Jem replied, then resumed our conversation about the staff member. I concurred with his assessment of Martin though.

I was a bit wary of challenging Meg when we were sitting on the sofa watching TV that night. I'd popped one of my pills hoping that I might get lucky and tempt Meg into some recreational sex for non-IVF purposes. She made it quite clear that she was having none of it.

I was as much put out by the wasted expense of the pill as I was by the prospect of another dull evening. I decided that if sex was off the cards, I might as well ask her about Martin.

'Where did you go out for food last week, was it that new Italian place? I can't remember you saying.'

'What? Yes, we went there, it was nice. A bit pricey, though!'

A lie. I'd caught her in a lie already.

'Only Jem said he'd seen you. He must have been mistaken, he thought you were in the Thai restaurant further along the High Street.'

I was watching her now, waiting for her to give it away.

She flinched when I mentioned Jem. Her answer was abrupt.

'He must be mistaken!'

She'd meant that to be the end of it. With sex off the cards, I was happy to push a bit further.

'He seemed certain that you were with a younger guy with a sculpted beard. Somebody from work?'

'Look, damn Jem and damn you, Pete! I was out with Martin, alright? We're not shagging, it's not Martin who I slept with, okay? I won't ever sleep with Martin, he's just a mate. I like him and he's helping me.'

He wanted to shag Meg though, that twinkle in his eye had made that perfectly clear to me.

'What about his code of ethics?' I asked. 'Is the little shit even allowed to do that?'

'I had to talk him around to doing it. He was really ethical about the whole thing, it was me who wanted to go out, not him!'

I'll bet he had an ethical struggle. Should I shag my client's wife or not? I bet he anticipated a lot of moral tussling with that little dilemma.

'What were you talking about?'

'You know, just things. Us. How we met, stuff like that.'

'Please tell me you didn't mention my erection problems? Not over Thai food!'

'No, of course I didn't, Pete. Anyway, that's over now, things are fine.'

'Why didn't you tell me about it, Meg? I've only just found out that you slept with some other guy, now you're sneaking off for meetings with Martin. I don't care what bollocks he spun about ethics, if his boss found out he'd met with you outside of formal sessions he'd be signing on at the

Job Centre. Or Super Job Centre Plus, whatever it's called these days!'

'I know, I know, I'm sorry, Pete. It's just that speaking to Martin makes me feel like it's going to be alright between us. I don't want this relationship to end, I want us to make it right. Martin helps me to feel like we have a future.'

'That's because he's trying to charm you out of your knickers! Can't you see it?'

'You said yourself that you'd underestimated him when you had your one-to-one with him. After my ... after I admitted having sex with ... that guy.'

She'd nearly said it. It was on the tip of her tongue. I didn't push further, the conversation that we were having was already delicate enough.

'You need to start telling me this stuff, I shouldn't be finding it out from Jem. I don't like you seeing Martin outside of our sessions, but it would at least help if you told me. We need to start building up trust here, Meggy. If we can't trust each other we're not going to make it.'

She looked sheepish, she'd been rumbled, she knew she was wrong. She put out her hand, touched my arm. I put my free hand to her cheek, moved towards her and kissed her, gently at first, then harder, more passionately. She reciprocated, moving her hand from my arm to my chest. She'd succeeded in defusing the situation, she'd distracted me from what had happened. And, in spite of my initial forecast, we both got some use out of my pill that night.

The fire alarm was a big pain for everybody. It took over half an hour to get back inside after the fire service had swept the building. There was a further delay when a couple of police officers arrived. They were deep in conversation with Bob for some time before we all got to move on back to our rooms.

I had been jolted by what Ellie had said.

'A stalker, you're kidding me aren't you?'

'Unfortunately not. I often get comments in the street, some of them a bit lewd, but it goes with the territory. Most of the nutters are harmless, just sad and lonely. They think you're their friend because you're on the TV.'

She paused, watching what was going on by the fire engine. There must have been thirty or so journalists in that crowd, every one of them trained to sniff out a story. All of us were watching the action intently, unable to detach from the fact that this wasn't our story to report on. Those instincts are hard to resist at times.

'This guy was a real nutter,' Ellie continued. She looked a little ashamed. 'If I'm honest, it's why I didn't ditch Dave sooner. He's a different kind of weirdo, but at least he's on my side. He frightened off Tony Miller on more than one occasion. I thought he was going to kill him once. I felt safe around Dave, even though I don't like him that much.'

Poor old Ellie, caught between a rock and a hard place. What a fix to be in. Even radio presenters have problems with the public sometimes. I knew one guy who had to shake off a woman in department stores because she would tail him from work when he left the office. I'd dealt with that one as his line manager, it had been deeply unsettling for him. The woman ended up in a psychiatric unit, the problem took care of itself. But Ellie was right, it was an occupational hazard.

'How frightening is this guy?' I asked, not entirely certain that I wanted to know.

'He broke into my flat several times. I found him naked

in my bed once. He thought we were married. Bloody hell, Pete, what a nutter!'

'What did you do? How did you get rid of him?'

'What, apart from Dave threatening to cut off his cock with a carving knife? Not quite Three Blind Mice is it? The police dealt with it. Well, that's the official version. My brothers sorted it in the end.'

I didn't like the sound of that. I sensed a vigilante story coming on.

'We got a restraining order, but it did bugger all. Dave is mental, but he'd never carry it through, he's all hot air. My brothers paid him a visit. I don't know what they did, but they must have put the fear of God up him. They wouldn't tell me how they scared him off. I haven't always been this posh you know, Pete. I come from a working-class estate in London. I'm the odd one out in my family. My brothers live in a different world from me. And they always take care of their sister.'

'I can't blame you,' I said. I'd seen enough shitbags beat the justice system in my career as a radio reporter. If it had been Meg that was being stalked, I'd have done the same. It's alright the police doing things by the book. Sometimes you have to scare people shitless, it's the only thing that works.

'Did it do the job?' I asked, eager to hear Ellie's story, my journalistic impulses getting the better of me.

'I haven't seen him in several months. It doesn't stop though, I'm always looking, expecting to see him lurking. I can't have seen him here, we're miles from home. He couldn't possibly know that I'm in Newcastle. I'm sorry, Pete. These little bastards get under your skin, it'll be a while until I get used to him being off the scene.'

We were in shadow in the car park, surrounded by other people who were all having their own conversations. I took a risk and squeezed Ellie's hand. It was the gesture of a friend, I wanted to reassure her. I liked Ellie a lot, we'd just slept together. And now she'd told me this. She was shaken, I wanted to help.

'Thanks, Pete, you're a good guy, I appreciate it.'

She smiled at me, I smiled back. Although what had happened between us in my room had only been a casual fling, there was a connection there. Maybe it hadn't been completely meaningless.

Ellie made her way back to her own room once we were given the go-ahead to return to the building. Some of her colleagues had started to chat to her as the crowd of guests began to move in a herd towards the main entrance. I dropped back, not wanting to alert anybody to what had happened between us.

I got caught up in the middle of the crowd as we filed slowly through the doors – it was difficult to escape the funnel effect. I wanted to break free, though. I'd seen something else that night which upset me.

Jenny was on her own, lurking away from the light of a street lamp, using the shadows for cover. She was crying, I could see her shoulders shaking. I wanted to go and see her, to make sure she was alright. She was such a bright young thing, it seemed impossible to imagine what might have brought her to tears like that.

Bob strode over to her, he was shaking his finger at her, clearly angry. Poor Jenny, what was going on? I wanted to go over there and defend her, but I couldn't escape the movement of the crowd, everybody was desperate to get back to bed. I looked over towards Jenny again, she was being comforted by Derek. Good old Derek, thank you, thanks for taking care of Jenny.

I squeezed through the door and made directly for room 123 along that long corridor. The fire door next to my room had been closed, it was as if nothing had happened. There was the smell of sex when I walked back into my room – of sweat and semen. I decided to open the window slightly, it was a bit of a giveaway.

My head touched the pillow, and I was out cold immediately. What a night! It wasn't even 3.00am on my fortieth birthday and there had already been more than enough action for one day.

But things were only just getting started.

CHAPTER SEVEN

There were some tired people when we started gathering in the conference room at 9:30am the next day. I skipped breakfast, I'd almost overslept. I hadn't set the alarm on my phone the night before, I'd been distracted, so I made the meeting by the skin of my teeth.

Ellie and I didn't sit together. We were in a room of investigative reporters, we weren't stupid. She smiled at me, said good morning and was warm and genial. We weren't blanking each other, I was pleased about that.

I must confess to surreptitiously looking at her during the meeting. She was gorgeous. I'm not sure I'd fully appreciated that in the heat of the previous night's passionate exchanges. I'd slept with that woman. If I hadn't been so ashamed of what I'd done to Meg, I could have enjoyed it all a little more.

But Meg had cheated on me. We were even. It wasn't revenge, that's not why I did it. Thinking it over, as Diane droned on about social media, listening figures and declining audiences, I had to admit that I felt better. Meg and I had levelled up. I could move on.

She'd cheated on me, I'd cheated on her.

She should have kept her mouth shut about her infidelity. It only hurt me because I knew about it. If she'd kept quiet, lived with the secret, learnt her lesson and moved on, I'd have been none the wiser.

If you're going to cheat, keep it to yourself. I would never, ever, ever tell Meg. It would change everything if she knew.

The teamwork activities were much as you'd expect, pointless and dry – and full of corporate speak. Expecting us to do more with less, and with the threat of redundancies and further cuts always in the background. Modern working life, in a nutshell.

I couldn't be blamed for being more interested in Ellie, running my eyes up and down her legs, filling in the missing pieces from my memories of the night before. I was jolted back into reality when violent shouting erupted in the corridor outside. Ellie looked horrified, she'd immediately recognised the voice.

'Where is the stupid whore? I don't give a shit what she's doing, I want to see her now!'

Ellie stood up.

'Excuse me, everybody,' she said, looking uncomfortable and annoyed.

She exited the room.

'Will she be alright out there?' someone asked.

'It's just her bloke,' another replied. 'He's crazy, he does this all the time. I don't know why she doesn't ditch the stupid idiot.'

For a moment, self-preservation made me wonder if I'd been foolish to get involved with Ellie. First a stalker, now this, some crazy boyfriend who was convinced she was sleeping with everybody. Maybe he was right. Did Ellie do what she'd done with me all the time? I didn't think so. It was only instinct, but it really didn't feel like she was that kind of woman. Besides, that would have made me that kind of man. I didn't make a habit of sleeping with people within hours of meeting them and I was certain that Ellie didn't either.

It was getting a bit heated in the corridor. Dave was sounding off and Ellie was trying to calm him. She was at work, these were her colleagues. What a prat. Broadcasters aren't the most aggressive human beings in the food chain, the main repository of testosterone is usually among the sports team. Unfortunately, although they were represented at a more senior level, we didn't have any of the younger guys available to get involved. When we heard Ellie getting upset, some of her work colleagues nearer the door got up to assist her. I felt honour-bound to at least show willing, I hadn't seen Dave at that stage, for all I knew he was massive.

I wasn't far off. He must have worked on building sites or doing some form of manual labour, he was way too fit to be an office dweller. That physique hadn't been created in a gym either, it was the result of hard, physical graft.

I should've been grateful that she'd even looked at me, let alone slept with me. I didn't fancy my chances with Dave, he looked strong and violent. I doubted if Ellie had told me the whole truth about him. It seemed to me that he knew how to handle himself. If I were Ellie's stalker, just one look at Dave would have warned me off.

Ellie's colleagues were trying to calm him down, encouraging him to walk away. Ellie was crying. I hate to see people cry. There's nothing more distressing than to see a genuinely upset person. That's how Jenny had looked to me the night before, after her mauling from Bob Hays. It's how Ellie looked now. This weekend was supposed to be an excuse to get away from home, but I was getting more drama here than I ever got from Meg.

'I know you're sleeping with one of these telly tarts!' Dave was shouting. 'Which one is it, slut? Which one are you shagging?'

'Dave, just leave, please, it's over!' Ellie was pleading with him. Dave was too angry, too wound up to pipe down. A male and a female police officer appeared from nowhere. I hadn't been aware of anybody calling them, they must have got there quickly. They knew exactly how to deal with Dave; he was quietened and subdued within a few minutes. A big bully boy who knew when he was out of his league. It was the WPC who got him under control too, no nonsense, she must have dealt with fools like Dave a hundred times before.

'You alright, luv?' the PC said to Ellie. She nodded, wiping the tears from her eyes.

'Lovers tiff?' he asked.

Ellie nodded.

'I'm sorry, he's a jerk. I never thought he'd come down here sounding off ...'

'It's alright, Ells,' one of her colleagues reassured her. 'He's a tosser, you're better off without him.'

'You okay, Ellie?' I asked, keeping away from the main huddle but anxious to express my concern.

'Yeah, thanks, Pete, thanks everybody, I'm fine. I'm sorry, I'm really sorry about Dave. I didn't think he'd do that.'

Two of Ellie's female colleagues took her over to the bar area for a coffee, the rest of us went back into the conference room to continue with the presentations. Our hearts weren't in it after that, we were going through the motions.

While Diane droned on through her second slide show of the day, one that I'd already seen in management meetings, I discreetly brought my phone out under the table. I wanted to figure out what Meg had been trying to say. There were no new messages from her. There was just one message from Alex, my TV friend. I'd look at it later, probably some daft joke or image, I wasn't in the mood for it.

My eyes darted from my phone to Diane. It wouldn't do for her to spot a member of the management team scanning their phone through her keynote presentation.

Live your! Got a specially surprised for your northeast. Seems you're laterally! xxx

I kept inputting my guesses into a new message, taking a look at the predictive options that were offered to me. We were on our afternoon tea break by the time I finally figured it out.

Love you! Got a special surprise for your birthday. See you later! xxx

What had Meg meant by that – see you later? She'd sent that message the previous night, Friday night, several hours after I'd left home for Newcastle. What was she saying?

I was distracted. Jem had just walked into the bar area where we were all helping ourselves to refreshments. He looked flustered, seeking out Diane straight away, obviously making his apologies to her. He did his duty, acknowledged some of the other people that he knew, then made his way directly to me.

'What happened to your neck?' I asked. He had a deep scratch running from under his right ear down to the collar of his shirt. 'Fall out with Sally again?'

'Something like that,' he replied, clearly not wanting to dwell on it. Then he thought better of it, everybody was going to ask him. 'I caught myself with a broken nail, looks like someone tried to murder me!'

He laughed. It was forced though. I thought that a fight with Sally was the more likely explanation. I decided to change the subject.

'Are you going to grace us with your presence now?'

'Yeah, sure, I'm here until Sunday afternoon. Sorry about the delay. Personal business – you know how it is at the moment. What were the cops doing in the lobby when I checked in? Something's going on out there.'

'We had a bit of a commotion with somebody's boyfriend kicking off, a couple of coppers came in to sort it out.'

'It's more than that. Looks like they've had a break-in or something. Too many out there to be anything else. Something's up. I couldn't get it out of them. I tried!'

'I don't know, I assumed they were here for Dave ... the guy who was kicking up all the fuss.'

People were beginning to make their way back to the conference room. I finished off making my tea and nodded to Jem.

'We're in this room, I'm over on the far side.'

As Jem started to move away, I caught sight of Jenny entering the bar area. She was looking for somebody. It was late afternoon, I assumed she'd just clocked on for her shift.

She continued to scan the bar area, then saw me as the crowd of people filtered into the conference room. She held her hand up to get my attention and walked over to me. She looked concerned.

'What's going on with the police out there?' I asked.

'I don't know. Something to do with the fire last night. Bob won't tell me. He's fed up that he has to be here on a

Saturday. I hope they get finished soon, it's going to be a long shift if he's here all night!'

'I'm so sorry, I completely forgot to tell you this last night,' she resumed. 'It was the fire alarm – and Bob – it completely slipped my mind. There was a woman here, it was really late, she said she was looking for you. She had a surprise for you or something. Said it was your birthday. Did she find you? I sent her down to your room. I shouldn't have really, but she seemed so nice. Only, I didn't see her again after the fire alarm. I got a dressing down from Bob because she wasn't on the fire register. I had to tell him about her, I couldn't just keep quiet about it.'

She must have seen my face drop. Now Meg's text message made perfect sense. She must have travelled down to the hotel to surprise me so that we could be together when I woke up for my birthday. She'd arrived, she'd spoken to Jenny and asked for me by name. Jenny had directed her to my room. We'd been in the same hotel at the same time.

So why hadn't she found me? Why hadn't she sent me any more text messages? Where had she gone? And what had she seen or heard if she'd been in the hotel the night before? Possibly at the same time that I'd been sleeping with Ellie.

Alex Kennedy was an old flame of mine. In fact, she was the closest anybody ever got to becoming Mrs Bailey before Meg swept away all my reservations about getting married.

Alex and I were old friends from university. Actually, it was a polytechnic when we went there, but nobody knows what you mean by that nowadays. It was the last year that it was a polytechnic, we were the last generation. It feels as if everything is a university now, even kindergartens will be giving out degrees before you know it.

Alex and I met on the first day of our course. We were going to be radio and TV journalism students. We'd done our degrees, I'd figured out that my English BA had no currency whatsoever in the world of job seeking and Alex had done the same with her ethics and philosophy degree. We were both there to avoid becoming teachers.

I fancied Alex from the minute I met her, but it took us a while to get it together. I'm not so sure that she felt the same about me. I like to think I've matured with age, I was a bit of a twit back then. Nevertheless, as friends, we hit it off straight away. Alex was tall, slim, funny and good looking. She could drink like a fish. She was an excellent journalist: sharp, incisive, observant and tenacious. We enjoyed working together in our student newsroom and loved social-ising together. The romance came later, it was slow to build.

We cut our teeth together as students, learning the ins and outs of libel law, public administration and reporting skills. We even helped each other get through the short-hand exams, though we both knew that we'd probably never use it again the minute we left the polytechnic. In fact, we colluded. We cheated. Neither of us was bad at shorthand, but you needed something like a 97 percent accuracy rate to pass. I'd only achieved 96 percent in my primary school cycling proficiency test, and that had been a once-in-a-lifetime result for me – and the school. Alex and I agreed to let each other copy during the test, it wasn't particularly strict exam conditions. We weren't so much cheating as checking. We both passed the exam – Alex got 99 percent and I got 97, achieving those scores by looking at each other's work. We were partners in crime. We were the Bonnie and Clyde of the shorthand world. We shared a dark secret about our journalistic careers.

It was only when we'd completed our coursework, and our postgraduate diplomas were in the bag, that Alex and I realised that we were about to be parted. We'd gone a whole nine months of the course without any romance, then it suddenly dawned on us that we weren't going to see each other anymore. And we were pissed off at the idea.

The truth about our feelings for each other came out when we were on our final night out with our fellow trainee journalists. We were all seated at a long table in one of those upstairs rooms in a restaurant where they shove the loud and boisterous groups. There must have been twenty-five of us, it was noisy, raucous and fun.

The chatter and laughter suddenly subsided as our ears picked up voices that were hostile, in conflict. It was Rosie and Mike, one of the many couples that had formed within our group. We'd all thought they were inseparable. We were wrong. Mike had slept with a male friend, and Rosie had just found out. As we all tuned into what was going on, I caught the tail end of a sentence which ended '... it matters to me where you stick your dick!'

Mike stormed out and there was an uncomfortable silence around the table. A couple of Rosie's female friends came to the rescue; they started to comfort her, and cautiously at first, the conversations around the table began to resume.

'You know, I didn't get together with you, because that's how I thought we'd end up,' Alex said, completely left of field.

'What, sticking my dick up some guy's butt, even though I'm strictly hetero?'

'No, nitwit. I figured that if you and I ever got together,

we'd end up having to go our separate ways at the end of the year anyway. I didn't want to mess up our friendship with that.'

Shit. I hadn't expected that one. I'd been in the middle of a story about my nan being rescued from her block of high-rise flats when Rosie and Mike had so rudely interrupted my flow. She'd been removed from her third floor flat via a turntable ladder. That would have been totally unexciting if she hadn't had to be given a fireman's lift to get her out of the flat. Only my nan never wore any knickers and the poor old firefighter had got the shock of his life when he placed his hand on her arse to make sure she was secure. It always got a laugh that story, and Rosie and Mike had messed up the punchline.

Was Alex telling me she wanted a relationship with me? Or was she telling me that she didn't want a relationship with me? I didn't know, it had taken me completely off my guard. She was being brave, she pushed at the door once again. Only there was an imbecile standing in front of it so it wouldn't open properly.

'You must feel it too, Pete. We're more than friends. I've always felt that we were meant to be together. We're much more than just mates, but I don't want to mess it all up.'

I looked at her. I could hear the chatter around us, but I felt as if I was in a cocoon, all I could focus on was our conversation.

'Wow! I hadn't expected that. I don't know what to say ...'

She was right. I'd never have dared to think it. I'd never made a move because I'd have been devastated to rock the boat and lose the friendship. I didn't know she felt like that. I certainly felt that way about her, but she'd been consigned to the this-will-never-happen-even-though-I-love-this-

person-deeply-and-I-value-the-friendship-above-
all-else pile.

I've had a few amazing relationship moments in my life.
Magical moments when something wonderful happens that
shapes your future. Meeting Meg was one of those
moments. It was as if fate had suddenly intervened in my
life and announced 'You must meet this woman'.

It was the same with Alex all those years ago when we
were cub reporters, still uninitiated in the world of radio
journalism. It was a realisation, a sudden flowing of water
after being held back by a huge dam. I just got it, sitting next
to her in that restaurant. Of course we were meant to be
together, we *were* more than just friends, there was a strong
bond between us.

'Have I made a fool of myself?' Alex asked. 'Please tell
me I didn't read this completely wrong.'

'No, no, it's fine ... you're right,' I replied. 'I never
thought you felt that way.'

'This is the last time we're all going to be together. I
don't want this to end, Pete. I don't want us to end.'

I touched her hand, which she'd placed on her lap. I was
charged with excitement, I hadn't expected this. I'd thought
the evening would end with me throwing up into the toilet
of my student digs. We looked at each other, and we understood. She was right, we were in love and we hadn't even
realised it.

I'm not proud of my romantic back catalogue. Many
people have love stories which involve falling in love with
people across crowded rooms or meeting on holidays while
in glamorous locations abroad. I have no such tale to tell
with Meg. And my romance story about Alex is just as
dismal.

Reading each other's mind, we stood up and left the

room. A couple of people commented about it, I heard them but barely acknowledged it. Holding hands, we walked towards the corridor that led to the toilets. There was a spiral staircase winding its way up to a third floor. It was an overspill area, the lights were off, I hadn't seen anybody going up there all evening.

Making sure that nobody had seen us, we rushed up the narrow staircase and surveyed the top floor. A long table filled the middle of the room, a pile of folded tablecloths at one end. There was just enough light from the corridor below to see what we were doing.

Alex was wearing a short summer dress, her legs were bare. They were long, smooth and sexy. I'd seen that, of course, I'd registered how great she looked, but I'd always considered that there was an out-of-bounds sign on her. There was no sign, there never had been, it had all been in my imagination.

She sat on the edge of the table and I pulled down her underwear. It was purple, skimpy, lots of lace. It was damp, she was as eager as I was.

I unbuckled my belt, pushed down my trousers and boxers to my knees and entered her as she drew her legs up higher from her position on the table. The forbidden fruit was ours for the tasting. It was over in seconds.

We were together for just over five years. Five happy years. We didn't even end badly when our time was up. Media careers are challenging. Alex simply got a job offer that was too good to resist. She had to take it. I knew that, she knew that.

We fizzled out. There was still a lot of love there, but as Alex had so wisely predicted at that fateful meal, we were always going to go our separate ways. We were media luvvies, we loved our careers, TV had beckoned for Alex and she'd gone running to answer the call.

Alex had always been a bone of contention with Meg. I didn't blame her for that one. It was obvious that Alex and I were still very close. We were mates above everything else. With Meg, the relationship had been born from passion and lust. With Alex, it started with friendship. We liked each other and we couldn't get enough of each other's company.

It had caused friction in the early days of my relationship with Meg. Alex and I spoke all the time, and that only got worse as social media began to dominate our lives and we could be chatting wherever we were. But here's the stupid thing. I hadn't seen Alex in years. We hadn't met up. I don't think we trusted ourselves after Meg and I got together. I loved Meg deeply, crazily, passionately, but you don't just switch off what I had with Alex. It doesn't become meaningless. Particularly because it never really ended, it just stopped happening. There hadn't been a big row like Rosie and Mike. There was no cuckolding like Meg and I had done to Daniel. There was no hate there. It just couldn't happen there and then, we both had other things to do.

So, it wasn't unusual or out of the ordinary when I'd seen Alex's text on my phone during the afternoon meeting. It was unlikely to be anything important, just a bit of chitchat between friends. Former lovers.

But Alex's message contained the information that was about to rock my life. And it was to be the thing that brought us back together again, after so many years of not seeing each other. Ironically, we'd be trying to save the person whose arrival had precipitated that distance in the first place. We'd be trying to save Meg's life and salvage our marriage.

It seemed to take an age for that final session of the day to finish. My mind was racing, and after what Jenny had told me about Meg a new social media strategy for the radio station was the last thing I wanted to hear about.

If there had been an exam after that final presentation, I would have failed miserably. It would have been A-level general studies all over again, a complete washout. I spent that final two-hour session texting and emailing Meg. I needed to speak to her, but she wasn't picking up anything. I was becoming frantic.

What could I do? I needed to know what Meg had witnessed, if anything. I shuddered at what she might have seen or heard. What a dimwit I'd been! I'd messed up everything. I had to speak to Meg.

I placed my phone on silent, then rang the home phone number. I wouldn't be able to talk to Meg, but if she answered at least I'd know where she was. I watched the screen on my phone as it dialled out. The ringing indicator kept flashing at me, finally dismissing the call with a bright red 'No answer' message.

The minute the session was over, I would go to reception. I needed to be certain it was Meg – could Jenny have been mistaken? Perhaps it was a colleague from work. I thought through the brunettes in the office. There were two who'd come to Newcastle for the strategy meeting, Amy was younger than Meg, Helen a bit older. Either could pass for Meg via a general description. Brunette, thirty-something, average height.

Jenny had definitely referred to her as my wife, though. She must see hundreds of people over the course of a week, perhaps she'd got confused. I was clutching at straws, I knew that jumping in the car and surprising me on my birthday was exactly the sort of thing that the old Meg would have done.

The session ended. I didn't hang around for pleasantries afterwards, I made my way through the bar area and headed over to reception. Jenny was there. There were police officers in the area too.

'What's going on, Jenny?' I asked. 'This looks like it's more than a smoker setting off the fire alarms.'

'They're not telling me anything,' Jenny whispered. 'I know what it's to do with anyway. Bob was ranting at me last night, but it wasn't my fault.'

'What is it? I saw he'd upset you? What's going on?'

'Our night porter disappeared last night ...'

'Not Derek?' I asked, concerned now.

'No, there are three of us on duty overnight at the weekend. They always put an extra person on in case we get football fans in, it can get a bit boisterous if they do. He's called Jackson. When Derek did the roll call last night there was no sign of him.'

'Did he go home or something daft like that?'

'He's a bit flaky, he's studying at the college and doesn't really have much idea about how to behave at work. He might have decided to knock off early and go home when the fire alarm went off. I wouldn't put it past him.'

'So why are the police involved? Has he actually gone missing?'

'I'm not really sure, they seem very interested in your corridor. You might get asked some questions when you go back to your room. In fact, they've probably been in your room already. Bob knows what's going on, nobody is telling me any details yet.'

I thought back to the open door next to my own room.

Even Derek had mentioned it. Had Jenny's colleague been taking a crafty fag in there? That would make sense. If he was a young lad, he might have been tempted to take flight if he'd set off the fire alarms. These millennials, they have no grit. When I was that age I'd have covered up my tracks and made it look as if someone else had done it. No need to give the game away by doing a runner.

But why all the police officers? If he'd gone missing, I suppose they'd have to account for him. If he'd done a runner, gone to a friend's house or something like that, the authorities would be duty-bound to account for him, especially after a fire drill. It seemed to be a lot of fuss about nothing, a daft teenager who'd got caught out having a crafty fag.

I needed to ask Jenny about Meg. That was my main concern.

'Jenny, the woman who was looking for me last night, what did she look like?'

'She had brown hair, was in her thirties, attractive. She came very late, she looked tired. She said she'd had a long drive.'

'Did she give you a name? Did she say she was my wife?'

Jenny looked as if she'd had enough of questions. It didn't stop me though. I was certain it was Meg who'd been in the building. I had to know what she'd seen. Was it over for us? Had she seen me with Ellie? Even worse, had she heard me and Ellie at the door? I began to sweat, I could feel that my face was red.

'You alright mate?'

It was Jem, back from the conference rooms, heading back to his room. Ready for the evening drinking session, no doubt. There would be no repeat of the preceding night for me, I had to speak to Meg. I'd drive back home to find her if I had to, I needed to find out what was going on.

'Yes, just sorting out something to do with my room ... That's one big scratch on your neck – I hadn't noticed how bad it was.'

'Yes, what an oaf eh? Everybody's asking about it. It was just a random thing, it'll heal soon. It looks much worse than it is.'

'I'm going to finish off here, I'll catch you in the bar later.'

I wanted rid of Jem. I was desperate to continue my interrogation of Jenny, but new guests had arrived and I'd have to let her go through her full check-in routine.

Jem took the hint and moved on. While Jenny was preoccupied, I sat down in one of the comfy chairs in the lobby and checked my phone. The battery was dying again, God forbid I should expect it to last a full day without keeling over.

CHAPTER EIGHT

Alex Kennedy had had a meteoric rise in her media career. I'd always been more cautious, I was probably too down on my own broadcasting abilities really. But Alex was a natural, she had a lot in common with Ellie in that respect.

Both women were fabulous on screen. They looked relaxed on camera, people were comfortable in their company, they were intelligent – and this never hurt in TV land, they were attractive. They were both the kind of women that everybody would have agreed were sensuous. Even other women would have acknowledged that they were sexy. That's why they did so well on the telly.

Alex and I had always intended to stay in radio. That was our plan at the beginning. After that night in the restaurant, we'd committed to staying together in our hunt for radio jobs. I'd already got a reporter contract at a Manchester radio station, and we couldn't believe our luck when Alex got a similar job at another station in the same city.

It meant that we were able to move in together and, even though we were often like the proverbial passing ships in the night, what with breakfast shifts, day shifts, overnight production shifts and all the other flexible working patterns that journalism throws your way, it worked great.

We'd see each other at various news events, each sporting a microphone emblazoned with the branding of our respective radio stations. For us, a traffic incident was an opportunity for a quick catch-up. We'd get our eyewitness reports safely onto our recording devices, then have a quick chat about domestic issues.

Alex was singled out for attention very early. She moved from routine reporting duties to breakfast show presentation. That's the crown jewels in broadcasting terms. To the listener, there's very little difference between a breakfast show and a drive-time show, except that one is early in the day and the other is around teatime. But to broadcasters, breakfast is the top gig, it's where the biggest audiences are. Until they're killed off by live streaming in cars that is.

Alex was an instant hit on CityNewsFM. She was bright, funny and engaging. I was so proud of her. I was a hack, I loved the news stories and the reporting, but Alex was showbiz on legs, she was a complete natural.

She was offered a lot of money to work for the local constabulary as their chief press officer. She agonised for days over that one.

'I don't want to move out of broadcasting really, but have you seen the money that the chief constable is proposing? I guess I can always move back, I'll get some brilliant experience there if I stay for a year or two.'

It turned out to be the best career decision of Alex's life. She was there for barely a year. Her performance on the TV cameras, dealing with all manner of topics from police corruption to sexual impropriety among senior officers, was exemplary. She was poised, composed, and her radio training had made her adept at dealing with the tricky questions that journalists threw at her.

Before we knew it, she was being courted for an amazing job in London. They wanted her to co-present Crime Beaters, a national TV show where they screened reconstructions of serious crimes in an attempt to gather new evidence and seek out witnesses.

Once again, there was doubt and uncertainty in our relationship.

'I can get the train up here at weekends, Pete. We'll still be able to keep things going.'

I think we both knew that wouldn't happen. And there was no way I was going to say anything that put Alex off that career move. In broadcasting terms, we were both relative newcomers, but her career trajectory had been astonishing. I wasn't jealous or even resentful, I wanted only what was best for her.

Needless to say, the weekend visits didn't happen. She was quickly overcome by the demands of fame and recognition. It went with the territory. Alex was an instant hit on Crime Beaters; it was a tired but established format and her combination of personality and professionalism had given the show a shot in the arm. The audiences grew, the suits at the top loved her, and before we knew it, she was everywhere. Alex got the *Famous Family Trees* treatment, she nabbed a guest slot on *Quick Action Throttle*, leaving the all-male presentation team gasping for breath, and she'd even been in the celebrity edition of *Glorious Garden Sheds*, almost beating some soap star to the top accolade.

Week by week we saw less of each other until our relationship became reduced to a daily series of texts and, later, social media messages. We never broke up, our relationship just stopped happening. We weren't married, we'd never discussed it, we just drifted apart. We hadn't even bought a house together, we'd found a rental, we were happy there, we didn't feel the need to get on the housing ladder. I think, at the back of our minds, we'd always known that our careers might force us apart.

I admired Alex tremendously. Her track was not the path that I would have chosen for myself, but I was so proud of what she'd achieved. I accepted that it was over, but because there had never been any great moment of break-up, it became how things were. It had happened so gradually – we just grew away from each other.

Romantically, nothing serious came my way for a few years after Alex. Not until Meg arrived, smashing through my life like a bulldozer. I'd never known a love like it. After Alex, I was ready for the whirlwind that Meg brought into my world.

I'd had casual relationships and several one-night stands in between. I'd had the occasional fling with younger reporters in the office, but nothing which ever caught my attention like those two women had. Alex was effectively back where she'd started. Out of bounds. She belonged in a box marked *This is over now*. When Meg arrived on the scene, the lid on that box was securely nailed down.

I didn't know what Alex got up to in her glamorous life in London, we never talked about the romantic side of it. Every now and then she'd be photographed alongside some perfectly groomed, beautifully manicured and coiffured celebrity. But nothing stuck. She never married, never had kids, never seemed to stick with one of those supposed boyfriends.

After meeting Meg, I didn't think that much about it. I was in love again, Meg was my life, Alex was like an old school pal. We shared history, we texted, chatted occasionally on social media. But mainly our relationship was in the past.

Alex was a handy contact to have. Being a regular fixture on Crime Beaters meant that she had access to the cream of policing and the very best in the legal profession. She'd often advise me on police procedures or give me snippets about the law. On more than one occasion, she'd helped me to land an exclusive interview on the radio.

I never spoke to anybody about our relationship. It was private, not just from an emotional point of view, but also in terms of preserving Alex's reputation. Jem was a bastard like that. If a reporter ever came on the TV and he'd slept with her, he'd announce it to everybody in the newsroom. Once he had naked pictures on his phone. I think even Jem sensed the gasp of horror when he began handing round his smartphone to anybody who wanted a look. If Sally had known only half of what he openly shared in the office, I wouldn't blame her for throwing him out. I think I'd have made his life a misery too.

Nobody knew about my relationship with Alex. I'd moved radio station and city since then. I kept it quiet. Occasionally people would slag her off as 'that tart on Crime Beaters' or 'the sexy bint on Quick Action Throttle' but I'd maintain my silence. They knew that I had some kind of past with Alex, but they didn't know quite how close we'd been.

I'd told Meg, of course, though I had glossed over some of the details. I needed to acknowledge the relationship, but I never actually told her that we'd lived together. She knew we'd had a sexual relationship, her feminine radar knew immediately that Alex was a potential threat to her, which was why I was grateful that I hadn't told her the whole story. She knew enough to explain Alex's texts on my phone and our connections on social media. But I think if she'd known the full truth, I probably would have had to end it forever with Alex.

It wasn't romantic anymore, it had long since been that. As much as I loved Meg, though, I wasn't prepared to cut off Alex completely just because of a bit of jealousy. So I kept Meg in the dark about the full nature of our relationship and continued to get daft texts and snippets of celebrity gossip from Alex. Our relationship was like a weak heart, a gentle beat just managing to keep the rest of the body alive.

So, as I opened up my text messages on my phone, I didn't have high expectations of there being any news. Perhaps it would be more gossip about the seventy-year-old gardening show presenter they had to sack because he kept farting on live television. The official reason was that he was retiring to care for his elderly wife. Or the other story that was creating lots of entertainment was the one about the TV show host who had to have a small microphone surgically removed from his arse. The gossip magazines hadn't caught onto that one, Alex had sworn me to secrecy before she revealed it to me.

So I was completely taken aback when I opened up her text. It jarred immediately, it was curt and straight to the point: *Shit Pete, have you seen Meg's Facebook feed? Is she alright? Call me.*

Damn it, I hadn't checked Meg's feed. I hadn't even thought to.

I moved my fingers over the screen of my phone, searching for the Facebook icon. I clicked on it and waited for the app to open up. Bollocks! My battery died, holding out for a day had proven too much for it and it had keeled over on me once again.

At last Jenny managed to clear the reception area of guests and their stupid questions: 'I've forgotten my toothbrush, do you have one of those vending machines?'... 'Does the restaurant cater for vegans with nut and broccoli allergies?' ... 'If I wake up because my husband is snoring loudly, does that entitle me to claim under your snug-at-night guarantee?'

Jenny liked me, I think. I was someone she could confide in. Certainly what she said next caught me off guard.

'Can I tell you something private? I'm really worried.' She had tears in her eyes.

She looked around, making sure that the reception area was still clear.

'What's up, Jenny? Has our mate Bob Hays been getting to you?'

If that middle-aged bully boy had been leaning on this poor girl, I'd have a word on her behalf. I'd seen him shaking his finger at her in the car park.

'It's not Bob, but he is being a bit tough on me. He's under pressure, the police are asking him a lot of questions.'

The police. I'd forgotten about them. They'd moved from the reception area, and it was out of sight, out of mind, as far as I was concerned.

'So what's up, Jenny? How can I help?'

She wiped a tear from her eye and took a moment, trying to stay composed, aware that a new guest might appear at any time with the latest in a long line of daft queries.

'I need to tell someone, but I can't speak to Bob or the police. Not yet.'

My mind immediately stopped churning over Alex's text message. Jenny had my full attention.

'Go on. Whatever it is, it's safe with me.'

'You know Jackson, the chap who's missing, the one the police are getting excited about?'

'Yes, you mentioned him. This is the young guy who probably went home from his shift early, yes?'

Jenny nodded.

'Only, he didn't go home early ...' Jenny looked around again. She didn't want anybody else to hear this. 'We were sleeping together ...'

It was finally out. She let it hang there, searching my face for a reaction. She wanted to know if I would judge her. How could I? I'd been doing the same thing the night before. Only I wasn't some twenty-something singleton. I was a middle-aged man cheating on his wife.

'That's not so bad – it's not as if someone's died.'

Jenny continued, her serious expression unchanged.

'We were using the room next to yours. We weren't supposed to. Bob would sack us if he knew. I always keep the block of rooms by the fire exit clear when I'm placing guests because it's quiet down there.'

I got the feeling I was about to find out why that door had been open in the room next to mine.

'After the bar closes and most of the guests are in their rooms, I put the sign up in reception.'

I'd seen it the night before. Only, according to Jenny, what it should have said was 'Nipped off for a shag. Back soon!'

I suspected that Jenny's misdemeanour would be the kind of thing we all get up to when young. But I was wrong.

'We'd got it worked out between us. Derek always takes a newspaper and goes to the toilet on the top floor at about

2am. That's our cue. He's in there for ages. Every night. God knows what he does in there.'

I couldn't help smiling at that one. Derek's toilet habits facilitating the sexual recreation habits of two youngsters. It sounded so romantic. He must have got cut off in his prime the night before. That's all you need, a fire alarm going off right in the middle of a night-time dump.

'So why the worried look, Jenny? Are you concerned that Derek might have constipation?'

'I need you to take this seriously, it's important!' she snapped.

'I'm sorry. Carry on. I didn't mean to make light of it. I don't understand the problem though.'

'Whenever Jackson and I were on shift together, I created a key card to open up whichever of the rooms hadn't been taken by a guest. It doesn't track on the system, it just shows that a staff member had to enter a room. It could be a cleaner, Derek with his toolkit, or one of us delivering an iron. It's easily hidden.'

'Go on.'

'Jackson opened the door early last night – it's easier to hide on the computer system if we vary the times. It was opened a bit before you arrived actually, that's why I put you down there. We're busy this weekend, I couldn't keep it completely clear. I thought you were nice, you'd be quiet, probably stay in your room all evening.'

If only she knew.

'Jackson left the door slightly ajar. The minute Derek disappeared with the newspaper, I'd put the sign up in reception, text Jackson and we'd meet in the room. So long as we didn't mess up the room, nobody was any the wiser. And whatever it is with Derek, he's always gone for at least half an hour.'

'So what's the problem?'

'I was supposed to meet Jackson. He sent me a text saying he'd gone in there early, he was waiting for me since he'd done all his checks for the night. Only we never got that far. The fire alarm went off. Derek checked the upper levels as he was up there anyway. I did a sweep of the ground floor, then made sure I called by the room to pick up Jackson. Only he wasn't there.'

Jenny's eyes began to tear up again, I was struggling to see what the problem was. I knew all this, it sounded as if Jackson had taken the opportunity to stop work a bit early. The only difference being that, if Derek needed to finish off his shit after the fire brigade had given the all clear, he was still on a promise from Jenny. At his age, with a beautiful young woman like Jenny wanting to sleep with me, I'd have hung on in there until the bitter end.

'I still don't get why this is a problem, Jenny. Has Bob caught you out? Is that why he was so cross with you?'

'No, he doesn't know yet, but it can't be long with the police here now. Jackson would have texted me, he wouldn't have just disappeared like that. He said he'd wait for me in the room, reckoned he'd got a surprise for me. The door was still ajar when I looked in to pick him up. Either he would have been in there or he'd have been making sure guests were heading to the fire exits. He wasn't there, though.'

'So what's upsetting you, Jenny? This seems like a storm in a teacup to me.'

'It's not, I'm really worried about Jackson. Something happened in that room last night. When I looked in, he wasn't there. It looked as if nobody had used the room, but then I noticed a piece of broken china on the floor. It had come from one of the cups on the tray. I walked into the room to pick it up, and then I saw it. There was blood on the carpet. A lot of blood. And no sign of Jackson anywhere.'

It seemed strange thinking about my relationship with Alex after such a long time. There was something that had happened during our five years together which had a profound impact on my relationship with Meg.

Alex and I had been living together for about three years, closer to four by that stage. There was no marriage on the cards, no talk of starting families. We had just picked up where we left off at the polytechnic. We were both working hard on our careers, and we had a good amount of disposable income, so time away from work was spent eating out, going to concerts, watching movies and travelling. It was a great time. We'd avoided the worst of the student finance shake-up so weren't looking at mortgage-level debt, and life was sweet.

When you're fully engaged in your career and loving every minute of it, you don't have to think that much about your life. If you're in love too and happy with your relationship, all is good with the world. That's how I felt, and I'm sure that Alex felt that way too, which is why it gave us both a jolt when Alex got pregnant.

It was only when I thought back that I saw how much I'd kept from Meg. Nobody tells their new partners everything, it would be too painful to hear, and I edited my past too. When Meg and I started having fertility issues, I was pleased that I had kept things quiet about Alex. I think it might have made things worse with Meg.

Alex and I were young, too young to be thinking about families, particularly because of the transient nature of our careers. People in broadcasting move around a lot, they're always chasing that next best job.

So when Alex came down to breakfast one Saturday and looked as if she had something serious to tell me, I braced myself for bad news. The look on her face made me question how things had been between us. Had I missed the signs? Was she about to end the relationship?

'I've got something to tell you, Pete. Can we turn the radio off?'

The radio was usually on quietly in the background – it's a curse of the job, you're always keeping one ear on the latest news stories. I turned it off, studying Alex's face for clues.

'I'm pregnant, Pete. Remember when we came back drunk from the pub that bank holiday weekend when I forgot my cap? Well, it *did* matter. We should have used a condom to make extra sure.'

I hadn't expected that. If you'd have asked me beforehand if I wanted a baby, I'd have told you no, I hadn't even given it any thought. But now that Alex was announcing that she was pregnant, my reaction was delight. I was really excited. Why not? We were in love, things were good. Neither of us would have opted to start a family at that time, but given that it had happened by accident, it didn't seem that much of a problem.

I stood up, walked over to Alex and kissed her.

'Me and my sweet-talking,' I smiled. 'I wonder how many couples have been caught by the it-won't-matter-just-this-once line?'

I think that Alex had been unsure how I'd react to the news. She seemed relieved that I was so delighted. Even I was surprised by that one, but it was fine, it was great, why not?

'How far gone are you?' I asked, ready to dig into the details.

'Almost three months,' Alex replied. 'I missed a couple of periods, but I've always been a bit irregular anyway, I didn't think anything of it. I've been really sick on my morning shifts so I decided to get a pregnancy test on the spur of the moment yesterday. I'm sorry I didn't mention it sooner, but with me on earlies, you on lates, I wanted to pick my moment.'

'It's fine, it's fine, I know how it is, it's hard work when the shifts aren't in sync. Will you give up work?'

'It's too early to say, Pete. I need to go to the doctor first. I've booked in for next week, we'll get a better idea of due dates then. And it's still early days, remember.'

Those words proved to be portentous. Alex got the pregnancy confirmed and was booked in for her first scan. We didn't share the news with anybody, it seemed prudent to wait for that first visit to the hospital. We'd celebrate it then.

For a couple of weeks we lived in a secret bubble of happy expectation and excitement. We bought some baby books, read and re-read the information about stages of development, speculating about what our own baby looked like at that time. I even bought a packet of sleep-suits from the supermarket. I couldn't resist it. I'd had virtually no direct experience of babies in my life. I wanted to get out a 0–3 months sleep-suit and see just how tiny they were.

For a short time, careers seemed unimportant. I honestly believe that Alex would have been quite happy to leave work, never looking back at the career that might have been. I wouldn't have expected that reaction from her and I certainly would never have asked her to give up her career if she didn't want to. We were parents-to-be, we were excited, it was our secret and we were as happy as we had ever been. Then the bubble burst.

To my eternal shame, I didn't go to the hospital with Alex for that first scan. The appointment clashed with my shift and I made the wrong call. I didn't want anybody to know about the pregnancy, so didn't want to show my hand by admitting that I needed time off to go with her.

Alex was matter-of-fact about it.

'It'll be fine, they'll just check everything is okay and I'll bring back a picture. You can come with me to the other check-ups, everybody will know by then.'

What she was saying made sense, so I went along with it. It was only when I emerged from reading the news bulletin to see a voicemail waiting on my phone that things started to fall apart.

'Pete, it's Alex. Can you call me? I've got some bad news, I'm afraid. I need you at the hospital if you can get here.'

She was choked up, having terrible difficulty getting her words out. With the bulletin delivered, I was into the last hour of that day's shift, so I made my excuses with the manager, saying I was feeling unwell. The hospital wasn't far from the radio station, and I was there within twenty minutes. I'd never seen Alex looking so vulnerable. She was on her own in a small waiting area, quietly sobbing. I walked over to her and hugged her. We held onto each other for several minutes, no words were needed. Eventually, she was ready to speak.

'The baby's dead,' she began. 'The sonographer started doing the scan and he went quiet all of a sudden. I could see he was struggling with something so I asked what was wrong. He said that the baby wasn't as big as it should have been, was I sure of how pregnant I was.'

I knew where the conversation was going. I'd done enough interviews about miscarriage to know that we were well and truly in that territory.

'The baby's dead, Pete. It just stopped growing. I've had a second test and they confirmed it. They need to get it out of me.'

It was over. We'd lost the baby. We'd never planned it that way, but when Alex had announced the news we'd both been ecstatic. Now our dreams for the future were being dashed. We'd gone from an amazing high to a devastating low. I felt completely deflated, God knows how Alex was feeling. Like a true journalist, I started asking questions.

'Is it definitely dead? How soon do they have to remove the foetus? Are you okay?'

That was the saddest time of my life. Up until that moment I'd never understood how completely desolating something like that can be. When we did eventually share the experience with close friends, people would say things like 'Well, it wasn't really a baby, it was just a foetus', and 'At least you can try again'. But that baby was all our hopes and dreams, and they'd been cruelly taken away from us. We'd never held the child in our arms so we didn't even get a funeral.

Alex had the required D&C and presumably whatever was left of our baby ended up in the hospital waste. We were given some leaflets about counselling and left to our own devices. For a few days it felt as if a death had occurred, but when Alex returned to work things got back to normal. We'd never intended to start a family, so we never discussed trying again. We picked up where we'd left off and carried our new emotional baggage with us on our way. What else could we do? Our loss was intangible and so difficult to articulate.

It wasn't long after that that Alex became unsettled and started looking for new jobs. The move to the press officer role followed soon afterwards, then the move to TV.

I'd never really thought about it before, maybe because I thought I'd dealt with it and put it in the past. There's a reason why I hated counselling so much. And there's a reason why I was ambivalent about starting a family with Meg.

Counselling took me back to that dark place with Alex. We'd attended one counselling session, decided it wasn't for us, and ducked out before we got too embroiled with the group. To be honest, we were a bit self-conscious about sharing everything – as journalists we liked to ask the questions. It's a good defence mechanism. As minor celebrities, we were recognised by some of the couples in the group. That put us off immediately, we decided to work through our problems together.

I'd never realised this previously, but looking back it's as clear as day to me now. I was scared to have a baby with Meg. It wasn't that I didn't love her or that I didn't want to have children. I was scared that I might have to go through that terrible loss all over again.

CHAPTER NINE

'Have you spoken to the police yet?' I asked Jenny.

'Yes, but I haven't told them what Jackson and I were planning. I keep thinking about it, but I don't think that helps Jackson, does it? I mean, if something has happened to him, they don't need to know that we were sleeping together, do they?'

I thought it over, but my mind was more preoccupied with my personal situation. I'd be joining Jenny in covering up my own bad behaviour very soon. Why did it have to happen in the room next to mine? There was no way I was getting out of that hotel without at least having some sort of conversation with the police. I'd have to do the same as Jenny, keep my mouth shut about Ellie and just tell them what I'd seen and heard – leaving out the adulterous sex.

'I think that if you tell them your exact movements and whereabouts, but miss out the bit about sleeping with Jackson, it won't mess up their investigation, but you won't get into trouble either.'

I was thinking aloud, working out my own dilemma. That's what I would do. The police didn't need to know that Ellie and I had been sharing the room. Nobody had seen us. Derek would confirm my whereabouts when the fire alarm went off.

'Do you have CCTV here, Jenny?' I asked, thinking through the options and potential slip-ups that might occur.

'Only in the car park. There's no CCTV within the building itself. We have a camera over the entrance too, but that's it.'

'So if you tell them what your movements were, they'll see that confirmed on the cameras. You need an excuse for checking the room next to mine when the alarms went off. Tell them it was ajar, that's true, let them know you were just checking it out. Derek did exactly the same after you exited the building, that'll back up what you say. Keep quiet about meeting Jackson for now ... unless you killed him, of course!'

Jenny looked horrified.

'Oh God, I'm sorry Jenny, I didn't mean to frighten you. Look, he's only missing at the moment, the chances are he finished his shift early. Keep an eye on your phone, he's bound to get in touch. You might want to check through your sent texts, to cover your back. Leave anything friendly on there, remove anything that could get you into trouble over the illicit meetings on company property.'

'It's okay, we use the Erazerr app for messaging, it deletes everything after it's been seen. We should be fine.'

I couldn't believe that I was helping Jenny to cover up her trysts with Jackson at the OverNight Inn. I thought it over again. So long as Jenny accounted for what she'd seen and done, it wouldn't divert the police from whatever they were doing. She wasn't being investigated, she didn't have to answer for her actions. It was the same for me. I'd tell them exactly what I'd seen and heard – very little – and it was none of their business about Ellie. I couldn't afford for that to be public knowledge, that's all I needed, it getting back to Meg via the rumour mill.

I needed to move on my own issues. Jenny seemed happy that I'd put her mind at ease. The blood that she'd seen on the carpet was troubling me, though. Could Jackson have done something stupid? Maybe cut himself on the broken cup, made a mess and done a runner? My journalistic sixth sense was kicking in. There were too many police officers around for this to be just about a missing teenager. Something was going on, and I couldn't avoid getting involved because of where my room was located. I'd have to talk to Ellie, give her a heads up about it. We'd need to stick to our story – it wouldn't mess up anything the police were doing, but it could screw things up elsewhere. At home, for instance.

'Jenny, I need to ask you more about the woman who was here last night. Was she definitely asking for me? What did she look like?'

'Yeah, I'm sorry, I've been distracted. I should have told you about that earlier. I shouldn't have let her through really, but she seemed nice and genuine. You get some weirdos coming in here who claim to be visiting another guest, but you can tell they're up to no good. I don't let them in, Derek usually sees them off the premises if they kick off. But she was nice, even showed me her driving licence to prove it was her. She had the same surname, Megan Bailey. I remember it because I like the name Megan. Why does she shorten it?'

'I've always called her Meg, I never really think of her as a Megan,' I replied. 'What time was this?'

'It was around midnight, probably just after, actually,' Jenny replied confidently. 'I know that because the late-nighters had come in from the bar and it had all settled down for the night. I'd put the sign up on reception while I nipped out to the loo. We do a tour of the hotel at around that time, to make sure there's no noise or windows open, anything like that. She came in as I was about to head to the second floor and do my sweep. Derek and Jackson had already gone.'

I thought through the timeline. Ellie and I had come back after closing time, some time after midnight, but reception had been empty when we returned. The sign was on the counter saying to wait five minutes and use the pager on the phone if necessary. Jenny would have been in the toilet then. Meg must have arrived after we got back from the pub. If she'd come before, she would have found my room empty.

If she'd come after we were back from the pub, that was getting serious. From what Jenny was saying, that sounded most likely. But nobody had knocked on the door. There had been some noise from out in the corridor, but I'd been preoccupied at the time. I thought back to Ellie. It had been good.

To my knowledge, Meg didn't knock at the door. Had she been outside? Could she have heard what was going on? We were both making a bit of noise the night before. If someone was listening at the door, they'd have heard all sorts. My face reddened, I could feel it, Jenny noticed it too.

'Are you alright?' she asked.

'Yes, yes, fine, I just came over really hot. It must be my age!'

I attempted to shrug it off, but I was feeling uncomfortable. What on earth had Meg done? Why hadn't she knocked at the door?

'Do you know what?' Jenny picked up. 'I've just realised something.'

Now it was her turn to blush.

'I may have sent her to the room next door to you. She asked what room you were in, but I may have told her the wrong number. I was thinking about meeting Jackson, he'd just told me which room we were meeting in. You're room 123, aren't you? I think I told her to go to room 121, not yours. I'm not sure now, I'm sorry, there's so much going on at the moment.'

I liked Jenny, but I was beginning to get a bit impatient with her.

'Did you see her again, Jenny? This is important.'

I thought about the blood in the room, and I considered the police presence. I was growing concerned about Meg. Could she be somehow connected with the blood that Jenny had seen?

'I didn't see her leave the building,' Jenny replied, sensing my urgency. 'I assumed that she'd join you in your room and that would be it. I don't remember everybody who comes here you know.'

She was getting jittery. She had her own subterfuge to hide. But we were tied together now, we had that room in common. If she'd sent my wife there, and her own boyfriend had been in the room, perhaps there was a connection? Had Jackson done something to Meg? I shivered at the thought of it. I dismissed it from my mind, it was crazy. There would be a sensible explanation, Meg was probably at home. The most likely option was that she'd tried to phone me when she realised that it was the wrong room and had no joy with my mobile number. If reception had been clear of staff when she came back through the building, maybe she'd headed home. No, it was a two-hour drive, she wouldn't do that. If I were in her position, I'd check into the hotel, wait until morning, then seek me out.

'Did she check in overnight, Jenny? Maybe Jackson or Derek booked her in?'

'It's possible,' Jenny said, turning to key in some information on her computer.

'I don't see her checked in as Bailey. Would she use any other name?'

'No, she'd use Bailey. Meg or Megan Bailey. I wonder where she's got to, I'm getting a bit concerned.'

'We don't see everything that happens here, of course. She could easily have left with another group. It's easy enough to get into the building if you walk in with a big group, but you couldn't get into a room without a key card, so it's fairly pointless.'

But what if the door was open already? I banished the thought immediately. There was a simpler explanation. For Meg and for Jackson.

'How easy is the CCTV to get to?'

'I can see the live feed on my screen, but I can't get into the archive. Besides, the camera at the entrance is faulty. That's why Bob was in such a mood with me – among many other things. I forgot to mention to him that the camera is on the blink. I never look at it, why would I? The police asked him about it earlier today, and then I had to admit that it's been broken for a while.'

We were stuck. Meg had gone AWOL, so had Jackson. The CCTV was on the blink, so that wasn't going to be any help whatsoever. I needed to get my phone charged, try to contact Meg again, then get my story straight with Ellie. All of a sudden a weekend of social media strategy seemed to be the least of my problems.

I don't think I'd ever really thought about how much I hadn't told Meg until circumstances forced me to think it through.

There was Alex for starters. Meg knew we'd had a relationship, she'd sensed our closeness. Of course, she was intimidated by the celebrity factor with Alex. Who wouldn't be?

To me, Alex was just a normal person, to Meg, I guess she must have been a threat. I understood that.

Meg wasn't aware that Alex and I had some form of online interaction on most days. Why was I hiding it? Was it because it would have been insensitive to flaunt it? I'm not sure now, but I was caught in my own silence, I would never have admitted to her that we'd lived together for so long. It never came up. I talked about those times in terms of work and where I lived, it was easy to airbrush Alex out of the picture. It made my life simpler too. I could feel the hackles coming up whenever I mentioned it, so it became a no-go area in our relationship.

I never mentioned the miscarriage either. If I'd been more open about Alex, the miscarriage experience would have been discussed long before Meg and I started having our problems. It was too late to share when we found that we were going to have difficulties conceiving. What was I going to tell Meg? 'Oh, by the way, I got that woman you hate on the TV pregnant by accident a decade ago!' I can imagine how well that would have gone down.

It was all in the past for me – Alex, the miscarriage – they were part of another life, one that took place before I met Meg. My life started again when I met her, and I'd loved every minute of it before things started to get difficult for us. I'd been with Meg longer than I'd been with Alex, and when Alex and I went our separate ways, we drifted apart. Neither of us fought for it, we just let it slip through our fingers.

I was ready to fight for Meg. I was battle weary, that was for certain, it's why I'd been tempted by Ellie. But I was ready to resume the struggle and push forward to a victory. I loved Meg with all my heart, it was our situation that I hated. Yet I'd realised, thinking again about my life with Alex, that it was fear that was making me so unsure about trying for a baby. I was scared. What happened with me and Alex was still having an impact on me over ten years since it had occurred. I'd pushed the thought of having children to the back of my mind. That was quite a shock to me. I'd just seen our marital situation with more clarity than ever before. Maybe I was more at fault than I'd cared to admit. And my dislike of Martin? Well, he was a prat, there was no denying that, but I'd shut him out, right from the start. Was it because of my previous bad experiences with counselling?

A mixture of guilt and fear made me crave Meg's presence. I wanted to see her there and then. It was a two-hour drive back home. Could I get there, spend the night with her, then be back in Newcastle in time for part two of the working weekend?

The decision was made for me. As I began to head out of the reception area, a police officer walked through the door.

'Are you Peter Bailey, sir? Room 123?'

I nodded. I was expecting this, but I hadn't thought that they'd seek me out first.

'I'm afraid we can't allow you to re-enter your room at

the moment, we've had to gain access as part of a preliminary investigation.'

'Oh?' was all I could offer. My journalistic abilities failed me at that moment.

'Nothing to worry about, sir, but we will need to have a chat with you at some point. You're not planning to leave anytime soon are you?'

'No, no, I'm here for the night. I was thinking about popping home overnight, but I guess that's out of the question now. What's up? Is anything wrong?'

I was getting increasingly concerned about Meg. I could feel Jenny's eyes burning into me at the reception desk, she looked petrified. We both had something at stake here, it was all beginning to feel a bit precarious.

'Do you have somewhere you could go, sir, while we're making our checks of the rooms? We won't be long. It's just routine. I'll need to send a colleague to have a quick chat with you and make sure that we have your contact details.'

'May I borrow a pen and paper, Jenny?' I asked, keen to be as helpful as I could. Jenny scurried around her desk, tearing a page off a memo pad and handing me her pen. I wrote down my mobile number, my home number and work phone details. I added my email address, then scribbled it out. The police wouldn't be sending me email updates any time soon. I added my home address too; if they needed to speak with me again, they might dispatch someone local.

'Thank you, sir. Will you be in the hotel all night?'

'Yes, I'll stay in the bar area. My mobile is dead by the way, I'll see if I can find a charger and get it topped up. I'll eat in the hotel this evening. How long until I can get back into my room?'

'No more than two hours, sir. The room has been made

up by housekeeping since this morning, there's very little that we need to look at in there.'

'Are you looking for anything in particular? Can I help?'

'No, no need, sir, so long as we can speak to you this evening we'll trouble you as little as we can. If this young lad shows his face, it'll all be over anyway. But until he does, we have to make sure everything is taken care of.'

The police officer took the sheet of paper from me and returned to the corridor which led towards my room.

I turned to Jenny. 'How much are they searching?'

'Everything from the final fire door and up to the fire exit,' she replied. 'That's seven rooms and a store cupboard. It's only you and one other guest affected, everybody else checked out this morning. They've been collecting guest names for the entire hotel. Can you see why I'm so scared now?'

'It's okay, Jenny, just stick to what I told you and keep chasing Jackson. You'll need to make sure he has his story straight when they find him. And give him a kick up the arse from me when they do.'

Jenny made a face. She was in no mood for anything remotely resembling humour.

'I need to find a friend's room. She has the same phone type as me, I need to borrow her charger. Can you tell me which room she's in?'

'I'm not really supposed to do that, but yes, what's her name?'

I stopped dead in my tracks. How embarrassing. What was Ellie's surname?

'First name is Ellie,' I blustered. 'She might have registered as ...'

What was Ellie short for? Eleanor? Ellen? Elisa? I

wasn't doing a very good job of covering my tracks, I'd have to perform much better when I spoke to the police.

'Try Ellie. She usually prefers Ellie.'

'I've got her. Ellie Turner?'

'Yes, that's Ellie!' I confirmed, relieved that Jenny had found her.

'Room 403, use the lift, it's to your left as you walk through the door.'

'What's that app you use to speak to Jackson, Jenny? Maybe we should connect on there ... in case you need to ask my advice again?'

'It's Erazerr, it's free. I'm JEN1995, you'll see my picture. I'm easy to find.'

1995. How could an adult have been born in 1995? That was a couple of years before I'd met Alex.

'Thanks, Jenny. Look, let me know if you hear anything about what's going on along the corridor. I'll get connected on Erazerr as soon as I can get some charge on my phone. I'll let you know when I'm back downstairs in case the cops need me. You okay?'

Jenny nodded. We were in collusion, but we weren't guilty of anything, at least anything that the police would get excited about. So long as we told them the truth about our movements and what we'd seen, we'd be in the clear and it wouldn't mess up whatever they were up to.

I forced a smile for Jenny, then headed up to Ellie's room.

I had to get some charge on my phone and start making calls. And I needed to see what Alex was talking about on

Facebook. It was unusual for Alex to send a message like that. And about Meg too.

As I headed upwards in the lift, I did a sense-check on going to see Ellie. I hoped that I could get to her room without anybody seeing me, that might complicate things. Normally I'd have sought out Jem, but Ellie and I needed to get our stories straight. Who'd seen us together the previous night? Only that nerd guy who wouldn't make himself scarce at the end of the evening. I hadn't even seen him that day, he must have been in one of the other working groups.

I stepped out of the lift and tried to figure out the numbering on the rooms. The corridor was quiet, that evening lull when everybody is back for the day but it's too soon to hit the pub or go for a meal. It would usually be the time that I'd check in with Meg, see how her day had gone, ask about that day's post.

I found Ellie's room and gently tapped at the door.

'Hang on!' I heard her call. There was some movement in the room. I saw the shadow underneath the door as she went to open it from the inside. She paused, I saw a flicker as she peered through the spy hole. Clever girl. After what I'd seen of Dave earlier that day, that was a sensible thing to do.

She opened the door in her towel, I'd obviously caught her just out of the shower. Had it been any other time and any other circumstances, I might have tried my luck again, but she obviously felt the same. Sex was off the cards, this was business. She quickly let me into the room.

'Everything okay with Dave?' I asked, genuinely concerned about what had happened to her earlier.

'Yes, thanks. What a pillock! They took him to the cells for a while to let him calm down, I haven't heard anything from him since.'

I spotted her phone charging on the desk. I was right, she was Android, like me, no iPhone for Ellie.

'Can I borrow your charger? I'm completely flat.'

The connection lead fitted into my phone and the charging icon appeared. I tried to switch it on, but it was too dead. I'd have to give it a few minutes.

'Have you seen the police activity downstairs?' I asked.

'Yes, something to do with a kid who went missing after the fire alarm last night. Seems to be a big deal about nothing to me. I suppose they have to go through the motions, though.'

'Well, it looks like I'm going to get involved in it. Something was happening in the room next to mine last night. They're in my room now.'

'Oh shit, was it anything serious?'

Ellie looked immediately concerned, she'd clocked the implications for the two of us straight away.

'I don't want to get all CSI about it, but the room was refreshed by housekeeping this morning. The sheets and towels will be at the cleaners by now. No one is going to stumble across the fact that we slept together, but we'll have to get our story straight.'

'Yes, yes, I agree. Do they think it's anything serious? Why are they doing the full Poirot if it's only a missing person?'

'They're just going through the motions at this stage. There is a bit of a complication, though. Apparently there were signs of trouble in the room, according to Jenny in reception. Did you hear anything?'

Ellie smiled. It was a weak smile, but it was there nevertheless. Like me, she was thinking back to the previous night's activities.

'I seem to remember you were going down on me at the

time. I wasn't really thinking about anything else. I did notice that the ceiling needed painting, mind you ...'

I smiled back. It was equally weak. I liked Ellie, she was funny. But I wasn't in the mood for it, I needed to get some answers. I tried my phone again. It had 5 percent charge, but it was enough to bring it back to life.

'Bloody thing! Excuse me, I need to get an app loaded on this.'

'Mind if I get dressed?' Ellie asked.

'No fine, I'm sorry to barge in on you like this.'

I went to the apps area and searched for Erazerr. It was easy to find, but I needed a wireless connection.

'Jesus, they don't half make it hard to get connected in these places. Do you have a code?'

Ellie had gone into the bathroom to get dressed. I guess it would have seemed strange to do it in the room in front of me, even though we'd spent the previous night in bed together. She poked her head round the door. I caught sight of her. She was wearing green briefs, a lovely colour, I'd not seen that before. I liked it. I caught the curve of her breast through the gap in the door. I pulled my gaze back to her face, she'd clocked my interest.

'It's on a scrap of paper by my bed. It's good for three devices, should be fine.'

I tapped in the code, confirmed the connection and downloaded the app. While that was chugging away, I saw that I had text messages on my phone. Nothing from Meg. One from Jem. Was I going out for drinks later? One from Alex wondering where I was.

Erazerr confirmed that it had successfully installed, so I registered for an account as quickly as I could. PBailey03, name and birthday, nothing fancy. Confirm email address, more buggering about, and I was in.

Ellie came out of the bathroom wearing figure-hugging jeans and a tight-fitting T-shirt showing the shape of her breasts. I could see the green of her bra straps too, the same green as her briefs. Matching underwear again. Damn it, Pete, focus on what's important!

I connected with Jenny via the app, then turned back to Ellie. Her long hair was still wet, and she was towelling it gently. How can that be so sexy when a woman does it?

'I'm not going to mention that we were together last night, we can't admit it. You've got to think about Dave, and I have to think of ... '

I hadn't even mentioned Meg. I felt ashamed for the first time. Ellie knew, though, she'd known the score.

'I have to keep what happened away from Meg.'

She didn't ask for an explanation. She simply accepted it. Thank you for that, Ellie. Thank you for not making me feel like even more of a shit.

'I'm going to tell them all my movements, everything that happened, exactly as it took place. Only, when we walked through reception last night, you went to your room, I went to mine. We saw no one. Is that okay?'

'Well, it's true. I don't see that it changes anything. It was only the usual noises in the corridor. A few knocks, doors being opened and closed, the fire door slamming shut. Nothing unusual. Did you hear anything?'

'Nothing! There's no CCTV in this place and there was nobody in reception. We're not messing up what the police are doing. I feel okay with this. Do you?'

'Yes, it's fine. So long as you tell them exactly what you saw and heard, nobody needs to know about what we were doing. It's fine, Pete, I'm as keen as you to keep this quiet. Not that I didn't enjoy it, you understand?'

She smiled. I smiled back. It hung in the air for a

moment. The silence was interrupted by an unfamiliar beep from my phone.

It was Erazerr. Jenny had sent me a message. I clicked on the icon and read what she'd sent me, expecting to see a welcome note. It was nothing of the sort. I felt the colour draining from my face as I read it: *They've found a body. They want to speak to you.*

CHAPTER TEN

'Shit!'

Ellie looked at me, sensing straight away that it was something that involved both of us. Maybe it was the way I was looking at her. Horrified and scared.

'They've found a body in the room next to mine.'

'You're kidding me.'

'Jenny on reception just messaged me. She said she'd let me know what was going on downstairs.'

'You're connected to Jenny on your phone?'

Ellie seemed surprised by that. I sensed a touch of jealousy – not jealousy exactly, but it was territorial. It felt like a 'WTF, you're chatting up the receptionist already?'

I ignored it, she was barking up the wrong tree and we had more important matters to consider.

'Jenny doesn't know much about what's going on, but she's upset and they've found a body. Her colleague, Jackson, has been missing. I hope to God it's not him.'

'You seem very friendly with everybody who works at the hotel.'

Again, the territorial questioning. I hadn't put Ellie down as somebody like that.

'I've been getting on well with Jenny. We chatted on my first night here and she's shared some stuff that's been going on in the hotel. I'm just some old git to her, but she's been seeking my advice.'

I wondered about the old git line. Jenny and I liked each other, but was there any spark? Put it back in your pants Pete, there's a dead body to think about.

'This could mean problems for us, Ellie. We need to think this through. We can't pervert the course of justice – but I don't want anyone knowing that we slept together last night either.'

'I don't want Dave to know anything about it, not after he was kicking off like that today. It won't help anything.'

'Agreed,' I replied. 'We need to keep it away from work too. I don't want the newsroom to know what's been going on!'

'Yes, if that bunch of tossers find out what we've been up to, they'll never let us forget it.'

'We need to retrace events, Ellie. Who saw us leave together? Did anyone run into us when we came back to the hotel?'

'No, the only person who knew that we were together at the end of the evening was that boring engineer guy. What's his name? Fergus?'

'Yes, he left the pub before us, he can't confirm that we returned together. Jenny told me that the CCTV is out over the entrance. There's no evidence there. What about the pub?'

'It proves nothing, Pete. Just that we left together, at the most. There's nothing to disprove that we went our separate ways when we got back to the hotel.'

'Okay, so nobody has to know about us going back to my room. Did you leave anything in there last night?'

'We're not going to be suspects, Pete. We don't need to do a complete DNA sweep of the area.'

'I know, I know. But come on, Ellie, we've reported on these things a million times between us. People make stupid mistakes, that's how they get caught out lying. We need to make sure we're telling a white lie here, we mustn't mess up the police investigation.'

'I didn't leave anything in your room, Pete. I was just carrying what I arrived with. When the fire alarm went off, I got dressed and picked up my bag. There's no toothbrush, no condom, no hairbrush.'

'Okay, so we're clear. Did we see or hear anything? Let's think it through.'

'There was nothing, Pete. Just normal noises. Comings and goings in the corridor. You were out cold after the sex anyway. I'm amazed you heard the fire alarm. Did you know that you snore a bit by the way? Sexy that!'

A smile from Ellie. She was teasing again. At least she'd dropped the innuendo about Jenny.

'I'm sure that we're clear, Ellie. I'll tell the story as if I came back on my own – there's nothing there that can mess up the police investigation. They're definitely going to need to talk to me, but your room is nowhere near the crime area, they're only going to ask you to come forward if you saw anything unusual.'

I saw a momentary change in Ellie's expression – if I'd blinked, I'd have missed it.

'What?' I asked.

'It's nothing, just a thought, it's nothing.'

'Are you sure we're good to go on this, Ellie? We mustn't foul this up.'

'I was thinking about Tony Miller. You remember I said that I thought I'd seen him in the car park?'

'You said you were mistaken—'

'I was ... I'm sure it wasn't him. What if it was, though? He's a nutter. And the police know about him already. If it was him, this will come back to bite us.'

'Think it through, Ellie. How likely is it? Did he ever follow you this far?'

'He must have been angry after my brothers got to him. But he backed off. I haven't seen him for a while. No, it can't have been him. It's just my paranoia.'

'I'll tell them about the door being slightly open, that's got to have something to do with it. The hotel guy – Derek – saw me leave my room on my own. Did you see him when you left?'

'No, I could hear him along the corridor, but he was on the other side of the fire doors. He didn't see me leaving your room, I'm certain of that.'

'Is there anything we've missed? I want to tell the cops everything, but they don't need to know about us. Nobody needs to know about us.'

'So long as that wasn't Tony Miller – and I'm sure it wasn't – we're clear.'

Her face changed again. She was used to being on TV, she knew how to control her facial expressions. But I'd caught a glimpse again, there was something troubling her.

'What is it, Ellie? Come on, I need to know. If it's going to cock this up, you have to tell me.'

She looked uneasy. I wondered what else could come out of the woodwork to make this weekend any worse than it already was.

'There's one more thing I need to tell you, Pete. I'm sorry, I didn't think it mattered. Not until you mentioned that something had happened. I've been trying to decide whether to tell you.'

'Go on, what is it?'

'You know when the alarm went off last night and I couldn't find my bra? You were out like a light after we'd finished that third time, I think you were still coming round while I was looking for it. Well, I think I must have left it in your room. I can't find it anywhere.'

I felt my heart sink. I'd used that phrase many a time, but as Ellie was talking to me, I finally experienced it for myself. My heart actually felt as if it was sinking. I must have looked like a man in shock. Things had just got complicated.

'What's up, Pete? Your face just turned white.'

'That was supposed to be a single occupancy booking, Ellie. If the police are searching all of the rooms on the ground floor, they're bound to find it and start asking awkward questions. It's going to cause us problems if they find that. We might have to admit to what we did.'

'It's fine, Pete, just say it had been left by a previous guest. It's easy enough to explain away.'

'But there's something I haven't told you yet. My wife came to the hotel last night. She was here to surprise me for my birthday. She must have been right next to my room. I don't know where she is now. But the police are going to know that she was here. They're soon going to link her up with what we did last night.'

___

As a radio broadcaster, I'm used to juggling a number of different things at one time. I have to be able to read a news bulletin while getting my timing accurate to the second, take a swig of tea while a news clip is running, and absorb the details of a breaking news story in the middle of it all. Even so, this situation was challenging me.

I had too many things to do, all shouting to be done immediately. I was becoming increasingly worried about Meg's whereabouts. There had been a death after all, it was probably this missing kid. But where had Meg got to? And why was Alex trying to reach me? It was unusual for her to communicate as directly and urgently as that. The police needed to speak to me as well. Of course, they did. There had been a murder in the room next to mine. Not a murder, perhaps, but certainly a death. And Ellie's bra was missing. The one thing that could place her in that hotel room with me.

'I have to go downstairs and find out what's happened. I need to contact my wife.'

Ellie hesitated, then nodded. I realised that was the first time I'd properly acknowledged to her that my wife was involved.

'I'm sorry, Ellie, but you knew the deal, right? You knew there was someone on the scene, didn't you? I know I'm a shit.'

'Yes, I ... I don't know, Pete. I assumed you were a free agent, like me with Dave. I know we'd only just split up, and it wasn't a great thing for me to do ... but I was a free agent. I assumed you were something similar. Divorced or separated or something.'

'I'm sorry. I know I'm a dickhead. It falls into the 'or something' category. I love my wife, but we're going through a tough time. What's happened will probably stop us separating. If she's okay ...'

'Look, get down there, Pete, find out what's going on. We can go to confession when we know that she's safe. Talk to the police and let me know what's happening. I'll stay here. I'm sure it'll be alright.'

I unplugged my phone and took it with me. I'd find out what Alex wanted on the way down in the lift.

'Check there's no one in the corridor, would you?' I asked Ellie. No point making anybody suspicious. She gave the all clear and I entered the corridor and headed in the direction of the lifts.

Fergus bloody Ogilvy was standing there waiting to get in. The geek from the night before. Engineering department, he had to be.

'Hi, how's it going?' he asked.

'All good, thanks,' I replied, hoping not to get too embroiled with him. 'How was your session today, as boring as mine was?'

Fergus smiled.

'Ours was good actually. The use of Voice Over Internet Protocol in broadcasting. Fascinating stuff!'

Yeah, I'll bet! I kept my thoughts to myself, but Fergus had something else that he wanted to say.

'Did that guy catch up with you last night, your mate?'

I looked at him, I didn't know what he was talking about.

'Which guy?'

'After I left you in the pub, he walked into the hotel with me. I told him that you were right behind me and that he'd catch you if he waited a few minutes.'

'What did he look like?' I asked. Surely it wasn't Jem. Who else could it be?

'Dark hair. Medium height. Tracksuit top. I haven't seen him again. Oh, actually, I did. Saw him briefly after the fire alarm. What a nuisance that was!'

I made a point of not knowing anyone who wore a tracksuit for anything other than exercise purposes. Who was this? Nobody I knew.

'Did he ask for me by name?'

The lift finally arrived on my floor and we stepped in.

'No, he didn't, now I think about it. Though I don't know your name either. It's Max isn't it?'

'No, I'm Pete. Pete Bailey. Who did he ask for then?'

'He wanted to know if I'd seen Ellie and her work friend. That lady you were speaking to, it was Ellie, wasn't it? He sounded like you all knew each other. I was a bit merry, I didn't think anything of it. There was nobody in reception – I left him waiting there. So he was gone when you got back? How long were you after I left you? They were just closing up when I left.'

Bloody engineer types. So analytical. Fergus was a potential problem. He knew I'd been with Ellie. Time to plant a white lie. I came up with one on the spur of the moment, no time to think it through, but it aligned with what Ellie and I had discussed.

'There was nobody there when we got back to the hotel. Ellie needed to use the toilets before we left, I wanted to hang back and walk her over. We went our separate ways when we got back, nobody was waiting in reception. Strange.'

A lie. A small one. Fergus would share his information with the police. Or he'd volunteer it when he heard about the death in the hotel. By telling him that Ellie and I had gone our separate ways, it would only confirm our story. Fergus could reveal the presence of this mystery man. It wasn't Jem, different hair colour. The police would need to know about him, but it wouldn't involve Ellie and me. The only thing that might cause some difficulties for me was Ellie's discarded bra.

The lift doors opened and we walked around the corner into reception. There were police all over the place, my corridor had become a crime scene. Jenny was telling a disgruntled middle-aged man that his room was no longer available and that he'd have to use a hotel elsewhere in the city.

'I booked this room online two months ago, and now you're telling me that it's no longer available? So much for your snug-at-night guarantee!'

One of the police officers standing nearby had clocked him kicking off and came to Jenny's rescue.

'This is the scene of a murder investigation, sir. The young lady is having to redirect you because we've had to close off an entire ground-floor corridor.'

The miserable git huffed and puffed a bit, then moved along.

I dismissed Fergus with a 'see you later' then walked up to the young police officer.

'What's going on in there?' I asked.

'I'm afraid there's a murder investigation going on, sir. There's been an incident in the hotel overnight.'

'Can I get back to my room? It's along that corridor.

'You're not Mr Bailey, are you? Room 123? We need to speak to you, sir.'

'I know, I know, that's why I'm here. By the way, you need to speak to a chap called Fergus. Fergus Ogilvy, I'm sure that's his name. Jenny – the receptionist – can find his room number for you. He just went to the bar. He might have some interesting information for you.'

The police officer took out his notepad and jotted down the information that I'd given him.

'We may well be able to release your property to you, sir, but we won't be able to allow you back into that room tonight. If you could wait here, Mr Bailey, I'll find some-body who can speak to you.'

'Can you tell me who was killed?'

'I can't tell you that yet, sir.'

I almost lost my patience but checked myself.

'Are you able to say if the deceased is male or female?' I tried again.

'I'm sorry, sir. I can't release any details of the investiga-tion just yet.'

'I'm a journalist, I'm quite used to all of this stuff—' I began, but he shut me down. He was only young, but he could still spot a bullshitter from that distance.

'Then you of all people will know that we can't release any details until the body has been identified and next of kin informed.'

I conceded.

'I'll wait over here,' I said, making my way to one of the chairs in reception. Jenny was busy redirecting customers who wanted to check in for the evening. I was desperate to know about Meg. I had to know about Meg.

My phone had a small charge, enough to make it useful again. I checked for messages from Meg. Nothing. I texted her again. I phoned home. I rang her mobile phone. Noth-ing. Just answerphone messages. It was infuriating.

Alex had called and texted again. Several times. I had to see what was up. Another text. *FFS Pete, check Meg's Face-book feed. Then call me. I need to know you're OK.*

I opened up Facebook. Loads of notifications. All about something Meg had posted.

You both okay?

WTF? Is that a joke? Bad taste or what?

Has someone hacked Meg's account?

I went to my feed and scrolled down fast. I passed it the

first time. It was sandwiched between a video of a dog singing along to a piano tune and an advert for a hair colouring product.

Meg had posted something via Facebook Live. I didn't even know she knew how to use it.

I recognised where the video had been shot immediately. The thumbnail made it obvious, I could tell from the colour scheme. Meg had made that video in one of the rooms at the Overnight Inn.

I will never forget the content of that video. It's stuck in my mind forever, I can repeat the dialogue word for word. It's a testament to Meg's quick thinking and strength of character that it ever got shot at all.

I ignored all of the comments, popped in my ear buds and clicked the play icon. It had been live-streamed at 1:13am, it was the recorded archive that I was able to view. Meg must have sneaked out her phone and tried to capture what was happening, until she was discovered and stopped.

The video was shaky, sometimes blurred and often pointing away from the action. However, the sound was clear and it was obvious what was going on. The lighting was poor, but not so bad that it made it impossible to work out what was happening.

The video started in the middle of something, it didn't have a clear beginning. I didn't know either of the two people who were being filmed.

'... the fuck up and keep quiet.' A man's voice, older I'd guess, definitely not a young man.

'Please, I won't tell anyone, just let us leave ...'

The second voice was younger, possibly a teenager,

deep voice, newly flowing testosterone. He was scared, very scared. The camera settled and the pixelation sorted itself out.

It was a room in the OverNight Inn. I could tell by the colour of the carpet, the bed linen and blue lighting at the back of the headboard. It was very distinctive. It was identical to my own room, only the orientation made everything on the opposite side. I guessed that whoever was filming was on the floor, by the radiator under the window.

I flinched. The fist of the older man went hard into the face of the younger man who was lying on the floor by the edge of the bed. The younger man began to sob – like me, he'd probably never seen any violence in his life.

He was OverNight Inn staff. This had to be Jackson. He was dressed in the same light blue shirt as Jenny and was wearing a gold name badge. The video wasn't sharp enough to catch the name, but it had to be Jackson. Poor kid, he looked terrified. He was whimpering.

'What time is this woman coming?' the older man asked again. He had dark hair. Was this the man Fergus had spoken to? There was a tracksuit top discarded on the bed. Shit, was this Tony Miller?

'She's meeting me at two. Please don't hurt her—'

Another punch. Jackson's head was on the floor, so when the blow came, it pounded into him, there was nothing to break its velocity. It was thrown by a violent man. It wasn't half-hearted or tentative, this man had used violence before.

'I'm going to show her a good time,' the older man goaded, 'show her what a real man feels like.'

Jackson began to struggle. The older man – Tony, it had to be – was kneeling by his side in the dominant position, able to throw a punch whenever he wanted. He put his hand to Jackson's throat, forcing it down hard. I could see Jackson's feet begin to move, he was thrashing around, doing his best to find anything that could give him an advantage.

'Don't want me to play with your girlie? The ladies love it when they get some attention from Tony ...'

Shit. So it was Tony Miller. Ellie's stalker had been in the building. He must have come for Ellie.

'... and I'm going to have your girlie. Now, you be a good boy and tell me her name. I like to say their name when I take them. Makes it personal. Romantic. I'm gonna release my hand, keep things nice and quiet now, okay? What's her name? She got a nice ass?'

Tony slowly removed his hand. All I could hear was Jackson trying to catch his breath, struggling for air. Tony's hand hovered over his neck.

'She's called Moira. Her name's Moira. Don't you dare hurt her—'

'Shut your mouth. What kind of a name is Moira? She'd better have a nice ass. Has she got a nice butt with a name like Moira?'

Behind Tony's back, I saw Jackson's left leg lift up and hook the kettle off the side of the desk. I'll give him this much, he was doing his best to protect Jenny.

The kettle must have been boiled recently. Jackson hooked it off the table and it bounced off Tony's back.

'Shit!' he called out, leaping off the floor and releasing Jackson from his grip. Jackson sat up fast, grabbed the kettle by its handle and smashed it onto Tony's head. It was only small and made of plastic, but it was a second, unexpected blow to Tony who was still recovering from the shock of the hot water.

'Are you okay? Come with me ...' Jackson said, looking in the direction of the camera. 'We've got to run, come on!'

Tony had recovered himself and, now standing, had picked up a cup. Using it as a knuckle-duster, he pounded it into Jackson's face, quietening him instantly. The cup smashed. Jackson reeled.

The camera moved slightly, away from the main action.

'And you keep quiet, you bitch!' Tony said, heading for the camera. Another fist. The camera dropped to the floor. Everything was black. All I could hear was a struggle between the two men. The camera was picked up again, it was pointed towards the fight. The hand holding the phone was shaking even worse this time, Tony's blow must have cowed the person doing the filming. I knew even then who it was.

As the camera settled, I could see Jackson on Tony's back, one arm around his neck, the other pounding his side. Tony was trying to shake him off, like a fly that he was unable to swat. Realising he was making no headway, Tony turned round and fell backwards onto the bed on top of Jackson. Jackson struggled to gain the upper hand again, but Tony rolled over, stood up and grabbed Jackson's head. He pulled it violently and threw Jackson onto the floor. I heard Jackson's head hit the ground. It had stunned him. His head was lying by the leg of the bed, it was too dark to see if he was bleeding, but it looked as if he was, his hair looked wet.

'Stay down, you bugger!' Tony snarled.

Jackson struggled to recover, he raised his head, but Tony booted it down with his foot. Jackson tried to move, he must have known that it was nearly over. He started to call out, Tony gave him a sharp dig with his boot, right in his teeth.

Jackson was half-sobbing, half-cursing as Tony knelt down once again and moved his face right up close.

'Moira isn't going to be interested in you now with a

face like that. She's gonna want to have a piece of Tony. She'll be here soon, I can't wait to show her what it's like to have a real man. Hey, you can watch us if you like. You might learn a few lessons ...'

Jackson made a last struggle, pushing his free hand towards Tony's eyes, trying to scratch, claw – whatever would give him an advantage.

'You bastard!' Tony squealed, moving a hand up to his eye. Jackson must have torn his eyelid – whatever it was, it had hurt him badly.

Tony placed his hand over his eye and moved his right hand out to punch Jackson once again. He punched a first time – hard and angry – then began to deliver the second blow. He stopped and looked towards the person filming.

'Is that on, you bitch? Are you filming this?'

He stood up, hostile, furious, and began to move towards the camera. Jackson grabbed his leg and bit into it. Tony cried out in pain, then turned to deal with him one final time.

'Will you stay down!' He punched him once again. Then I saw something that I could never ever have imagined.

Tony lifted the end of the bed up with his right hand and pushed Jackson's head with his left hand, his legs straddled over him as he lay on the floor. Jackson could see what was happening. The video was too dark to see his eyes, but he must have been absolutely terrified as he realised what Tony was doing.

Tony sank to his knees and lifted up the side of the bed with his right hand, putting his left hand around Jackson's throat. He fought as hard as he could, but Tony edged his head directly under the leg of the bed. Jackson made one last struggle as Tony pushed his head the final few inches, he was trying anything now, attempting to move his head to the side to avoid what was coming. Tony's grip was too fierce. He dropped the side of the bed, the wooden leg falling heavily into Jackson's mouth. He gave a short, sharp yelp as his head was pinned to the floor. Tony sat on the edge of the bed and forced the leg deeper down into his throat. Jackson's feet twitched, then there was silence.

Tony turned towards the camera. With Jackson now silenced, he was returning to whoever it was filming the events in the room. He must have thought that they were unconscious or restrained, he hadn't been concerned about them until he'd spotted the phone recording everything that was going on.

'And now it's your turn, you bitch!'

He stood up deliberately.

'Maybe you and Moira can share a bit of Tony's love later on. Let's not call her Moira. I prefer the name Ellie. Let's call her Ellie. You and Ellie get to sleep with Tony together. And what's your name, bitch? Better not be something ugly like Moira. Give me that bloody thing!'

The picture went blurred, then dark, as he grabbed the phone and threw it on the ground. I heard him stamp on it, but it was still recording audio.

'What's your name, bitch? You certainly look good enough to eat. What's your name?'

All I could hear was sobbing. A female voice. Petrified. Not knowing what was going to happen next, at the hands of a violent madman who'd just killed Jackson inches away from her.

'It's Meg. My name's Meg ...'

'Pretty name Meg. Meg and Ellie. Very tasty. Now shut your mouth, Meg, until Ellie gets here.'

There was a thud. The sound of flesh hitting flesh. Then just the sound of Tony breathing.

After that a voice, some distance away, probably from the next room. Muffled, but audible.

'Fuck me, Pete, harder ... oh God, that's good, do it again ...'

Then silence as the audio ended and Tony finished destroying the phone.

CHAPTER ELEVEN

I thought I was going to be sick. Then and there in reception. What a welcome that would have been for the family that had just walked through the entrance.

Oh God, what was I going to do? Ellie had been right about her stalker. And somehow he'd run into Meg. He'd got Meg in there with him when he'd killed Jackson. The police must have found Jackson. Were there two bodies? Had the bastard killed Meg too? I was frantic, I had to know if she was still alive. I'd have to talk to the police now, tell them everything.

I must have looked a state. Jenny was looking at me, concerned. Ignoring the family who were waiting to be checked in, she got up from her workstation, came through the door at the side and rushed over to me.

'What's happened?' she demanded. 'You know something, don't you?'

As a member of the senior management team at the radio station, I've developed something of a poker face. It's a non-committal expression which I use when I'm thinking furiously about how to deal with some piece of crappy news that a member of staff has just delivered to me. I deployed the technique with Jenny.

I needed thinking time. Ellie and I were on that video, as clear as anything. She even used my name. We weren't guilty of anything – not anything that the police would be interested in as part of their crime investigation – but all this had to come out.

Meg must have heard what was going on in the room next to her. I couldn't think of any way that the situation could be rescued. I'd have to tell the police about Meg, I had to know if she was okay.

I decided to lie to Jenny. There was so much deception involved already at that stage, what was another white lie? I couldn't face being the one to tell her about Jackson. The police would need to do that.

'It's nothing, Jenny. I've just received some bad news about my mum. Have the police interviewed you yet?'

'Oh …' She was disappointed. Poor girl must have been on tenterhooks all day wondering where Jackson had got to. I'd leave it to the police – or Bob – to break the news to her.

'Yes,' she continued. 'There's a couple of guys set up some interview rooms in the conference area through the bar. I'll need to go to the station at some point, but they got a statement from me earlier.'

'What did you tell them in the end?'

'I kept quiet about Jackson. For now. I told them every-thing I know, minus the bit about meeting up.'

Jenny's own secret had to come out now. She'd have to tell the police what they'd been planning. Now that Jackson was dead, it could hinder the investigation if she didn't. At least there was no doubt about who the killer was: Ellie's crazy stalker, Tony Miller.

'Jenny, you may need to tell the police about you and

Jackson. If it comes to that, you'll know when you have to admit it. I know it's hard, but don't lie about it. It's important.'

She looked at me, studying my face. She knew I was holding something back, but didn't know what.

'Any sign of your wife?' she asked.

She couldn't have asked a more pertinent question if she'd tried. I shrugged it off.

'Nothing yet, I think she must have gone straight home.'

My voice faltered.

'I'm sorry, I think I need a drink of water.'

'Excuse me, can we get checked in please?'

The dad from the family party was getting agitated. Get as stroppy as you want, mate, Jenny's about to tell you to sling your hook. Good luck spending the night searching for a new hotel with your fractious toddlers in tow.

'No, you can just piss off!'

Jenny turned on him suddenly, as if she'd stored up every snug-at-night guarantee that she'd ever had to offer, rolled it into a ball and shoved it down his throat. She stormed out through the door and into the night. I wasn't sure whether to go after her, but I was interrupted by the door to my side opening. A woman walked out, not uniformed, but very obviously police.

'Mr Bailey?' she asked.

I nodded.

'Are you happy to come with me to a temporary interview room so that we can talk in private?'

I nodded again. She must have wondered what kind of witness statement she was going to get. A series of nods wouldn't get the investigation very far.

'May I nip into the gents and get a drink of water before we talk? I'm a bit hoarse.'

It was her turn to nod. Bob Hays walked through from the bar, seeing a growing crowd of customers gathering at the reception desk.

'Where on earth is Jenny?' he muttered to himself, heading through into the reception desk area.

'The young woman just rushed out in tears,' said the dad. 'Told me to piss off!'

Bob began the unenviable task of placating the public, and I made my way to the main toilets which were just through from the bar area. I took a deep breath as soon as I was on my own again. I had to think through my story. Quickly.

I looked at my phone screen. Facebook was still open at the video, which had returned to the original thumbnail preview. I looked at the audience. Good old Meg. She hadn't shared the video publicly, it was a limited audience, probably just her friends. I looked at the comments. I knew most of the people who'd expressed concern about the video, it appeared to be friends, family and work colleagues only. Thank God it wasn't public, it would have been all over the internet.

I sent Alex a quick note via Messenger, that's how we usually spoke: *Going to call you soon. Your mobile number still the same? Got a problem here. Will need your help.*

I'd like to have spoken to Ellie about Tony Miller, but I didn't have time. Neither did I have any way to message her. It would have to wait. I'd speak to Alex as soon as possible, then catch up with Ellie. And I had to find out about Meg. I took a drink of water from the tap and headed back to reception.

The police had set up a makeshift interview area in the hotel. They'd have a lot of transient people to catch. I was semi-aware of the procedures involved, I'd reported on the process many times in my radio work, but had never experienced them first-hand.

There seemed to be a lot of fuss before we got started – procedure and arse-covering I guessed – but eventually we got to it. There were two people interviewing me, probably because I was slightly more important than other hotel guests as I'd been in the room next door.

Try as I might, they would not give me any details about the body – or bodies – that had been found. I knew enough about the process to understand that they'd need a clean run at my story, they wouldn't want it contaminated by any additional knowledge about what had happened. Tell the truth, Pete. Show them the video. Think only of Meg. Figure out the shitty bits later. Work through the process, you know how it goes.

The more senior cop excused himself for a moment as we were getting started: home address, contact numbers, workplace, availability, and so on. All the time, I was desperate to get more information about Meg.

'Alright if I check my phone?' I asked as he was leaving the room.

'Yeah, no problem, I'll be back in a moment.'

I keyed my password into my smartphone. The battery was about to die once again, the small charge in Ellie's room had only given me a temporary reprieve.

There were a couple of new messages, both Facebook. Alex, urging me to update her asap. And one from Meg. A Facebook message from Meg. She was safe!

The message had just been sent. I felt myself relaxing, I hadn't realised how wound up I was. I opened up Messenger on my phone: *Come home. Say nothing to police. Bring Ellie, cheating bastard. Talk to police and its over.*

The video was gone. It had been deleted from Meg's

timeline. All the comments were gone. It was as if it had never existed.

Meg hadn't written that message. It's a stupid thing, but it wasn't her language. She didn't speak like that. Even if she was pissed, she didn't speak like that. And she'd missed an apostrophe. She might have been crap at texting, but on Messenger, on a proper keyboard, she got things right.

Tony Miller must have taken her. Could he have got into her Facebook account on his own? There's no way, he'd have to be with her to get into her account. That meant Meg was alive.

He wanted both me and Ellie. He had Meg. The violent little bastard had killed Jackson, now he'd taken Meg. He wanted Ellie and me together. Was he lining us up for some kind of punishment?

I needed to go for a shit. They don't ever tell you that bit in films. I was so nervous and on edge, I had to get to the toilet. Soon.

'Mind if I go to the toilet?' I asked the young copper who was sitting in the room with me. 'It's an emergency. I wouldn't ask otherwise. Sorry.'

The young guy smiled at me.

'Sure,' he answered, 'I'll tell the DCI that you'll be back soon.'

How embarrassing. It was like sneaking off for a dump at school. Everybody knew where you'd gone. But I had to get away for a few minutes before I spoke to the police. I had to find out what was happening to Meg.

I made myself comfortable in one of the cubicles and got out my phone again. I read the message, looking for clues. I decided to take a chance and message back: *Tell me Meg is safe. I know who you are. Tony Miller. Leave Meg alone.*

Straight away I saw that the message had been read. I could see that a reply was being written: *The bitch is fine. Very sexy too. Come home or she gets it. After I've fucked her. We've had a nice day together, getting to know each other. I think she likes me.*

Anger surged through me, I wanted to shout, punch the sides of the cubicle, hit something hard. I wanted to smash Tony's face in. I had to think of Meg.

Leave her alone. We'll come. Both of us. No police. Do not hurt Meg. You hurt Meg I'll kill you you shit.

Possibly not the best words with which to talk a mad man down from a ledge, but I felt as if I had to make some kind of threat to him.

Whatever tough guy. She's wearing nice panties. Very sexy. Come fast. Before I do.

I wanted to scream. Dare I tell the cops? What would happen if I went back to the house? I didn't know what to do. I had to speak to Alex. I finished off in the cubicle, washed my hands, made the call. Her mobile number was the same. Good job. She picked up straight away.

'Pete?'

'Hi, yes, it's me.'

'What is going on with Meg? Have you seen the video?'

'Yes. Look, my phone is going to die, we'll have to speak quickly. I need you to keep a secret, Alex. And I might need your contacts. Can you help?'

'Of course I can, Pete. Just tell me what's going on. Is Meg okay?'

'I've landed myself in the shit. I'm at a works training event and I slept with somebody I met here ...'

I heard the breath. It was quiet, but there was a reaction. Alex didn't say anything.

'She's called Ellie and she has a stalker, Alex. She has a bloody stalker. Meg came down to see me. She got caught up with him in some way. He must have known about me and Ellie.'

'Okay. That's not Ellie Turner is it? I've seen her on the regional TV show reels.'

'Yes, she's on TV. You may have seen her. This stalker has taken Meg. He wants me and Ellie to come to him or he'll hurt Meg.'

'Jesus Pete! Do the police know?'

'He told me not to tell them. I'm in the middle of an interview with them now. What do I say?'

'Why are the police speaking to you?'

'This stalker guy – Tony Miller – he's killed somebody in the hotel. A young lad, one of the staff. It happened in the room next to mine. You saw it, that's what the video was showing.'

'Was that Meg's voice at the end? Was she filming it? Hell Pete, what's going on there?'

'It's a mess, Alex. Look, my phone can't hang on much longer, can you help?'

'Of course I can, what do you need?'

'Should I tell the police about Tony Miller? I don't know if we should go there alone. He's a nutter, you saw what he did to that kid. I don't want to put Meg at risk.'

'How far away from home are you, Pete? How long will it take you to get back?'

'Two hours, maybe more in the dark.'

'Look, get your phone charged. Finish off your interview with the police. I'm going to make some calls. I'll see if

I can get someone to the house on the quiet. I know a chap in your area, a private security guy who was on the show. I'll give him a call.'

'No names, Alex. He'll probably know who I am from the radio. We have to get Meg out safely. If I can get to Meg, then you can send the police in. We have to keep her safe. None of this is her fault.'

'Okay, Pete. Don't be an idiot though, don't go in there alone. And keep your bloody phone on charge, I'll ring you as soon as I can.'

'Thanks, Alex. I'm really scared. I've been a right shit with Meg. She doesn't deserve this. She drove over to surprise me on my birthday.'

'Just don't do anything stupid. Tell this Tony guy that you're coming. Alone.'

'Will do. Thanks, Alex. I appreciate this.'

'No problem, Pete. Stay safe. Love you.'

She put the phone down. She'd said 'love you'. Was it habit? Probably. There was too much on my plate to care. I needed to finish off with the police and make the drive back home. I returned to the Facebook app and messaged Meg's account: *We're on our way shortly. We'll be 2 or 3 hours. You keep your hands off Meg. You keep her safe. We'll come. No police. Just leave Meg alone.*

The message was read immediately. They were probably in the spare room, Meg kept her laptop on the desk there. A reply came back almost immediately: *See you soon tough guy. Bring Ellie. No funny stuff. Its Ellie I want to see. Bring Ellie and you get your bitch back.*

Another missed apostrophe. It wasn't Meg typing. He'd been with her all day. What had they been doing? There was a pause, but from the screen I could see that he was still typing: *Found a lovely knife in your kitchen. Any sign of police and I slice her neck.*

I rushed back to the makeshift interview room. They were waiting for me, impatient to get started.

'Apologies,' I said to the DCI. 'I had to nip to the toilets. How can I help?'

I was anxious to get it over with. I'd decided what I was going to omit and what would stay in my account of events. I had to protect Meg at all costs. I needed to get back to the house, with Ellie too. I hadn't figured out what we would do when we got there, but we had at least to show our faces. Alex was working on the detail, she had great contacts and lots of influence, I had to rely on her pulling a rabbit out of a hat.

The line of questioning was what you'd expect: times of arrival and departure; my movements up and down the corridor; had I heard or seen anything. I described everything in detail. The only part that I left out was Ellie's presence. I didn't mention that we'd walked back together. I airbrushed her out of the story.

Had I seen or heard anything suspicious? No. Was I aware of anything going on in the room next to mine? No. Is there anything else I'd like to add? Yes, the door had been ajar, I had noticed it a couple of times.

I did wonder if I was dropping Jenny in at the deep end with this snippet of information, but it was crucial to what had gone on. The cops only needed to know that Jackson was in there, presumably to meet somebody or have a quiet cigarette. Somehow Tony Miller had got in the room with him. I told them to speak to Fergus too. He'd mention the man that he'd let into the building when he returned from the pub. The police would then know that they were looking for a person who probably wasn't a hotel guest.

I had to keep reminding myself that I wasn't a suspect, I was a witness. Sure, I'd been unlucky enough to be in the room next door to a murder. They were investigating the murder of Jackson, nothing else at that stage. It was too late for Jackson, I had to consider Meg.

My mind wandered as I considered telling the DCI about Meg's abduction. I'd already seen what Tony was capable of, I daren't deviate from the plan. If the cops surrounded our house with Meg inside, it would become a siege situation. I'd covered two of those in my journalistic career. The first ended with the death of the two hostage family members, then the suicide of the hostage taker: an estranged husband and his two kids. What a way to show your love and put the marriage back together again.

The second was a guy who'd recently come out of jail. His girlfriend had moved in with someone else while he'd been inside. He decided to punish both his girlfriend and her new lover. He hanged them from their fifth floor flat balcony then jumped over the side to kill himself. Incredibly, he survived, ending up crippled. Another great bit of relationship management.

I'd seen how hostage situations went. I didn't fancy Meg's chances. I hadn't a clue what I was going to do to sort out Tony Miller. I only knew I had to help Meg.

My witness statement was soon over and done with. They'd probably want to speak to me again, they were very interested in the door being ajar. They'd already talked to Jenny, Bob and Derek. Derek would have confirmed my story about the door. That was the piece of information that they needed, that was the crucial thing that I had to tell them. Fergus would tell them about the man he let into the building. But would Jenny mention Meg? Hopefully not.

As I was getting ready to leave, there was a final question. It caught me off guard, I felt my face redden. They must have seen it. They don't miss a trick, these guys.

'One more thing, Mr Bailey. Derek Walker thought he saw a woman leaving a room in your part of the corridor. A younger woman, he thought, very composed and self-assured. Would you know anything about that?'

I stalled.

'Is Derek Walker the gentleman I spoke to from the OverNight Inn, the one who was checking the rooms when the fire alarm went off?'

'Yes, that's the one. He couldn't be certain because he was further along the corridor checking the rooms, but he thought he'd seen somebody through the glass in the fire door.'

They knew about Ellie. She'd said that Derek hadn't seen her. But he had. Damn it! She could have been anybody, I decided to stick to my story.

'There was a lot of movement in the corridor when the fire alarm went off. I could hear it in my room, but I haven't a clue who was out there. It was all clear except for Derek when I left the building.'

'You didn't mention why it took you so long to leave the building when you were so close to the fire door ...'

They were getting a bit too close to the truth. It was like having the dogs on my tail. I hadn't done anything wrong, extra-marital sex is not a criminal offence. I decided to throw them off the scent.

'I was a bit pissed, to be honest with you. I was fast asleep. I can sleep through virtually anything, I'm afraid. I didn't hear it.'

That did the job. I was good to go. They'd be in contact if they needed to speak to me again, which they were certain that they would.

'When can I go back to my room and get my stuff?' I asked. I'd need my car keys, and my phone charger would be a bonus.

'We've got your belongings in the room next door. We didn't need to retain anything, but your room will now be out of bounds for the remainder of your stay until the forensics team is done. We've locked off that entire corridor now. You'll need to sign for your things.'

I hadn't needed to bring much with me; a small holdall had carried my toiletries, a few changes of underwear and my tech. The DCI followed me into the adjoining room, although it was the constable who'd been tasked with giving me my stuff. That made me suspicious. He was lurking. I took my bag, signed the form on the clipboard that had been handed to me, and turned to leave the room.

'Just one more thing, Mr Bailey!'

Shit, what now? This guy and his theatrics were becoming a pain in the arse.

'Yes, what is it?' I snapped, perhaps a little too harshly.

'We found one more item in your room which didn't appear to belong to you.'

'Oh yes, what was it?' I asked, trying to appear as nonchalant as I could.

He had something behind his back. More theatrics.

'I don't suppose you recognise this do you, Mr Bailey?'

He held up the pink bra. The very bra that I'd removed from Ellie the night before. A bra that had somehow got discarded in the room. And missed when we had to evacuate for the fire alarm. How had Ellie managed to miss her bra?

'Well, it's not mine,' I laughed, perhaps a little too forced. The DCI stared at me. He was good at this game, he knew I'd have to follow up with something else.

'I don't know whose it is. If you found it in my room, I suppose it must have been left by another guest.'

'You're sure about that?'

'Certain. It's not part of your case, is it? I mean, does it really matter where it came from?'

The DCI looked at me, trying to make an assessment of what kind of man I was, I think.

'No Mr Bailey, it's not part of the case in question. We were just keen to return the item to its rightful owner ... whoever that might be.'

CHAPTER TWELVE

Were the cops suspicious about Ellie? I was certain they thought I was keeping something back. By staying quiet about knowing who the killer was and where he'd been hiding, I was now actively hindering their investigation. What choice did I have? He had my wife. I'd seen what he was capable of. I didn't trust them not to go in and bungle the job. I wanted Meg back. I wanted to make things right.

Alex was on the case. We'd put something in place, give Tony what he wanted, and send the local police in to overpower him. I had a couple of hours to figure out exactly what the master plan would be. And I had to break the bad news to Ellie.

I'd be interviewed again, there was no way they weren't going to squeeze me for more information. Meg's Facebook video had been deleted, presumably by Tony Miller, so there was no chance of that causing problems now. It was Ellie that he was after, not Meg. There was no way that I was sacrificing Ellie either, but in any scenario she would have to be used as bait. I had to talk to her, and we needed to jump in my car and head back to my house.

As I walked through reception, I wondered about Jenny. Did she know about Jackson yet? I was grateful that Meg had restricted the access on her Facebook video – it would have gone viral if it had been public. Jenny might well have seen it on her own feed if that had been the case. I'd need to get my phone charged, send her a message, check in with her. She'd be devastated when she found out about Jackson's murder, but there wouldn't be any point in telling the police what they'd been up to. They'd have to guess why Jackson was in that room; there were many reasons why a young lad might have sneaked off in the middle of the night to be on his own.

Derek had replaced Bob on reception, and things had quietened down as far as check-ins were concerned. I was sure that I wouldn't need a room that night, I'd stay at home with Meg. It was safe to say that I wouldn't be returning for day two of Diane's brainstorming weekend. Sunday was likely to be spent taking care of Meg and speaking to the police – with Tony Miller in custody by then, I hoped.

I headed for the lift and was taken aback when Jem stepped out accompanied by Ali, one of the young reporters from the office. She was nice. Clearly Jem had already clocked that.

'Hello mate,' he began, his face reacting immediately to seeing me outside the lift doors. 'Go on into the bar, Ali,' he continued. 'I'll be with you in a moment!'

Ali moved off, and we stepped away from the lift doors so that we could chat without obstructing the area.

'You coming down for drinks?' Jem asked. 'Look at all this going on with the police – we can't get away from it, even for a weekend.'

I wanted to be rid of Jem as soon as possible.

'Can't make it tonight, I'm afraid.'

I wondered if I should mention going home. It was unlikely that Jem would accept any lame excuses so I decided to tell another lie.

'I have to head back home. Meg is ill and I need to pick up some pills for her from the overnight chemist. I'll drive back early tomorrow morning.'

His face changed.

'What's wrong with Meg? Is she okay?'

'Who knows, some sickness thing, she's in quite a bad way by the sound of it. Thought I'd better do the decent thing and drive back and see what I can do to help. It's only a couple of hours, lucky that we're not in London for this one!'

Jem studied my face. He was fighting to stay cheery, but he looked concerned.

'Do you want me to come with you, mate? Keep you company? It's a bit of a drag having to drive all that way on your own. I wouldn't mind a chat, seems like a while since we caught up.'

I needed Jem to piss off. He was a best pal and all that, but I wanted him out of the way. This was a journey that I would be making with Ellie, if I could convince her to come with me.

'No Jem, seriously, it's fine. It'll all be a storm in a teacup. Nothing to worry about. I'll get up early tomorrow, I'll be here in time for breakfast, nobody will know I've gone. Besides, you look like you're getting on well with Ali ...'

Distraction. That was the name of the game. Jem was never happier than when he got the chance of a bit of innuendo about women. Since parting with Sally, it had become more pronounced. Ego probably. His pride had been hurt and he was keen to let everybody in the office know that he was still a player.

It suddenly seemed so unimportant. All I cared about was Meg. Why had I even slept with Ellie? Meg was the woman I loved, why hadn't I realised that without having to put us through all this crap? If I'd returned to my room after the pub, I'd have spent the night with Meg, and the death in the room next door would have had nothing to do with me.

'Ali's hot,' he smiled, distracted once again by the thought of that night's conquest. 'Very ambitious. I've promised to give her some career guidance, reveal the secrets to my success and all that. As usual, it'll require taking her knickers off.'

I'd always laughed along with Jem in the past, never challenging what he was doing. But in the context of what had been going on, it seemed predatory and calculating. I'd never noticed that, just chuckled along like Beavis and Butt-Head. What Jem was doing wasn't very nice. He was using his seniority as the basis for a sexual encounter. It had taken me a long time to see that and it made me uncomfortable.

'You enjoy the evening, Jem. I'll catch up with you tomorrow, okay?'

'Yeah, sure mate. Send my best wishes to Meg. Tell her I'm thinking about her.'

'I will, see you tomorrow.'

We parted, Jem heading for the bar to join Ali, me pressing the button to call the lift.

The lift arrived, the doors opened, my thoughts moved onto other things. Ellie. Charging my phone. Getting back to Meg. Talking to Alex. The lift seemed to take ages to work its way to Ellie's floor. I headed directly to her room, gently tapping at the door. I was anxious not to draw attention to myself. I was still hoping, stupidly, that we might be able to keep our casual encounter out of things.

There was no answer. No movement in the room. Ellie had said that she'd stay there. She knew how serious things were getting. I started to get agitated, annoyed that she'd messed up the plan. We'd agreed what to do, it had been the last thing we'd discussed. I tapped again, a little louder this time. Maybe she hadn't heard.

There was no movement in the room. Bloody hell, Ellie! I tried the door. It was locked. Maybe she was down in the bar, perhaps she'd got fed up waiting for me. I tried the door again and knocked once more. Nothing. I looked down to check if there was light shining under the door. There wasn't, but there was a piece of paper there. You'd have missed it if you were walking by, but it was sticking out enough for me to see it and pick it up. Ellie had left me a note. Good, at least she'd had the sense to do that before going wherever it was she'd gone.

She'd used the notepad in her room to scribble a message to me. I could see that it had been written hastily. My name was on the front, it was folded twice.

Pete — it's Tony Miller. I told you I saw him. He has your wife. The bugger texted me. He wants to speak to me. Smooth things over he says. He's weird as anything, but I don't think he'll harm your wife. I'm going to see him. He sent me your postcode for the satnav. I need to fix this, Pete. Follow me when you get this note. He said don't tell the police. I'm sure he'll be okay if I talk to him. He's just pissed off. Ellie x

Damn! Ellie had gone on without me. She'd scrawled her mobile number at the bottom of her note. Good, as soon as I got a charge I could call her. I hoped she was right about Tony Miller. She knew him better than I did. She'd be able to speak to him, get Meg released safely. Once everybody was out of danger, I'd let the police know straight away. It would all work out. Meg would be okay. Surely Meg would be okay?

As expected, Alex had moved fast.

I wasted no time in leaving the OverNight Inn and heading for my car. I didn't bother checking out of the hotel, my room was out of bounds to me anyway and the radio station was picking up the bill.

I had to get on the road and rendezvous with Ellie before she reached my house. I didn't want her messing things up for Meg. She was crucial to a solution with Tony Miller, but I had to think about Meg first. Perhaps I should have done that earlier.

I was able to start charging my phone via the USB unit, which plugged into the cigarette lighter. It was too dead to bring back to life straight away, I'd have to wait for it to replenish some basic charge so I could switch it back on.

I wondered if I'd be returning to the hotel. It was difficult to see how. However things played out, it would eventually involve the police. More statements, more questions, further discomfort. I hadn't done anything wrong. Tony Miller was the culprit, we had video evidence – if they could retrieve it from deleted items, that is.

It was dark and raining heavily when I left. Huge puddles of water lay on the road concealing potholes beneath. I needed to concentrate on my driving, but I couldn't stop myself reaching over to check my phone. Eventually it lit up. Glancing from the road, to my phone, to Ellie's note, I keyed in her mobile number. It went to voice-mail. She must have been half an hour ahead of me, in the rural bit of the journey where sheep replaced mobile signals. I'd call her when I thought she was nearing civilisation again.

Alex was next on the list. No, Tony Miller. I had to message him to let him know I was on my way. Like Ellie, I'd lose signal soon, I had to give him a timescale. Poor Meg, stuck with a madman like Tony Miller. How was he passing the time? They'd been together for the best part of a day. My mind flew into an unfettered panic. Would he rape her? Had he done so already? Would he threaten her? He'd already hit her, but she was unhurt enough to walk with him unnoticed from the hotel to one of the cars. I had to believe this was all about Ellie. Meg had been in the wrong place at the wrong time. It wasn't anything to do with her. She was just bait for Ellie.

On my way. No more than 2 hours. Ellie coming too. We'll give you what you want. Don't harm Meg, she's done nothing.

I didn't tell him Ellie was ahead of me. I hoped we'd be able to talk first. I didn't want her blundering in there on her own.

There was no reply from Tony. I tried to focus on what needed to be done, I felt sick whenever I thought of Meg. She worked with people like Tony Miller all the time. She knew what these guys were like. I had to trust that she'd be using her skills from work to keep him calm.

I heard the sound of a car horn. I'd veered across the carriageway into the path of an oncoming car while typing the message on my phone. I pulled the car back to my side of the road, cursing. I'd have the police after me if I wasn't careful.

Making much more effort to focus on the road, I scrolled through my phone contacts and rang Alex. I placed my phone on the passenger seat and put it on speaker phone. At least I'd be able to focus while I was talking to her.

'Pete, hi! Thank God you rang. I thought I'd never hear from you. Where are you?'

'I'm driving over to see Tony Miller now. He hasn't harmed Meg ... I don't think he's harmed her. The woman I slept with last night – sorry, Ellie, you know her name – she's driving over there. She went ahead of me. What do you know, Alex?'

'I've called some contacts, I can tell you what's going on. There's one body in the hotel, a kid called Jackson Deakin. Your guy, Tony Miller, had torn out the lining and concealed his body under the bed, that's why it took a while to find him. Miller has a police record – your lady Ellie is named on there, no surprises with any of that I guess. They don't know it's Tony yet.'

'Okay, we know that, it explains why the police took so long to find a body. What else?'

'Meg hasn't been placed in the room. They don't know what's gone on in there yet. Forensics will probably detect her eventually, but she's not in the picture at the moment. They'll find out it's Tony Miller too, at least he's known to the police already. It's a hotel room, there's all sorts of DNA in there ... it will take some time to process all that.'

'You've seen this more times than I have, Alex. I take it you actually watch the reports on your TV show? What are the chances of Meg getting out of there unharmed with a nutter like Tony Miller on the loose? It's Ellie he wants. However his crazy mind is working, Ellie is the one who can talk him down off the ledge. Has he ever hurt anyone before?'

'Nothing on his record. It's the usual thing. A loner. Lived with his mum. Mum died, he went a bit crazy. Forms unhealthy associations with women in the spotlight. He's never hurt Ellie. Done some crazy stuff, but not hurt her. No sign of him hurting anyone else either. This Jackson lad is the first.'

'I don't want the police to know yet. I want to keep me and Ellie quiet as long as we can.'

'Okay, so long as you're sure? I talked to my pal in CID, he thinks it's a hypothetical for a show idea, but the local cops could get someone round there very fast. Just give me the word.

'I did one more thing, I hope you don't mind. You remember that Special Forces guy we used to interview on the radio – when we were living ... when we lived in Manchester – Jason Davies. He's watching your house. He lives half an hour away from you. He'll see you when you go in. The minute you need him, he'll be there. I'm texting you his number. Why don't you dial into his phone when you go in? If you get in a scrape, he'll be there in seconds.'

'That's good, Alex, that's a great idea. He does know not to do anything until I get there? I don't want him messing it up.'

'He's good, Pete. He's there already, watching. It's all quiet at the house, lights on. Meg's car is in the drive, they used her vehicle to drive over.'

'Okay, great, thanks Alex. I'm shitting bricks about this guy, he's obviously got a screw loose. But Meg's dealt with people like him before, she'll know how to keep him calm.

Ellie knows him too, not in a good way, but he's never hurt her before. Do you think I'm doing the right thing – should I call the police?'

I never got my answer to that question. I was suddenly aware of two bright white headlights dazzling me. I swerved and undergrowth scraped all along the sides of the car as I veered off the road. The car came to an immediate and violent stop. The next thing I remember is coming round in the darkness, dazed and sore.

I can't remember the number of road deaths that I've reported on the radio due to the misuse of mobile phones. It's one of my pet peeves, alongside silly beards and vaping. Yet, ever the hypocrite, I was guilty of the crime that I so readily condemn others for.

Texting and driving at the same time. Not quite texting, but too busy concentrating on my phone call and not looking at the road. In the dark. On a wet, rural stretch of road. What a pillock! I got exactly what I deserved. We might have saved some lives that night if I'd pulled over to call Alex.

It was like waking up on holiday when you know something isn't quite right, but you have to remember where you are to figure out what's going on. My head was resting against the airbag when I woke up. I noticed I was dribbling first of all. All down the airbag.

I wiped my mouth. It was dark. Though my headlights were still on, I could see that I'd run off the road into an area of woodland. I could hear Alex's voice: 'Pete, are you okay? Pete? Pete?'

Slowly, my brain rebooted and I worked out what had happened. Shit, who had I nearly hit? Were they okay?

I started to move. I couldn't feel any blood. I wriggled my fingers and I could move my feet. Thank God for that. Slowly I found the seatbelt button and released the strap. The car had come to rest at an angle, it was leaning downwards, I had to prise myself out carefully. It was difficult to get my footing.

I could still hear Alex on my phone. Where had it gone? Moving up the bank where the car had come to rest, I worked open the rear door. I could see the light from my phone, it had landed in the passenger area. I picked it up, putting it upside down to my mouth.

'Alex, hi, I'm here. I just had a crash ...'

'Bloody hell, Pete! Are you alright?'

'Yeah, I'm just a bit dazed. I don't know what happened to the other vehicle, I need to make sure they're okay. This could make a mess of things if the police turn up. How long was I out?'

'Not long. A couple of minutes maybe. I could hear you breathing, it sounded horrible from my end. You sure you're okay?'

'Yes, fine Alex, thanks. I need to find out what happened to the other people. I'm going to ring off, then I'll call you back. Five minutes tops.'

I ended the call and began to orientate myself. I was standing in bracken. Wet bracken. Wherever I was, it was muddy and slippery. Great place to crash, Pete. I turned off the car engine – it was still running. I turned the lights off too, deciding to use the torch on my mobile phone to navigate my way back towards the road.

What had happened quickly became apparent. I'd veered off the road, across an overgrown grass verge and into a lightly wooded area. The car had gone down a small bank and hit a tree. I probably hadn't even been out cold, just shaken for a bit I reckoned. The front of the car was crunched.

The road was quiet, I couldn't see evidence of any other vehicle. Maybe the engine had stopped and they were out there in the darkness somewhere. The light from the torch on my phone was not a lot of use, and there was no way I was going to be able to reverse my car out of the wooded area. That was going to require a tow truck. I'd report the incident to the police in the morning, tell them I got caught by a deer running across the road. Meg would be fine by then.

I couldn't see anything on my side of the road, so I decided to cross over and take a closer look. There was nothing. No evidence of any vehicle there. I walked up and down, trying to figure out where the near collision had taken place. I found it soon enough. I could see tyre marks all over the verge. It looked as if they'd come to rest on the grass after swerving to avoid me. The little shits, though, they'd driven off and left me there. They might have checked to make sure I was okay.

Maybe they were pissed. Perhaps they had a reason for not getting involved. In the circumstances, that wasn't so bad, but leaving me on the roadside in the dark was a scummy thing to do. I might have been dead. However, it was good that my car would go undiscovered. I couldn't get a clear enough view in the darkness, but I reckoned I was deep enough into the trees to go unnoticed, even in daylight.

Okay, so nobody killed, nobody hurt. I needed to get my arse back to the house as soon as possible. I looked down at my phone. Two bars flickering to one bar, I was about to hit the dead zone in the journey across country. No data service available, so a quick check of Google Maps was out of the question.

My mind was still struggling to return to its normal ninja-like sharpness. I'd been shaken by the accident. I was wet and muddy and looked like a tramp. Not the best Saturday night out I'd ever had.

I needed to pee too. Desperately. The road was quiet enough to risk doing it there and then along the roadside. So I did. It seemed safe enough. I was in full flow when out of nowhere a set of car lights came on full beam, exposing me to the world in my urinating glory. There were calls of 'Screw you, arsehole!' and 'Don't tell me, it's the cold that made it so small!', the sound of a car horn, then the roar of an engine as a car sped off along the road into the distance.

I finished peeing and pulled up my flies. My phone was vibrating in my pocket. It would probably be Alex, wondering what was taking me so long, no doubt concerned that somebody had been hurt. It was Alex, but she had some worrying news.

'Pete, you need to get home fast. I was trying to check in with Jason, he was telling me there was activity in the house—'

'That's a good thing, isn't it? It means that they're still there, Meg's still fine?'

'That's what I thought, but I'm really worried. Jason went to get closer to the house to see what was going on and now I can't raise him on his phone. It just goes to voicemail.'

'He's probably turned his ringer off if he's up close to the house. He's special ops, he's not going to get caught out by a Nokia ringtone!'

'I know, I know. But he rang off when he said he heard raised voices. I'm worried, Pete, do you think we should let the police in on it? The last thing he heard was a woman's voice shouting. She was urging someone to stop—'

The adrenalin kicked in, my mind sharpened once again. Things had got tense in the house – was Meg in danger? Had Ellie gone storming in? I tried to work out if she'd had enough time to reach the house.

'Alex, what else did he say? Did he say who was shouting? Was Ellie there? Alex? Alex?'

Shit! I'd lost the signal. I'd hit the rural dead zone, where mobile phone signals go to die.

CHAPTER THIRTEEN

It was a strange time to be taking a trip down memory lane, but I remember being really calm when the phone signal died. I was in the middle of nowhere, it was only to be expected. I got one of those déjà vu moments, though, in spite of the stress of the situation. It was the rural location, it took me back in time to a place and moment many years previously.

It reminded me of a holiday that Meg and I had enjoyed in Cornwall, not so long after we were married. We were all loved up, our relationship problems had been a million miles away at the time.

Going to Cornwall had felt like driving to the end of the world. Just when you think you're there, you discover that the long, sticky-outy bit takes forever to drive across. Why couldn't they have stuck Penzance closer to the top, surely it would have been better for tourism?

This was the days before satnavs, or at least devices which were affordable by mortals. We thought nothing of reading maps then, in fact, it was part and parcel of a nice journey together. Meg would read the map and tell me which turn-offs to take. I loved listening to her voice as she outlined the turns and roundabouts coming up ahead, and we'd work together to navigate to the ends of the earth. Penzance.

We'd had a well-timed moment of excitement when we saw Falmouth signposted. It turned out we'd both nearly gone to college there. We were beginning to flag, we'd been on the road for close to seven hours by that stage. Meg spotted it on the map first, then the signposts started to appear.

'I was going there to study journalism years ago,' I announced, 'but I didn't fancy any of the girls in the prospectus.'

'You're kidding me, aren't you?' Meg had asked. 'You seriously chose your college based on the pictures of the other students?'

'Yes, there were some right uglies in the brochure. Universities need to learn to wheel out their best totty for the prospectus photo shoot. And I'm not being sexist here, I mean male and female totty. Didn't you even consider the hotness of the guys?'

'Never, you pervert!'

'If I'm going to study somewhere, I don't want to be stuck on the set of The Addams Family. Anyway, what put you off going there?'

'Well, the distance for starters. I made the right call on that one, it's bloody miles from where Mum and Dad live – lived.'

It was still catching her out. It's hard to make adjustments when people die. Things stay the same in your mind, you have to keep reminding yourself that people are gone. Meg had told me early on that she'd lost her mum and dad really young. In her teens. It's cruel that. She was an only child too. Her family just disappeared off the face of the planet, there had never been anybody for me to meet. There was nobody left except for some distant relatives whom she'd never met. I didn't dwell on it, I was enjoying the conversation about Falmouth. It was a simple slip on her part, no big deal, she was enjoying the conversation too.

'Now I think about it, Pete, my reason for not going is as ridiculous as yours. Only not quite so pervy!'

'Go on then, why didn't you go there? If you'd been in the brochure, there would have been at least one bit of totty on the prospectus and I'd have certainly gone to track you down. A hottie like you would pull in the crowds!'

Meg laughed, flattered I think that I always found her so attractive.

'It was actually the photos in the prospectus that put me off. You must have noticed it too? It was the days before computer graphics and fancy software. But it was still crap. They'd got this photo of four students – two geeky blokes and two bland-looking girls—'

'Ah, so you admit it! It does matter how people look!'

'It's true the guys didn't do much for me, but it was more that they'd taken the same picture and stuck it in front of different backgrounds. Same students, same picture, terrible cutting out. But there they were. In the library, in the lecture theatre, in the college grounds. Looking exactly the same! It was like they only had four students in the whole place. It put me off. I went somewhere where the lecturers looked hotter!'

We laughed at that one. A silly thing, but it was very revealing. I hadn't thought about it for years. There were a lot of harsh truths in that memory.

Most importantly, it showed how much we loved each other's company. Sure, a lot of our relationship was based on sex and mutual attraction. I don't see anything wrong with that, it's only a problem if that's all you have. Meg and I loved hanging together. We could find joy in the simplest of things. A boring, seven-hour journey to Penzance? We should have been bitching at each other over Meg's map-reading skills. But we didn't. We found our pleasure in the simple things. The lack of sex was a symptom of our relationship difficulties. It was the closeness I was missing, the comfortable feeling of being with someone. I missed my pal. It had all got so serious. I wanted my best friend back. Maybe that's what I'd seen in Ellie. Of course she was sexy, but she was easy company too.

I don't think I'd ever made the connection before, and it was funny that it should take being stranded in the middle of nowhere and a random memory to make me realise it. I finally understood why Meg was so desperate for the baby. I saw why it was such a burning force in her, something that she felt we had to achieve. She felt exposed. She had nobody left. She was on her own. If we ever split up, she had no sisters or brothers to console her, no mum and dad to run to. It was only Meg. And she wanted to make a baby. With a child, there would be something more than her in the world. Of course, it was all the other reasons why people want to start families too. But I suddenly got it, the penny had finally dropped.

As I started walking along the roadside, checking my phone for a signal and looking behind me in the hope that a car or lorry might come along, I realised something that I should have thought about a little more carefully before I'd risked messing everything up by sleeping with Ellie.

I loved my wife deeply. I wanted to protect her and give her the child that she so desperately craved. I wanted more than anything to make her happy. Happy, like being in the car on the way to Penzance. Happy, like we'd been so many times in our lives. I'd been a dickhead sleeping with Ellie. I should have been working on my own relationship, not finding solace elsewhere with the first woman who gave me a smile and let me into her knickers.

I'd been a fool. I despised myself. Alone in the darkness, heading back home towards who knows what, I resolved that I would make it up to Meg. If I had to die for her, then I would. My wife meant more than anything in the world to me. I was going to sort out Tony Miller, then we would get on with the rest of our life together. There was still time to put it all right.

I was beginning to feel stiff as I walked along in the darkness. The car accident had taken its toll and I was experiencing some physical discomfort. I wasn't certain how long I'd been walking. A few cars had passed me, but the only person who'd pulled over was heading in the opposite direction.

It was a vicar of all people. At least she was practising what she preached.

'Are you alright? You look like you've been in the wars. Can I call someone for you? Where are you heading?'

'No, I'm good – thank you for stopping. My car's broken down, and I have a friend coming to meet me along the road. I decided to start walking to meet her. I look worse than I am. I got in a mess trying to bump-start it.'

'Are you sure I can't call somebody for you? Would you like a chocolate bar?'

What a strange thing to offer. Maybe she'd been

watching too much Bear Grylls on the TV. I took it – a sugar boost was exactly what I needed.

The vicar went on her way and it wasn't too long afterwards that a van driver pulled over.

'You alright, mate? Want a lift or something?'

Maybe the vicar had put in a good word for me with Him upstairs and sent a bit of help my way. The van driver was a shop-fitter who'd been working late in Newcastle, grateful for a bit of company to keep him awake on his way home after a long day. He didn't ask any questions about why I was covered in mud, neither did he seem to notice the grazes on my arms. Even I hadn't clocked those in the darkness, they didn't hurt at all.

I was grateful for the distraction of a bit of generic conversation – and for the fact that he listened to the other local radio station so wouldn't recognise my voice. Now that might have been tricky.

As we neared the outskirts of the city, the signal bars began to reappear on my mobile phone. I didn't want to risk a phone call in the van, but I needed to communicate with Alex.

What news from the house? I got cut off. Bloody phones.

Where have you been? Nearly called the police. Still no word from Jason. Call me?

Can't call yet. Soon. Nearly at the house. Don't call police yet. Be ready though. I'll tell you what's going on.

Don't do anything stupid Pete. You see anything dodgy, call the police. Don't put yourself at risk. Or Meg.

It's Ellie he wants. I need to contact Ellie. BRB

There were still no messages from Ellie. I was getting really annoyed with her. She'd been impetuous and stupid heading off like that. Of course, she hadn't seen the video, so she didn't know what Tony had done, but she did know what he was like. We should have tackled him together. I decided to try her mobile again.

I texted, I couldn't risk that call with White Van Man listening in: *Ellie! Call me! DO NOT go in there alone. Need to tell you something about Tony. Don't tackle him on your own. I'm on my way. With you soon.*

A text came in. It was all kicking off now I had a signal once again.

I did a double-take on the text. It was Martin Travis. What was Martin Travis doing texting me so late on a Saturday night? I opened it up, trying to keep my positive but non-committal responses about that day's football match to the minimum. Conversations between men always get to football eventually.

'How's the wife and family?'

'Great!'

'Work alright?'

'Fine!'

'Did you watch the game?'

Cue an hour of enthusiastic and highly detailed conversation. Maybe that's why I got on so well with women – I always hated football.

Martin's text made me panic. The conversation with my driving companion had taken my mind off what was happening, at least a little. But Martin's text was blunt and out of character: *Hi Peter. Is Meg okay? I'm worried about her. Call me please. Any time.*

Why would Martin Travis be texting me about Meg on a Saturday night? I was desperate to get through the city and home. I'd plumbed the depths of the football conversation already. I'd shared my profound thoughts on how 'the boys done good' and 'they were cheated' and that was all I had to offer. I think the driver sensed it as we got closer to the agreed drop-off point.

'Just drop me off at the end of Dundee Road, that'll be great, thanks.'

I could feel myself tensing as we got closer and closer.

'I'm happy to drop you outside your house, it's no problem, we've come this far!'

'No, I'm fine thank you. Don't want to startle my wife with the sound of the van pulling up the drive. Can I give you anything for the diesel?'

'No, you're alright mate. I'm pleased for the company, it gets really boring driving along that road at night.'

We exchanged final pleasantries and I jumped out of the van. I was home at last. It would be over in a matter of minutes now. I'd finally be reunited with Meg.

I waited for the van to drive off before I headed towards our road. I hadn't been entirely honest with him, we didn't live on Dundee Road, we were a bit further up in what the locals would have called 'the posh houses'. They weren't that posh, but they had short drives and a bit of garden, and you generally needed a bit more money than average to live there.

We were a working, childless couple. It was a bit of a stretch financially, but we liked it there. You could come and go without neighbours popping out from behind the fence. It was good for Meg because there was little chance of running into the clients there. And it was good for me because I liked to keep out of things away from the office. I wasn't keen on being spotted in the street, I liked to leave work and be anonymous outside it.

I checked my phone. Nothing from Ellie, nothing more from Alex. I wanted to call Alex, but I was more anxious to get to the house. Martin Travis could wait.

I walked up the road. It was lined with trees, there were very few street lights. Those that we had were older, they didn't give out much radiant light. My phone was on 10 percent charge. I decided not to make any more calls. I had to save enough juice to call the police, if it came to that. We had a landline in the house, I'd return all my calls from the regular phone once Tony had been sorted out. And Meg was safe.

I reached the end of the drive. There was only one car. Meg's car. No sign of Ellie. Had she got lost? I didn't know what car she drove, but there was nothing parked along the street either. Where on earth was Ellie?

I walked towards the front door, trying hard not to crunch the gravel which we'd spread in front of the house. Meg had insisted we do that, it's a great deterrent for thieves apparently. It's also a pain in the arse when you're trying to creep up to your own front door.

The lights were on. All over the house. The front door was open – it was just slightly ajar, but I could see that it was open. That wasn't good.

I looked around for Jason Davies. It was only to be expected that he wouldn't be so careless as to leave his car where it might be spotted. He'd probably be hidden in the undergrowth like a character from Dad's Army. Would he make himself known to me? Or would he stay watching in the distance, as Alex had suggested? I pulled out my phone again, wondering if I dared risk a text. Six percent power.

No, I'd have to go in. I couldn't wait any longer. I took a look around the garden, trying to spot Jason. He was good at hiding, I couldn't see him anywhere.

I walked up to the door and gently pushed it open. The house was quiet. No TV, no radio. No voices. Strange.

I remembered as a kid coming downstairs in the middle of the night. All the lights were on, but there was nobody there. I waited in the sitting room for a bit, looked around and went to bed. I assumed my parents had gone upstairs and forgotten to turn off the lights. It reminded me of that moment. Years later, they'd revealed that they'd been having sex behind the sofa when I'd come down. My dad had been in the middle of some sexual manoeuvre when I turned up out of nowhere. They were there, holding their breath, as they waited for me to piss off. Praying that I wouldn't investigate any further.

This scene reminded me of that situation. It wasn't quite right, and I couldn't put my finger on it. At that moment I'd have breathed a huge sigh of relief if my dad had emerged from behind the settee with his trousers round his ankles and everything had turned out to be okay.

I stepped into the hallway, listening – for any sound. All I could hear was the hum of the boiler. I decided to announce my arrival. I didn't want to spook Tony.

'Meg? Are you here?'

Then again, only louder this time.

'Meg? Ellie? Tony? Is anybody here?'

There was nothing. Silence. I walked into the sitting room. Nobody there. My mind was racing. Was it all over? Had Jason sorted it all out while I'd been talking football with White Van Man?

Then I saw it. I'd missed it at first. You don't really expect to see a chunk of bloodied skin caught on the side of your coffee table. It had hair attached to it. Not Meg's hair. Not Ellie's. I moved around the coffee table so that I could get to the second sofa.

Shit! There was a bloodied hand poking out from behind the settee. I pulled it out, away from the wall. I threw up, I couldn't hold it in. I didn't want to hold it in.

It was Jason Davies, or at least the man I remembered from years back. His throat was cut. He was still bleeding out behind the sofa. Shit.

I was desperate, frantic with worry about Meg.

'Meg! Meg!' I called. Nobody in the dining room. Nobody in the kitchen. The kitchen drawer was open. There were wine glasses on the worktop, one empty, the other hardly drunk. This was the place where Meg and I had enjoyed that last hug before I headed off for Newcastle.

I ran upstairs. There was blood in the bathroom sink. Lots of it. More blood than I'd ever seen before. No attempt had been made to clean it up.

I was heading for the main bedroom but had to pass the two spare rooms first. I looked into each one, terrified of what I might find there, all the time calling out: 'Meg! Meg!'

I reached the main bedroom. There was blood on the carpet. It was everywhere. How could there be so much blood? I saw it straight away. There was a body on the bed, covered by the quilt. I couldn't see who it was. I was desperate to pull off the quilt but at the same time I dared not look. I couldn't bear it if it was Meg, what would I do if it was Meg under there? I was sobbing now, cursing and begging.

'Don't let this be Meg, don't you dare let this be Meg.'

I grasped the top of the quilt and slowly drew it back. So much blood everywhere.

'No! Do not let this be Meg!'

It was hard to see, there was so much blood that I couldn't make out the clothes, the hair was badly matted. I retched as I turned the body over.

I looked at the face. It was strangely calm, showing none of the horror that must have led up to those final minutes.

I started to sob. I've never cried like that before. It was a mixture of fear, horror and adrenalin. I looked down at the body and collapsed to my knees.

It wasn't my Meg. It was the last thing I'd expected to see. The body on the bed was Tony Miller.

CHAPTER FOURTEEN

I've never fainted in my life before, but there's a first time for everything. I'd already vomited once, now I felt light-headed and had to sit down on the bed. I thought I was going to pass out, it took a few minutes to steady myself again.

Tony Miller was dead, in my house. Jason Davies was dead downstairs. Jason had had his throat cut, Tony had been stabbed several times. Their deaths had been frenzied and violent. The stab wounds were all over Tony's body, as if somebody had been wielding the knife inexpertly, doing anything they could to bring down the victim.

Had Meg killed these men? I had to consider that possibility, but there had never been a violent bone in her body. Maybe she'd killed Tony Miller in self-defence ... but what about Jason Davies? Had she mistaken him for an accomplice? If she was frantic and in a state of panic after killing Tony Miller, she might have lashed out at Jason Davies if he'd suddenly burst into the house. She'd never seen him in her life before, never heard his name.

Oh God, poor Meg, what terrible things had happened

in our house? We'd had our last cuddle in the kitchen before I left for Newcastle. Our domestic issues seemed so petty all of a sudden, we'd had the whole of our lives together to sort them out, we'd have got there in the end. Instead, I'd had sex with Ellie and brought a maniac into our lives.

And what about Ellie? Her car was nowhere to be seen, there was no evidence of her in the house. No phone, no bag ... no body. I had to think the situation through. The police would be hunting for a killer now – Meg had gone from victim to fugitive. I had to speak to her, I had to find out what had happened.

My mind snapped back into focus, the journalist in me found his feet once again. I forced myself to roll over Tony Miller's body. His hands were lacerated, he must have tried to defend himself from the knife attack. There were several wounds on his body, some quite shallow. He had been killed by an inexperienced killer, this was no Dexter Morgan masterpiece. The pathologist would figure out what had killed Tony Miller, but it didn't take an expert to see that there had been a fight here. Tony had put up a defence, but been killed by a fatal stab. It was a mess, the killer would be covered in blood.

I made a thorough search of the bedroom and the rest of upstairs. No more dead bodies, but my home had turned into a Saw movie. I took a second look at Jason's body. I hadn't seen it before, but Jason had been hit forcefully on his head. The wound was at the back, that's why I'd missed it.

I've only seen two dead bodies before. The first time was when I'd been doing a series of interviews for the radio about what happens after death. I was recording at an undertaker's and the chap showing me around accidentally walked me into an area where there was an old guy laid out in his coffin. My guide apologised for his error, concerned that he'd taken me by surprise. But the old guy looked peaceful. When people say 'at rest', that's exactly what it looked like. An old guy who was no longer alive.

The second time was my dad. He'd died from a stroke a few years before. I'd been reluctant to see him at first, why would I want to look at my dead father? There was an emotional connection that time, I wanted to take care over my final memories of him. My mum finally convinced me to go and see him, and I'm pleased I did. It was just my dad, nothing scary. He looked calm, peaceful, and – those words again – at rest. It was fine, I'm pleased I did it.

I'd never seen anything like the bodies in my house, though. I suppose TV prepares us for murder, but in real life it's so brutal, and the mess, the blood goes everywhere.

I pulled out the sofa a little further so that I could get a closer look at Jason's body. My inexpert guess was that he'd been struck on the head, then had his throat cut afterwards. The wounds were messy and random once again, this was no accomplished killer.

My amateur sleuthing seemed to be correct. Everything pointed to Meg killing these men. These looked to me like frenzied attempts at self-defence. She must have been terrified, scared for her life.

I thought through my options. The men were dead, it wouldn't require a paramedic to confirm that. There was no need to call an ambulance; if there were lives that could have been saved, I'd have made the call.

Meg was my main concern. Had she gone on the run? She must be frightened out of her mind if she'd killed those two men. I had to track her down and find out what had happened. I'd comfort her and we'd go to the police station together. There was no need to call the police, not until I found her. It wouldn't change anything.

I scanned the room. My mobile was dead again. I headed for the house phone, picked it up and pressed the button. No dial tone. It had been unplugged from the wall and the cable cut. There were more phones at various locations in the house, and I checked them all. All disabled. Tony Miller had had plenty of time alone with Meg in the house – any half-decent maniac would make sure that she couldn't raise the alarm.

How had they passed that time? Had he hurt her? Had he raped or tortured her? Would there be any evidence of that? How would I know? I'd have to talk to Meg. Oh God, please don't let him have hurt her.

And where was Ellie? Had Tony sent her to the wrong address? Maybe Meg had given an incorrect postcode. She'd be panicking and desperate to speak to me. I had to find a phone.

I'd lived in that area for several years, but I couldn't think for the life of me where the nearest payphone was. Did we even have one still? There was no way I could use one of the neighbours' phones, not in my current state.

I looked around again, there had to be some way to get in touch. I walked into the kitchen. The drawer was open. It was a crazy thing to do, but I pushed it shut. Tidying the place up. We might have looked a little more presentable once I'd removed the corpse and blood-soaked carpet from the sitting room.

Interesting. The drawer had been opened, presumably to find a weapon. The biggest, nastiest knife had been removed from the wooden knife block on the worktop opposite. That must have been used to kill Tony and Jason.

However, Meg knew where the knives were, why had she gone for the drawer first?

I shuddered, thinking about the missing knife. I'd actually laughed with Meg once that it looked more like a murder weapon than a cooking implement. Those words were coming back to haunt me now. It was long and had sharp serrations along the blade. I'd cut myself on it once, and it hurt badly. I'd stopped using it afterwards. It explained the mess made by the wounds, though. They'd been hacked rather than sliced, it must have been that knife which did it.

I liked to think that I knew Meg well. Surely she was incapable of such violence? Yet, there was the evidence, in the sitting room and the bedroom. She must have been running on pure terror to be forced into making such a mess of those men.

I needed a phone. I had to speak to Alex too. She'd be mortified about Jason, she'd feel guilty and responsible. Then I thought about Tony's earlier messages to me. He'd used Facebook – maybe the broadband was still working. The router was in the hallway. It was cold in there, the door was still slightly open.

The router was on, the broadband working. I ran up the stairs, taking them two at a time, and got the laptop. The lid had been closed, but it was in sleep mode. After a few moments, the screen was live. The browser had been left open at Facebook, the messaging window still open. I sat down at the small desk, and pulled in the wheeled chair, ready to take a closer look.

My foot touched something. I looked under the desk to see what it was. It was Meg's brown leather handbag. Tony Miller must have thrown it under the desk, probably to keep it out of her way. There was a single bed in the room. Had he raped her in there? I walked over and checked the quilt cover, pulling it back, examining the sheets. No signs of a struggle or any sexual activity, I even checked around the bed for a condom, it looked okay. If he'd held her in that room, there didn't seem to be any signs of violence or struggle.

I walked back to the desk and opened up Meg's bag. No sign of her phone, but there was a coloured envelope in there with a card inside. It was probably for my birthday. But it was what was concealed behind the card that troubled me most. It was a pregnancy test kit and the box had been opened.

I knew that Meg was working her way through a lot of pregnancy kits at the time. She'd test and double check every month, it had become a bit of a routine.

'Anything to report this month?' I'd ask, aware that a month must have passed since she last gave me an update. I almost dared not ask the question, there was always so much hanging on the answer. When we'd first started trying for a baby, Meg had given me a cheery 'Not this month!' fully expecting that it might take a month or two, then there would be no problem.

As the months turned into a year, the monthly pregnancy tests became more anxious, the feeling of disappointment heightening each time. Once we'd started the IVF treatment, any enquiry would be greeted with a snap. Meg was tired and worn out, our lack of success was taking its toll. I didn't know whether to keep my mouth shut until she told me or make sure that I asked regularly to show that I was still committed to the process. I realised as I held the opened box in my hand that I had neglected to ask her the question recently.

Another wave of guilt washed over me.

I couldn't face looking into the box at first. I opened the envelope instead. She'd got me a funny card, it had a great joke on it, one from my favourite newspaper cartoonist, a news-related joke and ideal for a journalist. Inside she'd written a message: *To my dearest husband, best friend (and hot lover!) Pete. With all my love on your 40th birthday. I hope you enjoy my birthday surprise! I love you, Meg xxx*

What a shit I'd been. Here was Meg planning a birthday treat, probably plotting it from the moment I announced my weekend away. And where was I when she arrived at the hotel? In bed with Ellie. I couldn't have felt more wretched if I'd tried. And now Meg was in terrible danger. Something horrific had happened in our home. What a mess!

Tucked beneath the envelope and pregnancy test was a small plastic bag. I pulled it out and recognised the shop name immediately. It was from a classy lingerie shop in town. I'd always drooled over the sexy underwear on display in the window. I'd joke with Meg, in a very passive-aggressive way, about her own mismatched underwear preferences.

Inside the bag was a lacy thong and a provocative bra. In my favourite colour too. For a moment my mind drifted to an image of Meg wearing the undies and walking over to the bed to seduce me in my hotel room. That's what she must have planned. It was what I wanted, it was exactly what we'd needed.

What a fool I'd been. If I'd waited a little longer, we would have course-corrected. If I'd gone to bed alone, at a decent time, I'd have been alerted by a gentle tap at my door late at night. My gorgeous wife would have stepped into the room, wished me a happy birthday, and said that she had a little surprise for me. She'd have slipped into the bathroom to emerge wearing her new lingerie. We'd have kissed and caressed, my hands moving closer to her bra and panties. I'd have snapped open her bra, my hands making their way to her breasts with an electric excitement as if I were touching them for the first time. My hands would have slid into her thong, I'd have torn it off and we'd have stood there, kissing passionately. I would have looked in the mirror to see our bodies entwined, the sight of Meg's toned, curvaceous body. Then, we'd have rushed to the bed to make love, our bodies wrapped up in a glorious fusion of lust and love.

Only I'd screwed it up. I'd done something similar, but with Ellie. If things had gone as Meg had planned, we'd have made love again, fallen asleep, then woken up in the morning to a mixture of comfortable chat and companionable silence. It would have been perfect. When the fire alarm had gone off I wouldn't have needed to hide what I'd been doing. Meg would have joined me in the car park, she'd have seen a few of my colleagues that she knew, it would be no big deal. And Tony Miller would never have come into our lives.

I dared not open the pregnancy test. I couldn't face what I might find in there. I picked up the packet once again, turning it around in my hand, too scared to take out the plastic packaging and discover what was in there.

I was startled by a noise downstairs. There was a creak of the front door. What now?

Whoever it was, they were keeping quiet. Anybody who should have been in the house would have called out to make themselves known. Suddenly I heard someone cry out. I couldn't make out the words, but they weren't calling my name. Perhaps there were there two of them down there.

I heard a movement on the stairs. Bollocks, I wasn't going to be able to hide and hope they left. Maybe it was a casual robber casing out the neighbourhood and spotting my open door?

I quietly unplugged the heavy metal lamp stand at the side of the spare bed, taking great care not to make the floor-boards creak. I had no experience of violence, it was not a part of my life, I was terrified of a physical confrontation. How must Meg have felt when she'd seen Tony Miller murder Jackson?

There was something about the way the person was moving. Had it been a friend, they would have made their way confidently through the house, calling for us by name. This person was moving stealthily, trying not to make a noise. It must have been a man, the movements were too heavy for it to be a woman.

I positioned myself at the side of the bedroom door. If I was lucky, whoever it was would peer in and pass by. Would they see the laptop and want to grab it? Electronics are good to steal and easy to sell. I was tense, standing straight and alert, hardly daring to breathe. I saw the shadow first, then the carpet on the other side of the open door moved as he stepped carefully along the hallway.

I waited, I wondered if he could sense me there waiting for him. I could feel my palms sweating. I moved the lamp stand into my left hand, wiping my free hand on my trousers, then passed it back again.

Walk on, I said to myself. Go on, you bastard, walk on.

He didn't. He stepped into the room. I was so hyped up, my reaction was inevitable. I didn't even look at him. He was bigger than me, a male and wearing a coat. There was no way I'd come off better in a confrontation, so I struck him with the lamp as hard as I could. He let out a cry. I recognised it straight away, but I was committed to the second blow by then. He sank to his knees, then dropped to the ground.

I've seen it done a thousand times on TV, but I hadn't got a clue how hard you had to whack somebody to knock them out. I also didn't know how long someone stays down when they've been struck like that. It didn't matter, this man was no danger to me. God knows what he was doing in my house creeping around like that. Why hadn't he called out? It was his own fault – I hoped I hadn't hurt him badly.

I dropped the lamp onto the floor. It hadn't drawn blood, but it had done a good job. I put my hand to his neck, feeling for a pulse, not really knowing what I was looking for. Eventually I felt a rapid beating. Thank God for that, at least I hadn't joined my wife on her killing spree.

'You stupid git!' I shouted. It was Jem. Not so long ago I'd seen him about to cop off with that young journalist. Funny, he'd been a bit concerned about my whereabouts when we spoke last. And here he was in my house, creeping about – as if he was up to something.

'What is going on here, Jem?' There was no reply. I was about to find out how long it takes somebody to come round after two hard blows to the head.

I picked up the lamp once again and placed it on the desk. Although I knew Jem, I wanted to keep the upper hand when he came round. It didn't feel good that he was in my house. What was he up to? Why did he have that scratch on his face? I'd knocked him out. I could ask myself as many questions as I wanted, but I wouldn't get any answers until he came round again.

I'd forgotten about the pregnancy test, it was where I'd

left it, next to the laptop. Nervously, I tipped it sideways so that the plastic tray slid out into my other hand. The plastic stick was the wrong way round, I couldn't see whether it had been used or not. I knew the answer before I even looked. Why else would Meg travel over to Newcastle to surprise me in the middle of the night on the eve of my fortieth birthday? She was pregnant, of course. She'd saved the news for a special occasion, she'd planned the most incredible birthday that I could ever hope to experience.

———————

There had been something off kilter about Jem's behaviour at the time, but I couldn't for the life of me place my finger on it. I'd assumed that he had his own shit going on, and it was messing with his life. I had an uneasy feeling about him turning up on my doorstep like that. It didn't feel like something that he would do, marriage breakdown or not.

As he lay on the floor, unconscious, I sat in the desk chair waiting for him to come round. I had to get my phone charged before I did anything else.

The desk in the spare room had a drawer which was full of leads belonging to tech and kit dating years back. I managed to find a USB lead with the correct attachment and plugged my phone into the laptop to give it yet another top-up. I had to speak to Alex, try to contact Ellie, and keep trying Meg's phone.

I looked at Jem while I waited for the phone to charge enough to switch it on. What did I really know about this man? He'd bailed me out at work a few times, he'd always had my back in the office. We got on well, had a laugh, enjoyed taking lunch together when our shifts allowed. But were we really best friends? I'd never given it much thought before.

When Meg and I moved in together, a lot of my attitudes changed. I'd had the odd one-night stand with young reporters before I met her. I was a single guy with no girlfriend on the scene, there was no reason why not. I always took care not to make any advances on the work premises, though a bit of mild flirtation was often part of the cut and thrust of life in a journalistic environment.

I recalled one encounter that I'd had with a recent graduate called Anna, shortly before I'd first met Meg. She was on a period of work experience from her university, with us at the radio station for just two months, and the source of much lusting by the majority of the news team.

The funny thing is, Anna wasn't your usual broadcasting totty. She was extremely talented, had a great voice for radio, and was an astute and capable reporter. She was the kind of work experience student who should have ended up with a job on our radio station, she fitted in really well and everybody liked her.

Anna and I had a short fling together, but it was a bit more than a one-night stand after a boozy works do. I thought that it might have gone somewhere. It was early days, we were still getting to know each other, but it was fun. She'd be heading back to university so it was time limited. Who knew what would happen then?

I'd had a fallow run without much sex or female company, and Anna came along just at the right time. She was fresh from a split from some young dickhead from her journalism course who'd played her around. She was in the market for an older guy, like me, who knew his mind and had the ability to stay focused on one woman for more than five minutes at a time.

Anna was a bit more inhibited in bed than I would have liked, but we had a lot of fun. She was easy, undemanding company, and the mixture of cinema, DVDs, meals out and sex worked just fine for the nearly two months that she was around. But it all took a sudden turn.

I'd thought that things were going fine. She hadn't moved in or anything like that, but we saw each other maybe three or four times a week, and she'd stay over when sex was on the cards. One night, though, she texted me to say that she wouldn't be around that night. She was working a late shift and had arranged to go out for a drink with the news team to chat about career options, paths to full-time employment and the like. That was fine by me. Anna was a grown woman, I was not her keeper.

As I walked into the office the next morning, I was immediately hit by the tense atmosphere. Newsrooms are usually irreverent places. There's a lot of laughter in them and much dark humour. You deal with all sorts of human shit and tragedy as a journalist, and I figured it was a defence mechanism to help to cope with that.

The boss at the time, not Diane, it was a chap called Leo, had his office door closed, which was unusual. You could generally catch Leo for a quick informal chat at that time of day, it was only after 10 o'clock that he'd become embroiled in meetings, strategy calls and budget reviews.

'What's going on in the boss's office?' I asked to no one in particular.

'Who knows?' … 'The old man is in a right mood' … 'Stay well away!' were the answers that I received. Heads were down. It felt as if someone had died.

I never found out what had gone on. I know that I never saw Anna again, not in our radio station offices. And I know that Jem wasn't around for a couple of weeks afterwards.

The official explanation was that he had been signed off by the doctor with stress.

The HR team were very present at that time too. They often appeared, like vultures, when there were HR-type matters to deal with, such as hounding the long-term sick back to work, dealing with staff misdemeanours and reassuring us all that our jobs were safe after the latest announcement of budget cuts.

Usually they came and went like rats scuttling in sewers. But something was up, there were too many of them. And they kept coming back to speak to Leo.

I took it at face value. I didn't think much about Jem. I sent him an email to his home address, ribbing him about the stress and saying we'd catch up when he returned: *Don't know how you're off with stress, you never do any work!*

That was the gist of my comforting words.

I was more concerned about Anna and why she'd had to leave the radio station so suddenly.

I couldn't raise Anna. It was as if a veil of silence had fallen over the radio station. As a journalist, I'm not used to taking no for an answer, so I tracked down her university tutor. He wouldn't be drawn either. The official version was that Anna had decided not to pursue a career in journalism. That must have been some crappy careers advice session with the late production team in the pub.

'But she's brilliant, she has a great career in radio ahead of her. She does know that doesn't she?' I pleaded down the phone.

'Anna has a lot of talent, Mr Bailey, but I'm afraid that her decision about her choice of career is final.'

I was unable to get a reply via her phone, it looked like she'd changed numbers. She didn't reply to emails, and besides her temporary email address at the radio station was soon removed.

Only years later, when I was comfortable in my life with Meg and had got the hang of how things work at management levels, would I realise that the shit must have hit the fan in a big way. Leo looked like a troubled man. When Jem returned to work, he was chastened and cautious.

I only ever saw that type of behaviour one more time afterwards. It was when we'd had to issue a formal written warning to a member of staff who'd been using a staff vehicle to visit prostitutes on a local council estate. It was his journalistic patch, anybody who'd seen the car would have assumed that he was working on a story. Instead, he was getting blow jobs from teenage girls who were fuelling their need for drugs.

When he returned to work, after a short break to distance himself from a gruelling disciplinary procedure, he was quiet, timid and on his best behaviour. He was a man keeping his head down, working hard to keep his job. After a short time on parole, he left the radio station to reinvent himself as a broadcasting lecturer at the local college.

I got one of those odd feelings after I'd been involved in his disciplinary hearing. I realised that Jem must have been going through a similar process at the time Anna left. I wasn't in love with Anna; we hadn't exchanged rings, eternal promises or set up an expectation on either side that our relationship was anything other than fleeting. But we did like each other, the sex was okay for both of us, I think. I was certain that she wouldn't have rushed off like that without ending it more tidily.

Once I'd understood what must have really happened with Jem, I assumed that Anna had slept with him after receiving valuable careers guidance. Maybe she'd regretted it and made a complaint, perhaps Jem had said or done something inappropriate – it wouldn't be the first time – and it had come back to bite him.

There were a few years in between Anna leaving under a cloud of secrecy and me realising the nature of what must have been going on. I'd long forgotten about Anna by then, Meg and I were completely distracted by the heat of our own relationship and the events at that time were just a memory.

But it made me stop, momentarily, to wonder how far Jem was pushing these young women, how much he was leaning on them to get them between the sheets. Because I knew him, I assumed him to be incapable of hurting anybody. He was married to Sally, he might have been unfaithful, but surely he must have been reasonably okay if Sally had stayed with him? Their marriage had seemed fine, and they'd produced enough children between them.

It was only looking at Jem, heavy and unconscious on the floor, that the uneasy feeling from years previously had returned. How well did I really know this man?

CHAPTER FIFTEEN

Jem had been out cold for a few minutes, I didn't know how long it would take him to come round. I had struck him hard. Surely he ought to have been conscious by now?

I knelt at his side again, checking for signs of life. It looked as if he was beginning to move, his eyelids were twitching.

'Jem? Are you awake? Jem?'

Nothing. I wondered if he was playing dead, but there was no response from him. I tensed my legs, ready to return to my chair and check my phone again, but something made me pause. There was a green pill on the floor next to him. It looked as if it had fallen out of his pocket, but it might have been left over from Tony Miller's earlier activities. It was nothing to do with me or Meg, I'd never seen a pill like it. Most of them are white and round, and if they vary from that, they're usually in capsule form. My erectile dysfunction tablets were blue. What were green pills?

I could only assume it was something herbal. Stuff like that usually has bits in it to make it look more healthy, but this looked like a pharmaceutical product, not something that a bunch of hippies would cook up in a peace camp. Besides, Jem wasn't exactly your herbal kind of guy.

I returned the pill to his pocket, assuming it was a drug that he had to take. It could have been an anti-depressant for all I knew. I'd never used them. Maybe they were all green?

I pressed the power button on my phone, it had just enough charge for the screen to light up once again. I waited for it to find the phone signal. A few more moments and then the text messages started coming in.

There was an electronic beep to my side. It hadn't come from my phone, it was a message from my mum, sent via Skype. Of course ... I was being an idiot. I could use Skype to speak to Alex, she was easy enough to find, I didn't need a phone.

There were three texts from Alex. What you'd expect, given the circumstances.

WTF Pete! Call me!

Call me asap

You there? Call me please.

A notification appeared on my Erazerr app, it was from JEN1995. An update from Jenny. Still nothing from Ellie.

I decided to prioritise Alex. I texted her, not sure if my phone would cope with a call: *I'll Skype you. Long story. What's your ID? Don't call. Phone is fucked.* She must have been anxiously waiting for my message as she was straight back to me: *Skype is AlexK1981 x*

I sent her a contact request and we were speaking within minutes. There were no welcomes.

'What's going on, Pete? I can't raise Jason. What is happening? You need to get the police involved.'

'It's not good, Alex. I'm at the house now. Meg isn't

here. I haven't seen her. There are no phones. My mobile is buggered.'

'What about Jason? Did you meet up with Jason?'

'Jason's dead, Alex ...'

I let it hang there, waiting for her reaction. We were audio only, I was relieved about that. I didn't want Alex to see my face.

'What happened, Pete? Jesus Christ, what is going on up there?'

'Tony Miller is dead too.'

Her face appeared on my screen, she'd activated the video feed. I fired up my webcam too. I hadn't seen Alex for some time, only in passing on the TV.

She was white, drawn, shocked. I'm sure I was looking pretty shitty too.

'What are we going to do, Pete? Who did it?'

'It has to have been Meg. She must have been defending herself. Maybe Tony Miller killed Jason, then Meg killed Tony in self-defence. I don't know how it happened, but Meg has to be responsible for at least one of those deaths. She must have fled. She must be shitting herself. I can't contact her, she's not answering her phone.'

Alex looked into her webcam. I don't think she knew what to say. I was at a loss myself. Eventually the silence was broken.

'We have to call the police now, Pete. They have to find Meg, work out what happened. She'll be okay. She'd have killed Tony Miller in self-defence, they'll see that, won't they?'

I'd worked in journalism all those years, yet I hadn't got a clue how it would be viewed by the law. Was it manslaughter? I'd heard of reasonable force, but Tony was carved up badly. He'd been stabbed several times, he was a mess. It had been a frenzied and violent attack. I wasn't so sure that Meg would pass that particular test.

'I really don't know, Alex. I need to find Meg and hear it from her mouth, then we'll go to the police. I don't know where she is.'

'Did you think of the hospital, Pete? She might have gone there. Maybe she's gone to the police already.'

'They'd be over here like a shot if she had,' I replied. 'Maybe the hospital, though. I hadn't thought of that. Wherever she is, she's been able to walk, her car is in the drive still.'

There was an electronic beep to my side. I looked at my phone, but it hadn't come from there. I turned round to look at Jem lying motionless. I felt in his jacket pockets and detected the outline of a phone. It would be a text or a notification, something like that. I turned back to Alex. She looked like shit, but she was still beautiful. I could still see why we'd fallen in love.

'You need to contact the hospital, Pete. That's the first place she'd go if she was hurt. She might have got a taxi – strange that she didn't use her car. If you can't find her there, you've got to call the police. You can't put it off any longer.'

'It doesn't change anything if I call the police!' I snapped. I knew immediately that I shouldn't have. 'Sorry, sorry, I didn't mean to say it like that. But Jason and Tony are dead, they're not going anywhere. I've disturbed the crime scene by moving the bodies. The police are going to curse me for that. I just need to find Meg.'

'Okay, okay. But look, it's a little after two o'clock now. If she doesn't turn up by 8 o' clock, you've got to call it in, Pete. Leave it to the police to find her. You'll land yourself in trouble if you don't call it in.'

'Yeah, I know, I know. Jesus, this is a mess. Some fortieth birthday!'

I'm not sure if I sensed the movement first or if it was Alex's shocked face which alerted me. I was right about Jem, he'd been playing dead. Whatever message had come in via his phone, he'd quietly eased it out of his pocket, read it and decided it was time to make a move.

I heard Alex shout 'Pete!', caught a fast movement to my right side, then felt a blow to my head. The bastard had just repaid the favour, he'd whacked me with the same lamp stand that I'd used to hit him with earlier.

'Fucking hell, Jem!' I shouted, turning to defend myself. He struck me again. This time he missed and it hit my shoulder. Christ, it hurt.

'Sorry mate, I'm really sorry ...' Jem began, turning to leave the room. I grabbed his jacket by the collar. It must have looked ridiculous. Like the Chuckle Brothers having a scrap. I was pulling off Jem's jacket, he was thrashing at me with the lamp stand, only he had his back to me. We were both cussing and Alex was listening to everything off camera via Skype. Jem was strong, it hadn't been an issue before. I'd never thought that we might end up in a fight. Was this a fight? Or a scuffle? I didn't know, I certainly had no intention of hurting him.

Unfortunately, he had a different agenda. Whatever had forced him to make a move needed to be done without me on his tail. After several thrusts of the lamp stand missed their mark, he finally landed one directly on my nose. I felt the bone crack and could see the blood dripping onto the carpet. I moved backwards, instinctively backing away from Jem and the source of the pain. It gave him his window. He hesitated for a moment, deciding whether or not to pick up his jacket, which I'd managed to work from his arms. Not quite a Steven Seagal move.

He looked at me, saw that I was down for a few seconds, and ran. I sank to the floor, giving it up. My face felt as if it was on fire, all I could do was feel it with my hands, assess the damage that had been done and try to stop the bleeding.

'Pete! Pete! Are you okay?'

Alex's voice came through the laptop, anxious, panicking.

'I'm okay, Alex!' I called from the floor. 'Just give me a minute!'

I sat on the floor, cradling my nose. On the road outside the house, I heard a car door slam violently and the roar of an engine as Jem disappeared into the night.

'Who was that?' I heard Alex asking from the laptop. 'Was that Jeremy Denning? He's put on some weight!'

I struggled up to the desk chair and turned towards the laptop webcam. I saw her flinch as I came into focus.

'What happened, Pete? Are you okay? That looks painful!'

'God, it hurts! And yes, that's Jem.'

Alex had met Jem briefly, many years ago, on a training course in London.

'Where did he come from?'

'I forgot to tell you, he was out cold on the floor. I thought he was an intruder, so I hit him.'

'Bloody hell, Pete. It just gets worse. What's going on for Christ's sake? It's like Game of Thrones over there!'

I had to laugh at that one. I winced as I moved my face to smile. How could a blow to the nose hurt so much?

'I don't know, Alex. Something's up with Jem, but I can't figure it out. We only spoke a few hours ago in Newcastle, he was about to cop off with some gorgeous young journalist from the radio station. The next thing I know, he's creeping around my house.'

I paused a moment and thought back to our earlier encounter.

'He had a scratch on his face too. Didn't say where it came from. Something is going on, that's for sure.'

'Any idea where he went?' Alex asked, clutching at straws.

'I have no idea what that was about,' I replied. 'I have to find Meg. I'll figure out what's going on with Jem later.'

I knocked my phone screen with my hand and it lit up. The battery was holding a decent charge once again. It reminded me of Jenny's message.

'One minute, Alex. I want to check my phone.'

I opened up the Erazerr notification. As I read Jenny's messages, they disappeared from my screen.

Came back to hotel after I calmed down. It's all kicked off here.

Bob is going spare, he's got Head Office onto him and everything.

What did police say to you? Jen

That had come in as I'd been driving back from Newcastle. There were later updates.

Police were just looking for you. Wanted to know which room we'd put you in. Where are you? I told them you'd gone into town. They're asking questions about you. Want to know who you were with. Didn't say anything. Message me pls.

Shit, they'd be looking for me before I got a chance to find Meg. We'd be out of time if I couldn't get to Meg soon.

Events were closing in on me. There was one more message.

They've been asking me about Jackson. I started crying, couldn't help it. They must have an idea what was going on. But I didn't do anything. Can't stop thinking about Jackson. Working double shift tonight. Knackered. Police asking about you again. I won't say anything. Please don't you say anything either.

I was exhausted. I was desperate for a rest, but I had to locate Meg. I was almost on the verge of handing myself in, maybe it would be the easiest thing to do. Alex looked busy at her PC, I could see her working away via her webcam. She sensed that I was back with her.

'I'm contacting one of my legal chums,' she said. 'There's not much I can do here now, but I can at least find out what is likely to come Meg's way. Shit Pete, you know this is probably going to end up on the show don't you?'

The irony of it. It would make a great reconstruction for Alex's TV show. I wondered if the budget would stretch to buying in Brad Pitt to play the part of Pete Bailey. I scolded myself for wasting time. I had to get moving. My phone had charge again, I had a car, Alex was up to speed. Still no sign of Ellie. I remembered Martin Travis's text from earlier. What had he said? I scrolled through my messages, I hadn't deleted it: *Hi Peter. Is Meg okay? I'm worried about her. Call me please. Any time.*

That message had come in late. It was one more thing that didn't sit right.

There was Ellie to think about too. Ellie can't have had an accident, she was ahead of me on the road home, I'd have seen it. Where was she?

I looked at Jem's jacket on the floor. Was his phone in there still? I felt in the pockets. It had been moved, the sly bastard must have checked that incoming message while I was talking to Alex. I was about to take a look when I heard a knock at the door.

'What now?' I said aloud. 'It's the middle of the night for Christ's sake!'

'What's the matter?' asked Alex. 'What's happening now?'

'Stay online will you, there's a knock at the door, I need to see who it is.'

I slipped Jem's phone into my pocket and ran down the stairs. Jem had closed the door when he left, he'd done me a favour.

'One minute!' I shouted. 'Who is it, please?'

'Police,' came the reply. 'Is everything alright, sir?'

'One moment, I need to get some clothes on!'

I had blood on my face. There were two dead bodies in my house. Were they onto me already?

I rushed into the sitting room, moved the sofa to conceal Jason's body, then ran up the stairs, taking three at a time. I pulled the sheets over Tony's body, rearranging some pillows to conceal the blood. I hated all those blasted pillows which Meg insisted on scattering on the bed, but now they were coming in handy.

I pulled off my trousers and shirt, threw on my dressing gown and headed for the stairs. I caught my reflection in the bathroom mirror on the way across the landing. I looked a state. I'd have to lie. There was another knock at the door. Not loud enough to draw attention from the neighbours, but more impatient this time.

I ran down the stairs and opened the door. There were two Specials on the doorstep, a man and a woman. The man was an older guy, my sort of age. The woman was younger, twenties maybe. The guy took the lead.

'Is everything alright here, sir? We just saw a vehicle departing from outside your house – the driver seemed to be in a hurry. You look like you've been in a fight.'

They'd seen Jem. I had to think on my feet.

'Thanks for coming, I appreciate it,' I began, playing for time.

'That was my brother you saw. We had a row. A fight, upstairs. I came off worse, as you can see. It was a stupid thing. It was over money.'

'Are you alright, sir? Do you need us to run you to the hospital?'

Funny she should ask that, that's where I intended to head next. But I'd do it without the police in tow.

'I'm fine thanks, it hurt my pride more than my face. I used to be able to kick his arse when we were kids. No chance of that now, he's much bigger than me.'

'I take it you won't be taking any action against him, Mr ... Mr?'

'Bailey. Pete Bailey. No, no, of course not. These things happen. It was my fault. I borrowed money off him, should have paid it back weeks ago. He needs it for a holiday now. He's getting grief from his wife. It's my fault, I need to pay him back.'

The constable was peering inside the door.

'Did you say your fight was upstairs?' he asked.

'Yes, in the spare room. I had to show him my bank balance online, convince him I'm broke.'

'There's quite a lot of blood on the carpet, do you mind if we come in and take a look?'

Yes, I did mind. That's all I needed, someone auditioning for a role in CSI on my doorstep.

'I think I've troubled you enough already, officers. I'm so sorry about this. I need to get myself cleaned up—'

'If you don't mind, Mr Bailey, it would be helpful if we could come in. I'd like to make sure everything is okay here.'

I looked back to the sitting room. There was blood on the carpet, it might have been mine it might have been Jason's. I'd lost track. It's not every day you get to host a couple of corpses in your house. I didn't have a choice, I had to let them in. Stall them. Convince them it was my blood.

'Come in,' I said. 'Feel free to do whatever you need to. I'm really sorry for causing all this trouble.'

They gazed into the sitting room, then walked along the hallway into the kitchen. Jason was reasonably well hidden, but it wouldn't prove the most challenging game of hide and seek I'd ever played. He'd bled so much – I'd pulled the settee over the mess as much as I could. It depended how suspicious they were.

Alex's voice could be heard from upstairs. She was still connected via Skype.

'Are you still around, Pete? Pete?'

The two Specials rejoined me in the corridor, attracted by the sound of a female voice in the house.

'Do you have company, Mr Bailey? Is there somebody who could corroborate what happened here earlier?'

This guy was a pain in the arse. He could smell that something wasn't quite right, but he was struggling to put his finger on it.

'Oh, it's just a friend on Skype. She's on the computer upstairs. Go up and check if you want.'

I knew that there was less chance of them finding Tony's body in the bedroom. I'd managed to conceal it better with the cushions. I'd pop into the sitting room and double check Jason in case they looked in there on their way out.

As they headed up the stairs, their radios crackled into

life. Police radios aren't usually the best source of high fidelity sound, but I managed to catch the basics of this message.

'Any units in the Fairview area?'

That's where I lived. My ears pricked up. As they stepped into the spare room upstairs, I heard the male officer respond that they were in Fairview.

'We need you to make a call at number eleven Ashbourne Drive ...'

I'd heard enough. That was my house. It would take them a moment to figure it out, then they'd come for me. Dressed in only my underwear and dressing gown, I grabbed Meg's keys from the shelf in the hall and slipped out of the front door. They were onto me. I had nothing to hide, I'd get a rap over the knuckles, but they weren't taking me into the station until I'd found Meg. There was no way I was going to let Meg down again.

It's extremely difficult to drive in bare feet. For some reason, the pedals feel much harder to push when you have no shoes on. I'm not sure why that is, you'd think it would take the same leg strength to do the pushing. I drove up the road from my house like a ninety-year-old, kangarooing and stalling as I got used to the feel of barefoot driving.

I hadn't got a clue where I was heading, all I knew was that I had to get away from the police and as close to Meg as I could. What a pillock! My great escape kit comprised a set of underwear, a dressing gown and Jem's mobile phone. Not quite Steve McQueen.

I was driving a car which would take no time at all to trace. If I left the car, it would be a piece of cake to apprehend a man running about town in his boxers and night-wear. It wasn't looking good.

As I was driving up the road towards the town centre, I passed a charity shop with two large bin bags deposited outside. Clothes. Probably quite horrible clothes, but better than what I was wearing.

I pulled over into a narrow alleyway further along the row of shops, and I drove Meg's car right to the end. It was a great hiding place, the car should be fine there until the shops opened in the morning. That's if they even opened at all, it being a Sunday.

I walked to the end of the alleyway, back towards the shop. I peered up and down the road. It must have been around 3am, maybe later. The late night revellers had gone to bed, the early shift workers hadn't started to emerge from their front doors. It was the perfect time to be running around town in my nightgown, although I'd bet that Wee Willie Winkie wasn't on the run from the police.

When I was sure that the coast was clear, I ran up to the charity shop entrance, grabbed the two bin bags, and like a rat returned to the dark alleyway that had become my temporary sanctuary. I just missed being seen by a police car that was on the prowl. They seemed to be checking for flashing alarms and broken shop windows rather than a fugitive.

I retreated to the blackness of the alleyway. It was too dark, I couldn't see a thing. I was surrounded by industrial bins and flattened cardboard boxes awaiting recycling. I felt in my dressing gown pocket for Jem's phone. Did it have a torch?

I fumbled around with the controls, the screen lit up. It was a standard smartphone, nothing complicated, it didn't take long to find the torch function. I shone the light at the first bin bag. Bollocks! It was full of summer dresses, wide-brimmed hats and old handbags. I was better off with the nightwear.

The second bag was a different colour. Hopefully, that meant it had been dropped off by somebody else. Eureka! It was packed with old plain work shirts, work trousers and a couple of belts. Someone had left a pair of Y-fronts in one of the trouser legs. Disgusting! I didn't know anybody still wore underwear in that style. I threw them to the side of the pavement. At least they'd frighten any rats away.

The trousers were a size too big for me, but they'd stay up with a belt. The shirts had been worn by somebody with a bit of a beer gut. There was plenty of excess material in them, but at least I looked half normal.

I emptied the contents of the bag onto the ground. There were a few goodies in there. Three black sports caps for starters. I took the one that looked cleanest in the dim light and put it on my head. I'd read countless radio news bulletins giving descriptions of people that the police wanted to question. They usually had no useful detail in them. I'd gone from a bare-footed man wearing boxer shorts and a dressing gown to a normal guy wearing regular clothes. Granted, I looked like I'd just completed a successful diet, but nobody would notice the ill-fitting clothes. The cap would help too, it would disguise my facial features and hair colour. It was a good start.

I emptied the bag of dresses onto the ground too. There was a pair of plain plimsolls in there, smaller than I would have liked, but it was better than nothing. At least I could now walk about without looking completely obvious. I wouldn't be winning any fashion awards, but I didn't care. I had to find Meg.

I bundled up all of the clothing and threw it into one of

the large waste bins. I was no master of disguise, but if the police located my car they'd still think that they were looking for a man dressed in night-time wear.

So how was I going to find Meg? I'd left my phone in the spare room, the cops were looking for me, I'd done a runner. And there was the small matter of two dead bodies in my house. It wouldn't take long to find them, the house would not bear any level of scrutiny. I'd be caught with my pants down. Maybe I'd been too hasty, it might have been better to come clean with the police. No, they'd have taken me to the station, I'd have been out of circulation for who knows how long. Meg was somewhere in the city. She hadn't taken her car. I hadn't thought about that. If her car was still at the house, where was she? That suggested she was on foot. Or, maybe she was with someone else.

I sat on the pavement in complete darkness, turning over Jem's phone in my hand, wondering what to do next. I'd come to a dead end. The irony of being at the end of the alleyway wasn't lost on me.

Then events moved again. Jem's phone vibrated. It was a message. I hadn't even thought to look at his messages, I'd just used the phone. It was ridiculous, I'd been trying to preserve his privacy. The bastard had just whacked me with a lamp stand. I looked at the screen of his smartphone. There was a strong phone signal and data too. His battery life was good, well over 50 percent. He'd been receiving a lot of messages. The fool hadn't put a PIN number on his phone.

I navigated around his screen. It was a bit of a mess, but at least all the basics were there. He hadn't got Skype, but if I could download it over his mobile data, I'd be able to get in touch with Alex. I began the download and let it chug away in the background while I took a look at his text messages.

There were several texts from Sally. Some opened and read, others had come in more recently. Unusual that they should be texting each other in the middle of the night. I decided not to intrude there at first, scanning for other names. One caught my eye immediately. Martin Travis.

What was Martin Travis doing messaging Jem? Martin had been texting throughout the evening. I worked my way through the messages, starting at the first message.

We need to speak in private Jeremy. Can you make it 10am on Monday? I'll clear a slot for you. Martin.

At least Martin's constant use of Peter, rather than Pete, wasn't reserved for me alone. Nobody referred to Jem as Jeremy. Probably his mum. And Martin Travis.

Was Jeremy in relationship counselling with Martin? He'd never mentioned it. Then why would he? I moved along the messages.

Just heard from Sally. We need to talk. Could you make it tonight? I think it should be sooner rather than later.

Interesting. There were a couple more, increasingly urgent.

Jeremy, call or text me. Worried about Sally. Martin.

Then, the first time I'd seen Martin ruffled.

Jem. Call me now. Urgent.

By that stage, I didn't give a shit about Jem's marital privacy. I had to understand how he knew Martin Travis and what was so urgent that Martin had to speak with him straight away.

There were a lot of texts from Sally. There was some horrible stuff in there, going weeks back.

Get stuffed you shithead.

Nice. I'd never heard Sally use language like that in my few encounters with her.

Why do they all like your dick so much? It never satisfied me you prick.

This was horrible stuff. The mood of the texts changed soon afterwards.

Who was the bitch? I know you love her. Tell me the name of the slut. You'll never see the kids again.

Meg and I had had a few arguments in our time, but never anything like this. The messages became increasingly obsessed with one person.

I know who it is you bastard. I finally figured it out. How could you do it with her, of all people? Does he know? I'll tell him. You shit!

Just for a moment, it occurred to me that Meg might have had her affair with Jem. No, there's no way she'd do that to me. It had to be someone else. A family friend, probably. Whoever it was, it had hurt Sally badly. The tirade of hostile messages was disturbing.

But it was Sally's last message which finally jolted me into action. It made much more sense, in the context of what I'd just seen and read. The message had come in while Jem had been lying on the floor of my spare room, supposedly unconscious. No wonder he'd leapt up and fought so fiercely with me to make his escape.

Come to Martin's office now. I've got your slut with me. It's time we settled this.

CHAPTER SIXTEEN

So there it was. Martin's text to me. Jem's suspicious behaviour. Was it Jem who'd had the affair with Meg? I'd thought I'd known him. I'd thought I could trust him. How had it happened? He must have exploited our shift system, he knew exactly when I was on earlies and when I was on lates. Unless one of us was on a day shift, some days we'd barely see each other.

Martin's office was not that far away. That text had come in some time ago. I was constantly running to keep up. I was certain that I'd find Meg there. It must have been Jem she'd had her fling with. Why else would Sally be so irate?

Skype had finished downloading. I didn't have time to mess around logging in and trying to connect to Alex. I put the phone in my pocket and started running towards the counselling offices. My head was pounding and my broken nose was making it hard for me to breathe. I cursed my lack of fitness. I was out of breath after a few minutes, and the ill-fitting plimsolls didn't help.

There was very little activity on the streets, but when I

saw pedestrians walking towards me, I put my head down and tried to cross the street before we passed each other. Eventually I arrived at the offices, breathless and in need of a rest. Adrenalin kept me going. I was so close to Meg now, I'd see her in the next few minutes, I'd be able to make everything alright again.

The building was almost in complete darkness. There was just one light on. I tried to figure out where Martin's office was, mentally retracing my steps through the building from my previous visits. It was his light which was on. The blinds were shut – I couldn't see what was going on. It was on the second floor, it wasn't as if I could tap on the window.

Having recovered my breath, I headed for the front door. It was locked. The interior door of the entrance had been propped open, suggesting that somebody was inside, but the front door was locked, or at least on the catch. Damn!

I walked around the building, wondering if there were any other doors. There was a fire door at the side, but it was closed.

I had Jem's phone. If I called Sally, would she answer? Would she let me in? I assumed that Jem was in there with her already. Jesus, if Sally, Meg, Jem and I were left in a room with Martin Travis, it would have all the makings of the world's worst ever counselling session. Jeremy Kyle would pay a fortune to get us all together with the cameras rolling.

I tried calling Sally on the phone. There was no answer, it just went dead. I typed a message.

It's Pete Bailey using Jem's phone. I'm outside. Let me in. We all need to talk. I pressed send on the text, I couldn't think what else to do. I moved around the side of the building, scouring the ground for small stones. I threw some up at the office window. I didn't want to attract any unwanted attention by making a noise; the cops were after me, and to be arrested for causing a disturbance was all I needed. No response. No movement. I began to feel a sense of dread. I thought about the bodies back at my house. Had it all turned to shit up there? I panicked, thinking once again about Meg's safety. Was Sally with Meg, is this what it was all about?

I could see from Jem's phone display that the message had been received, but there was no reply. Damn it, I was breaking in.

How do you break into a modern building? They're airtight. Double glazing on the windows, reinforced locks on the doors, alarms all over and usually wired with CCTV. At least there was no CCTV at these offices, I suppose security wasn't a huge issue. All there was to steal was lost dreams and broken relationships.

I walked around the building once again, closely examining each window. They were all closed. I did another circuit, looking upwards. As I came to the pipework which ran up and down the walls, marking the location of the toilets, I took out Jem's phone and switched on the torch function again. There were cigarette ends on the floor. My guess was that some member of staff had been smoking with their head stuck out of the toilet windows, probably when it had been raining and they didn't fancy being banished to the pavements outside.

I shone the torch upwards into the darkness. The window was slightly open. If I could climb up the plastic piping, I'd be able to reach it. With any luck, I'd be able to prise it open from there and climb in. It was a very long time since I'd climbed anything. I wasn't even sure if the plastic pipe would take my weight. Only one way to find out. I had to get into that office.

I must have looked like the most cack-handed burglar ever. It took me several tries to get started, there was nothing to grab onto. I reached up, I tried to jump, I attempted to lift my leg up as far as it would go. Useless. Then I figured it out. The plimsolls worked great. They helped me shimmy up the pipe because they didn't slip against the plastic. After a few tries, I'd reached the diagonal pipes that were connected to the back of the toilet units inside the building. Once I'd made it that far, I was able to hoist myself up, grip the windowsill of the adjacent toilet, and work my fingers around the open frame. There wasn't much of a gap to play with, and I cursed when I felt that there was no window stay that I could flip up. I moved my hand around to the right-hand edge of the frame. There it was – there would be two of them. As my fingers explored blindly, I felt a loosely closed latch. Whoever the secret smoker was, they'd done me a huge favour. Probably left the window very slightly open to be sure there was no residual smell of smoke. I flipped the latch. Brilliant, halfway there.

It would be harder for me to reach over and get the second latch. I would have to move my steadying hand to allow me to lean right across the frame. I was precariously balanced as it was. I could hear the plastic piping creaking as I shuffled about trying to position myself correctly.

Why wasn't Sally answering my text? If she'd looked at her phone, I could have avoided all of this nonsense.

Cautiously, I moved my hand over, clutching the windowsill next to me. I tried to lean over, testing the angle

I'd have to maintain to get my hands anywhere near that second latch. My first attempt was aborted: I moved my foot at the same time as I leant my body over, but there was no pipe for my foot to rest on and I almost fell off. I swiftly moved my furthest hand back onto the windowsill, holding it firmly while I steadied my body – and my nerve.

The second time, I did it. I'd had to stretch my arm so far that I strained it. Wincing, I pushed through the pain. My fingers explored the gap between the frame and window and eventually came to rest on the latch. My arm felt as if it was about to pop out of its socket, I wasn't sure that it would stretch any further. Then I got it. I worked the latch out of its retainer, the window swung open, and I went flying to the ground below.

What a dunce! I should have loosened the furthest latch first, then I could have hung onto the window while it was still secured. Instead, it flew open and I fell onto the paving slabs below. My head cracked as it hit the ground. I was struggling to stay conscious; something made me hang on for a few seconds before I dropped back down onto the hard concrete floor. It was the sound of voices. Raised, angry voices. I heard Jem. He sounded scared, as if he was pleading with somebody. And then I heard her scream. I couldn't do a thing about it because the blow to my head had finally taken its toll. As I slipped into unconsciousness, I heard Meg cry out with an anger that I'd never heard before.

'You bastard! You fucking bastard! How could you do that to me!'

I don't know how long I was out. Probably only seconds,

maybe longer. It was enough time for everything to change again. When I came round, it was quiet. No voices, no shouting.

I tried to raise my head off the slabs. It was sore and I was disoriented. It was like those Tom and Jerry cartoons when the birds fly around their heads. That's how I felt. Dazed.

I was consumed by an overwhelming sense of self-loathing. I was an imbecile. Why couldn't I have worked out that the window frame would send me flying when the latch was worked free? I pulled myself off the floor. I felt as if I was twice my normal weight, my body seemed so heavy after the fall. There didn't appear to be any blood, but my hands were scratched, and one of my knees was incredibly sore.

I hobbled round to the front of the building, hoping that the door would be open. It wasn't. However, the internal door was now closed. There were also more lights on. And the car that had been pulled up around the front had gone. I hadn't even thought about that. I didn't recognise it, whoever it belonged to.

I pulled Jem's phone from my trouser pocket. Shit, I'd broken the screen. It was still readable, but it made life tricky in the darkness. I had to get inside the office. I'd already opened the window, Martin's office light was still on. There was something on the blind now, not much, but a splash of something, a silhouette. Was it blood?

I ran towards the drainpipe, forgetting about the soreness in my leg. I pulled myself up, balancing once more on the plastic pipework. I cursed myself again for falling, then began to pull myself through the narrow window. I scraped my stomach on the bricks in the wall and on the window frame. I put my hands on the rim of the toilet to pull myself inside – it was none too clean.

Eventually I managed to haul my entire body into the room. It took an undignified roll to get my legs through the window without my head landing in the shit-plastered bowl.

I was cautious now, nervous of what I'd find in Martin's office. I'd used these toilets before, I saw where I was as soon as I stepped out into the corridor. I couldn't hear a thing. No voices, no shouting. Yes ... there was something. A quiet sobbing. A man. It wasn't Jem. It was a really whiny cry. It had to be Martin Travis.

I moved towards Martin's office door. There was blood on the handle. I burst inside and rapidly scanned the room. There was more blood on the white blinds, as I'd thought. Two people were sitting on Martin's settee, both with heads bowed, a man and a woman. They looked up as I entered, terror in their eyes.

It was Ellie and Martin Travis. Martin's face was bloody. It looked as if he'd been shot a couple of times, but he didn't seem to be at risk of dying. The blood must have been his, there were no bodies anywhere. And no Meg either.

They were bound together on the settee, their legs fastened by parcel tape, a figure of eight weaving in and out of their limbs. Their hands were also taped, not together like the legs, they had some small degree of movement. Each had tape around the mouth too. Ellie looked scared and sweaty, her long hair was drenched. Martin was cowed and badly hurt, his wounds looked deep and sore.

I looked around for something to cut the tape with. Martin started mumbling something.

'Sorry,' I said, stepping over to remove the tape from their mouths.

'This is going to hurt, Martin,' I warned, as I pulled the tape that was stopping him from speaking. It had caught up in the facial hair that I hated so much. At last I was getting to give Martin Travis a partial face wax.

He took deep breaths, he'd been struggling I think. Ellie looked calmer. I removed her tape more gently than Martin's. She gasped for breath too.

'Thank God, Pete. Christ this is a bloody mess!'

'There are scissors in my top drawer,' Martin interrupted. 'Get my blue asthma inhaler out of there too, please.'

Ellie and Martin had started to work the tape with their fingers, but it was securely if inexpertly applied. I put them out of their misery, cutting through the tape and giving them their freedom. Martin took two deep breaths from his inhaler, it seemed to relax him immediately.

'What happened here?' I asked.

Martin and Ellie both began to speak at once. Martin let Ellie lead.

'Jesus, Pete. I got to your house and all hell had been let loose. Tony Miller dead and some other guy too. There were two women in the house, one of them has to be your Meg. I walked right into it. One of them had a gun for fuck's sake ...'

'That was Sally Denning. You know her, Peter, I think?' said Martin.

'Why does Sally have a gun?' I asked.

'It's some kind of air pistol,' Ellie said. 'It looks like something off the TV. A Beretta, something like that. It's not a real gun, though. She shot Martin a couple of times ... are you okay?'

Ellie looked guilty, as if she'd completely abandoned her fellow captive.

'She shot me twice in the face and once in the foot. It hurts like mad,' Martin answered. I could see the small hole in his shoe, I hadn't noticed it previously. There was a small patch of blood on the carpet.

'It's one of these CO_2 air pistols, I think,' Ellie resumed. 'We've done stories on them on the bulletins. Usually teenagers shooting at cats. They don't kill, but they can mess you up pretty bad.'

'Is Meg alright? Is she hurt?'

'She's alright, Pete, but I don't know how safe she is now. This is really messed up. I don't know who's been shagging who, but this is one big bloody mess!'

'Where is she?' I asked, anxious to move on, to bring the whole sorry story to an end.

'I don't know where they went,' Martin said. 'She has Jeremy with her too, Peter—'

'Will you please just call me Pete!' I shouted, then immediately regretted it. He looked like a scolded dog.

'I'm sorry, Martin,' I said. 'I think we're all feeling the stress a bit.'

'It's okay, Pete. I need to tell you something about Meg. This would normally be confidential, but under the circumstances ...'

Oh God. I wasn't sure that I could take any more revelations. I had a feeling I knew what was coming.

'Go on,' I said, sitting down in Martin's armchair. 'I know you fancy her, Martin. You don't need to confess that.'

'For heaven's sake, Pete. Meg said you could be a prat sometimes. I'm gay! I love Meg as a friend, but I'm not into women. I think women just find me safe to talk to ...'

My face reddened. I would not have guessed at that

one. I was embarrassed. It was just one more blow to add to my feelings of humiliation and stupidity.

'It's nothing to do with that, anyway. That night when Meg and I went out for food, she wanted to tell me something. Something that she didn't want you to know, Peter – Pete.'

I looked at him, I was too ashamed to open my mouth.

'You must have worked out who she slept with? It's why we couldn't tell you.'

'Jem?' It had to be that bastard.

Martin nodded.

'But it's not what it looks like, Pete. That night we went out, Meg wanted to confide in me. She admitted that she had been out with Jeremy, once, and in secret. They'd gone out for drinks. She felt that you and she had been growing apart. She wanted to talk to Jeremy, see if you'd said anything to him. She was trying to save your marriage, Pete.'

'So why did she sleep with him? Why did she sleep with a mate from work of all people?'

'That's just it, Pete. You were on a late shift that night. She went out with Jeremy, she knew you wouldn't find out. She wanted to see what was on your mind, push him for some information. She remembers having a glass of wine. She has memories of him touching her hand in the pub. She recalls thinking that he was being overfamiliar. She only has flashbacks after that. Driving back to your house in Jeremy's car. Her skirt pulled up above her waist. The bedroom in your house. Jem's face next to hers. Him breathing deeply.'

Martin must have seen the pain on my face. I needed to listen, but I couldn't bear to hear the words.

'Did she want him to do it, Martin? Was it consensual?'

'She doesn't know, Pete. She came round later that evening. Jeremy had gone. There was semen on the bed.

Her pants were at the top of the stairs. She panicked, Pete. She thought that she'd led him on. She thought that she was to blame. It was killing her. The first time she said anything was when we met up that night. She was confused. She didn't know what to do or who to tell. She thought that nobody would believe her.'

I felt a creeping chill move through my body. I knew what Jem had done. I understood now how the bastard had betrayed me.

———

Before I met Meg, Jem and I had been commissioned by our then boss to research a week-long series of broadcasts on date-rape drugs. A student from the local university had reported a lecturer to the authorities and it had shocked everybody in the community. The concept of date rape was new and unfamiliar at the time.

When you're a journalist, you can get away with a lot in the name of research. I remember a story about a local girl who'd secured a slot in a porno mag. We'd all assumed that she'd got her kit off and done some tasteful shots. In the interests of in-depth research, when that issue of the magazine came out, we dispatched a young reporter with a fistful of petty cash to buy it from the nearest newsagent. She'd done a full gynaecological number. There was no crevice left unexplored by the camera. I got to interview her too. I like to think of myself as a man of the world, but it's difficult to have a formal conversation with someone when you've taken a glance up their arsehole.

It was a similar thing with the date-rape story. We were working closely with the police; they supported our public information radio reports, and we were educating vulnerable women about the risks that they faced. We were given access to some of the drugs so that we could see what they looked like. It was important for the reporting to get the details right. We needed to describe the tablets, the boxes that they came in, the websites that supplied them.

It seemed to make Jem quite excited. He'd make taste-less jokes about deploying the drugs at home. 'I might get Sally to give me a decent blow job!' he'd say. Or once, worryingly, he talked about working his way through the latest crop of students on short work placements. 'I might finally get a threesome with some fit students!' he'd laughed.

I'd shrugged it off at the time. It's not my sort of humour. I love sex, but it has to be completely consensual, that's the fun of it as far as I'm concerned. Nothing beats hot, passionate, fully consensual sex.

Jem must have sensed my distaste at the jokes. It was as if he was testing my limits. Well, I'd drawn my line. I hated the thought of the date-rape drugs, it made me feel sick. As far as I was concerned, it was rape. No ifs, no buts, none of 'I was just having a bit of fun', it was rape and there was no excuse for it. Jem's jokes stopped, but his fascination didn't. He couldn't believe that these things could be bought online. Or even better, at clubs in the city.

As I sat in Martin's office listening to him describing Meg's experiences, I saw how naive I'd been. It was all beginning to make sense. Anna. Meg. The other young students who came and went. And Sally's terrible anger.

'Did Sally know?' I asked. 'Did she know what he was up to?'

'She suspected, Pete, she didn't know. You know that I dealt with their marriage break-up don't you? Did Jeremy tell you?'

'No, he didn't talk about it,' I replied. 'He used to curse

Sally and how she was squeezing him over the kids and the money. He's done this before, Martin. Meg is not the first. I should have seen this. I should have known this is what he was doing.'

'Jeremy is the only one to blame here, Pete ...'

Martin was slipping into counsellor mode.

'No, I should have seen this. I laughed him off, thinking he was my best mate. I let Anna down. I should have known. If I'd done something, I could have helped Meg.'

Ellie's face was white. She could probably see where I was going. My wife had been raped by my best friend. She'd been coming to visit me on my birthday and I'd been shagging Ellie. She looked as ashamed as I felt.

'Who killed Tony Miller and Jason Davies?' I asked. 'Was it Meg?'

'I don't know,' Martin replied. He looked at Ellie.

'I walked into the house in the middle of it,' she said. 'I very nearly ended up like Tony. Sally was doing her nut at the time. I can't say I'm unhappy about Tony. He deserved what was coming to him, but I don't know how he got killed. Sally pointed the gun at me and Meg and drove us over here. I wasn't going to argue.'

'What happened in here? I heard shouting. I heard Meg, didn't I?'

'Jeremy came straight from your house,' Martin answered. 'He looked like you'd beaten him up – I see that he got a few punches in too. Sally went crazy when he came in. She'd asked him to come. I don't know how many pellets she has in that gun of hers, but he took a couple in the groin.'

'Sally's insane, Pete,' Ellie said. 'I think she reckons Jem and Meg were having an affair. I don't think she even knows about the date-rape thing. God knows what she's planning to do!'

She saw my face change.

'Look, I'm sorry, Pete, but this woman is nuts. Believe me, I've been stalked by Tony Miller, I know all about nutters, she's got a screw loose. The real question is: what is she going to do next?'

CHAPTER SEVENTEEN

'We've got to call the police now, this is getting too complicated!' I said. I had to get Meg away from Sally.

It seemed that Sally was putting two and two together and making five. Jem had taken advantage of Meg and had been a total dickhead with Sally. He must have pushed her over the edge.

'How much did Sally know about what Jem was doing?' I asked Martin. 'I know it's all supposed to be confidential, but come on, we need to end this now.'

Martin didn't hesitate.

'She knew he was having casual flings with young reporters. She could smell it on him when he came home at night. They'd had a sexless marriage for years. She was happy that he left her alone and didn't make any sexual demands on her. She was staying with him for the kids. And she needed the money, of course — she'd given up work when it became cheaper to stay at home than to pay the childcare. She told me that she felt trapped but that she couldn't leave. She'd been very depressed. She was on medication.'

It was as if he was reading out their case notes. Martin knew more about us than anyone else, even our own spouses.

'Did she suspect what he was doing, though? Did she know what he'd done with Meg?'

'She suspected Meg. She told me once in one of our one-to-one meetings. She came to see me several times after she threw Jeremy out of the house. She knew that his latest conquest was different ... I'm sorry, Pete. I shouldn't have used that word.'

'It's okay, it's fine, carry on ...'

'Sally thought Jeremy was in love. She knew that he'd slept with someone, but it was more than the usual fling. This one seemed to mean more to him. She couldn't take that, it was the final humiliation for her.'

'Okay, look Ellie, I need you to make a call to the police. Don't tell them that you've seen me. We need them out looking for Meg. If they can get to her before I can I'll have to settle for that. Tell them that it's connected with the death of Tony Miller. They've got you on their records, they'll believe you. My address is 11 Ashbourne Drive. Mention that, it'll get their attention. Tell them that Meg is in danger.'

I thought about the gun that Sally had used.

'Can she hurt someone with that gun? Could she kill with it?'

Ellie considered this for a few seconds, no doubt thinking through her TV report.

'It's possible, but it's unlikely, Pete. You could blind somebody, certainly hurt them. But killing, no.'

'She had that knife, though,' added Martin, 'covered in blood. It had some flesh caught in the serrated edge. It was horrible.'

Martin wasn't helping to put my mind at ease.

'Shit. That's the knife from our kitchen. It's what was used to kill Miller and Davies. She won't use it on Meg and Jem, surely? What do you think she's after?'

There was silence from Martin and Ellie.

'Revenge, I think,' said Martin after a while, 'but I don't know what that will mean. She got Jeremy over here by threatening the safety of the kids, said she'd left them in a hotel room in town on their own where he couldn't get to them. She wanted him with Meg. Sally wanted to hear the truth from both of them together.'

'Ellie, you'd better mention the children when you call the police. You don't think she'd hurt the kids do you, Martin?'

'I don't think so, but she's been increasingly irrational at our sessions. I tried to get her to talk to her doctor, I was concerned about her mental health. Her anger was directed at Jeremy – and whoever he'd slept with. Now she knows it was Meg I don't know what she'll do.'

'Okay, here's the plan. Ellie, call the police. Tell them about Sally, Meg and Jem. Let them know that the kids may have been left somewhere. They should check Jem's house. They live at 19 Oswald Close.' I scribbled that address and my address on some notepaper from Martin's desk. Ellie wasn't local, these streets would mean nothing to her.

'Are you okay, Ellie? I'm sorry, I didn't ask you. Have you been hurt?'

'I'm fine, Pete, honestly. This is not my idea of a great Saturday night out, but we need to end this. Martin's the one who got hurt. She has a baseball bat in the car too, she left it in on the front seat when we met Martin here. Be careful of that too, Pete.'

I felt a pang of remorse for the way I'd treated Martin. Poor bugger had been shot by Sally. He'd been held captive, summoned to his office late at night by a woman who'd flipped. And his knowledge of what was going on had already helped to make some more sense out of this crazy situation.

'Martin, you should call a taxi to take you to A&E.'

He nodded. I looked at his facial wounds. They looked sore and bloody, but I couldn't see how someone could be killed with a gun like that. It would be good as a threat, I certainly wouldn't want to be shot by one, but it couldn't kill. Sally's knife was more of a concern. And that bloody baseball bat.'

'Who killed Tony and Jason? Do you know?'

Martin and Ellie looked at each other. It was the second time I'd pushed them, I had to know.

'They were dead when I got to your house,' Ellie said. 'Meg and Sally were covered in blood when I arrived. I don't know who did it, but Sally was in control of the situation, it must have been her.'

Martin spoke.

'I met Meg and Sally here, Pete. It was me who let them in. I thought it might help, I was wrong about that. I got a voicemail from Meg yesterday telling me she needed to speak to me. That's why I texted you, Peter – Pete. She sounded tense. I tried to contact her on her mobile, but couldn't raise her. When you didn't get back to me, I started to get worried. I wondered if you'd had an argument. It was Sally who asked me to come here. She said she needed to speak. Urgently. I didn't know she had Meg with her. I didn't know what she'd done ...'

'Thanks, Martin,' I said, and I meant it. I was beginning to wonder if he was the only decent person in any of this.

He'd been nothing but discreet, supportive and a good friend. And I'd got him so wrong.

A phone rang. It was somebody's mobile. We looked at each other. I didn't recognise the ringtone at first. It was Jem's phone, ringing in my pocket.

Shit! It was Sally. I answered the call.

'Sally?'

There were no pleasantries.

'I've got your slut of a wife here, Pete, and my bastard of a husband. I'm trying to get to the bottom of what they've been up to. I've put a few bullets into Jem, but he doesn't seem to want to share very much. I've got about six shots left. I'm saving them for Meg. I think you might want to hear this.'

'Where are you, Sally? You've got this wrong, Meg is nothing to do with this—'

'Shut up!' Sally screamed down the phone. It shocked me, she sounded like a toddler who can't control their tantrum.

'If you bring anybody – *anybody* – Pete, I swear I'll slit her throat. We're going to sort this out between us. It ends tonight.'

'I won't bring anybody, Sally, I promise. Just don't hurt Meg, there's an explanation for all of this. Where are you? Tell me where I can find you.'

I heard Meg shout something towards the phone.

'Be careful, Pete—'

There was the sound of a shot. I heard Meg scream, then crying.

'What are you doing to her, Sally? Leave her alone, your bloody husband is to blame for all of this.'

'Just shut up, Pete. You're all so used to gobbing off on the radio. Well, listen to me. I know Meg is pregnant. For all

I know, it's Jem's baby. You get here fast and don't bring anyone with you. You do, and my last pellets get shot into your slut's stomach. You understand me?'

The baby! Oh, for God's sake, don't hurt the baby!

'Jesus, Sally, leave Meg alone! You've got this wrong ...'

I could hear my wife sobbing in the background.

'Come to the cathedral. We're in the bell tower. Shout when you get here. You bring anybody with you, and it's over.'

Sally ended the call.

'What did she say?' Ellie asked.

Sally's got Meg over at the cathedral. She wants me to go over there now. She's threatening to shoot her stomach. Meg's pregnant ...'

Martin looked guilty, I saw it in his eyes as soon as I said those words.

'What?' I asked. 'What aren't you telling me?'

'I'm sorry. I told Sally that,' he said, not looking me in the eye. 'She forced it out of me. That's how I got these wounds.'

I couldn't blame Martin. I'd shit bricks if Sally was waving a gun at me, even if it was just an air pistol.

I had to get over to the cathedral. I knew why she'd gone there. It's where they'd got married. Sally was one of the bell ringers there. Or she had been before she got tied down with the kids. It made perfect sense that she would go there to try to figure out who had ruined her marriage and her life.

'I need to use your car, Martin,' I said. 'You do have a car?'

I'd had my fill of bad news that weekend.

'I'm sorry, Pete, there's no car.'

'For Christ's sake, the cathedral is right across the city. I need to get there fast.'

'How about a taxi?' Ellie suggested. 'You'll get one fast now the clubbers have all gone home.'

'No taxi,' I replied. 'I did a runner from the police, I daren't take a taxi now.'

'There is something I can offer,' Martin said, sheepishly. 'It'll be faster than walking ... if you want it?'

'Go on ...'

'It's a Brompton. I keep it here so that I can take exercise during my lunch breaks.'

'What on this planet is a Brompton?' I asked.

'You know. It's a bicycle. It's a folding bicycle.'

I wondered if this man could do anything in a straightforward manner.

'If it's the best we can do,' I said, trying not to show my exasperation with him.

'Where is it?'

'In the storeroom downstairs, behind the reception desk. I'll help you if you want?'

'No, it's fine. When you see me leave the building, call a taxi, get yourself looked at in A&E.'

'Should I still call the police?' Ellie asked. 'Do you think it will make things worse?'

'I just don't know.' I was weary, both mentally and physically exhausted. 'What do you think?'

'I think we need to alert them, Pete. In case things turn bad. They can have an ambulance ready. She's really angry, Pete. Take care with her.'

'Okay Ellie, call the cops, but tell them not to go into the cathedral. Tell them what Sally said she'd do, let them know that Meg is pregnant. And yes, tell them to get an ambulance over there. No sirens, though, they'll just make the situation worse.'

Ellie nodded.

'I'll catch you later,' I said. 'Let's get this sorted now. Only call when I'm clear of the building, I need to get out first.'

I rushed down the stairs to the reception area and immediately found the storeroom that Martin had been talking about. I looked around. I didn't see a bicycle. Had he been mistaken?

I turned on the light to get a better look.

'For God's sake, Martin!' I shouted aloud. It was one of those folding bikes. The type that you see middle-aged men taking on trains. The type of middle-aged man who thinks you can only ride a bike if you're wearing a ridiculous pair of shades and uncomfortably tight Lycra.

I picked up the folded contraption and began the process of assembly. Out came the handlebars, I tightened the nut. So far, so good. Move out the front wheel, tighten the nut. It was beginning to look like a bike. A wanker's bike mind you, but a bike nevertheless. I couldn't figure out the back wheel. How did the back wheel move into position? I messed around, pushing it, pulling it, trying to figure out how it moved into place. I got it eventually and tightened the nut. The seat was way too low, I moved it up and made sure the bolt was tight. I was good to go. Precious minutes lost because Martin Travis couldn't just buy a regular bike like everybody else rides.

I shouted up the staircase, not sure if they'd hear me.

'I'm off now!'

The doors opened easily from the inside, I wished it had all been that simple on the way in. I wheeled the bike away from the building. Ellie and Martin were looking through the blinds. Ellie waved to acknowledge it was safe to call the police.

I rode off into the night, wobbling at first because the Brompton took some acclimatisation. I must have looked crazy, it's a wonder I didn't get stopped. I was cycling as fast as I could, dressed in trousers and shirt that were too big for me and a sports cap that had seen better days, powered by a pair of too-small women's plimsolls, rushing to save the wife I loved from a mad woman. In all my years reporting on the bizarre and unusual, I'd never covered a news story quite like this one.

The cathedral was some way away, of course it was. I cursed the Brompton's smaller wheels, why do people ride those things? I thought through the scenario in the bell tower. I'd been up there a few times reporting on stories for the radio station.

Once it was a retiring bell ringer who'd been ringing bells there for fifty years. A great guy. The second time was to talk about how one of the bells was being removed and replaced. They were massive, really heavy. The bell tower itself was amazing, it was quite something to look around. It was high too. Not scary high, but you had to climb a ladder or two to get up there.

What was Sally up to? I was damn angry with Jem too. I wanted to punch the git. If Sally didn't get to him first, then I might do that. I wanted to hear what he'd done from his own lips.

Who knew what Sally was doing, what twisted scene was playing out in the bell tower? It took me about ten minutes to cross the city. I stopped outside the cathedral doors and threw the Brompton to the ground. In the distance I could hear police sirens. Was that Ellie? Was it some other incident? Either way, the police would be at the cathedral soon. I had to get to Meg. I had to set Sally straight. The police could take care of Jem.

The cathedral doors were open. I'm not sure how Sally pulled that one off, maybe she had a key. Then I got my answer. The verger was out cold on the floor. Some gaudy bit of church gold had been discarded on the ground next to him. He'd been hit over the head but he was still breathing.

Which way to the bells? I'd forgotten where to go. There was blood on the floor, not much, but enough to give me a direction. I remembered that the door to the bell tower was tucked away at the back of the building. You had to walk along a gallery to get to it, then up a further two levels. The drops of blood helped me to navigate. Perhaps it was nothing serious, it looked like a nosebleed or something like that. It was fresh though, still wet.

I made my way up the spiral staircase and walked along the gallery. The last time I'd made that trip I'd been laughing and joking, recording equipment in hand, fascinated by the free tour that I was getting. Now I was terrified of what I might walk into. I'd heard Sally on the phone. She'd lost it, she was unhinged. She was a woman who'd been pushed too far. Whatever I did, I'd have to stay calm. I'd have to keep her calm too.

I approached the first of the ladders. I was sore, aching, still out of breath and my head hurt like crazy from the earlier fall. My nose felt like it had exploded on my face.

In the distance outside, I could hear the far-off sound of a helicopter. Surely not the helicopter? Ellie must have mentioned Sally's gun – they'd deploy the firearms officers if any kind of gun was involved. A helicopter was all we needed.

I gave a shout, anxious not to startle Sally.

'Sally! It's me, Pete. I'm alone. I've come to talk.'

No answer.

'Sally? It's Pete. I'm coming up.'

Cautiously, I started to climb up the stairs. As my head came level with the wooden flooring, I paused a moment. I was nervous of that gun.

'I'm coming up, Sally.'

There was nobody there. Just a circle of ropes, all tied up, ready for the ringers. No, there was one that had been cut off. It was a rough cut, Sally's knife probably.

They must have moved up into the bell room itself. I headed for the door, calling up the narrow passageway. We were back to a short spiral staircase now.

'Sally! I'm coming up!'

I could hear a sound above me. It was a muted sobbing. Jem's voice. No sound from Sally or Meg. I stepped out into the bell room. The bells were massive, heavy metal objects each one attached to a huge wheel. When the bell rang, the wheel would rotate to almost full circle and back again.

I didn't see him at first. It wasn't very well lit, and it was the sobbing that drew my eyes. It was Jem. Bloody, broken and with his head and arms pulled through one of the wheels. His hands were tied. He was stuck and secure.

'Pete! Pete! Thank God you're here, she's gone crazy! She won't listen to me—'

'Shut up, Jem!' I shouted. 'Where's Meg? What's she done with Meg?'

'Help me, Pete. If these bells ring, they'll take my head with them—'

'I don't give a shit about you at the moment, Jem. As far as I'm concerned, you'll get what you deserve. Where are Meg and Sally?'

'They're up on the roof, Pete. She's really angry. Tell her Pete. Tell her she's got it all wrong!'

I looked at Jem's mobile phone. It was almost 7am, the bells would ring soon, silenced through the night but summoning the great and the good to worship for the first service of the day.

There was no time to release him. I had to get to Meg.

Without knowing exactly what was going on in the cathedral grounds below, I was aware of cars arriving, doors slamming and voices giving instructions. They were distant sounds, we were high up, and it was windy and exposed out on the roof. It would be the police, called by Ellie. But I knew that this situation had to be played out between the three of us.

I stepped out into the night. The helicopter was buzzing round the tower. I could hear Sally's tense voice.

'Sally, it's me, Pete. Come on, we need to talk about this. It's not what you think!'

Sally had Meg precariously perched on one of the turrets. She looked scared out of her wits. There was so much blood, both women were covered in it. Their hands, their clothes, their faces.

'Meg! Look at me, Meg! This is going to be over soon—'

I rushed towards them. It was too much too soon. Sally raised the pistol and shot. It hit me just above my eye. I could feel the blood running, blocking my vision.

'Okay, okay Sally! It's okay.'

I held up my hands and stepped back. She kept looking up at the helicopter, and she was aware of the activity on the ground below. She knew her time was nearly up, she had to decide what she wanted to do.

'Sally, I can explain. You're not the only victim here. Meg is a victim too—'

'Piss off, Pete. You're bound to take his side. Both of you have screwed young reporters in your time, you're like a bloody double-act!'

'Sally, it's alright, you're right to be angry. I knew about Jem and the young reporters, but this is different—'

'You're bloody right it's different! Do you know she's pregnant? Do you know that, Pete? Not content with humiliating me, he's now made this slut pregnant!'

Sally looked absolutely broken. I could have cried for her if Meg had not been standing so dangerously at the edge of the building. If she fell, I was certain that she'd die. It was too high to escape with a broken neck. If she fell, she was dead.

'Sally, I didn't know what he was doing with those girls. If I had, I'd have stopped it.'

She looked away from the helicopter, which was buzzing above us like an annoying fly. Would they have a marksman in there? Sally had a gun, it was quite likely. It looked like a proper firearm.

'Sally, why don't you put the gun down? There might be armed officers in the helicopter, I don't want you to get hurt.'

'Don't you come over all concerned now, you wanker! You might have thought more about me and the kids while you two were off shagging in the office.'

Meg looked at me then, doubtful for a moment.

'Meg, it was before I met you. You know what I used to be like. I haven't done anything since you and I got together ...' Only I had. The night before. With Ellie. Did she know? Had she worked it out?

'Sally, listen, even Meg doesn't know the situation yet. I

only just worked it out myself. Jem has been drugging women. Meg didn't sleep with Jem. He drugged her. She went to him to try and get some advice to save our marriage. We've been going through a rough time recently. Did Martin Travis tell you that?'

Meg looked at me, searching my face to see if I was telling the truth. This would be the answer she was seeking, if what Martin had told me was right. Sally was watching me too. My face was bloody, I was finding it hard to see. All the time we could hear the helicopter in the distance.

'Is it true, Pete? Did he drug me?'

'It's true, Meggy. I found a pill in his pocket this evening at the house. It all makes sense. We did some reports on it on the radio years ago. He's been drugging and raping girls, Meg. Sally, listen to me. Meg is a victim in this. It's Jem who's the guilty party here. He's the one that the police need to talk to.'

Sally began to cry, the gun lowered in her hand. Meg kept looking between me and Sally. The helicopter seemed to be getting nearer, I could sense the activity on the ground below us, even though I couldn't see it. Where was the knife? Did she still have the knife?

'Sally, it's alright, you're not to blame. This is Jem's fault. He hurt you, and he hurt Meg. He'll get his punishment. The police are here now. Put the gun down and let the police know that it's over. We can end this now.'

She looked so tired, so worn out. She stepped away from Meg. Meg looked at me, watching for a sign that it was okay to step down from the turret. I held out my hand, signalling to her to stay still. I didn't want to spook Sally, she seemed to be listening to me. Her hand tightened around the gun, she started to wave it between me and Meg.

'What about the baby!' she screamed. 'Is that his?'

She spat out the words as if she was trying to get poison out of her mouth. Her eyes became wild again.

I looked at Meg. Was it our baby? It had to be. How pregnant was she? Meg held my gaze for a moment, then looked away. Did she even know whose baby it was?

'Whose baby is it, Meg?' I asked. She looked up towards the helicopter, which was creeping closer in response to Sally's waving of the gun.

'Sally, you need to put the gun down. They don't know it's only an air pistol. If they think you have a gun, they might shoot you—'

'Fuck them!' she screamed. 'Let them shoot me. I don't care anymore. I want to know if it's his baby ... is it, Meg? Is it his?'

Meg hesitated. She should have just spat it out, said 'No' and given Sally the answer that she needed to hear. Instead, she paused. Maybe she didn't even know herself. She should have lied.

The helicopter moved in closer, Sally looked frantically between me, Meg, the helicopter and the turrets. I sensed it before I saw it. She raised her gun towards Meg and fired into her stomach. Three times. I rushed towards her. From the helicopter I saw a weapon raised, pointing directly at Sally. She just stepped up on the turret and jumped. The police officer never made his shot.

Meg stumbled on the turret, shocked by the sudden pain of the pellets. Her foot slid on the wet stonework, I watched her disappear over the edge.

'Oh no, not now! Christ not after all this ...'

The helicopter buzzed across the top of the cathedral, I could feel the blast of air from the blades. My eye was bloody and sore, my hair was blowing over my face. I was crying now, begging for Meg to be okay.

Then I saw it. A hand. A bloody hand, hanging on to the stonework of the turret. As the helicopter moved away, I heard her shouting. She'd managed to catch the turret. I rushed over, that was what the guys in the helicopter must have been trying to signal to me. I grabbed Meg's hand. It was wet, cold and slippery with blood.

'I can't hang on, Pete. Grab me, please grab me!'

'Reach your free hand up to me ...'

'I can't, Pete. It hurts, it hurts so much ...'

Her free hand was clutching her stomach where the shots had entered her body, she looked as if she was about to give herself up for dead.

'Hold on, Meg. Don't you dare let go!'

I was aware of a flurry of activity below where Sally's body was dashed on the aged paving slabs that surrounded the cathedral. It was growing lighter now, the darkness of night-time finally subsiding to bring in a new day.

I reached over the stonework and put my hands under Meg's armpits.

'I'm going to pull you, but you have to help me. You have to help, Meg. Do you hear me? I can't do it alone. You've got to help me pull you up.'

She was sobbing, resigning herself to what she thought was the inevitable conclusion. She looked down at Sally's body below. I could see her trying to work it out. How quick would it be? Would she die instantly?

'Focus on me, Meg. Look at me! I'm going to count to three, then I need you to try to pull yourself up. I've got you, but I can't hold you on my own.'

'I can't do it, Pete, it hurts so much, I can't hang on.'

I watched as her grip loosened. She was slipping away from me.

'Hang on, Meg. Don't let go!'

Leaning over the turret, the hard, cold stone pressing into my side, I took her weight, but the strain was too much for my back.

'Meg, come on, please, grab the side.'

She looked into my eyes. I was sorry for everything that I'd done to her, I was sorry that it had come to this. I just wanted my Meg back.'

She must have seen it. One moment she looked as if she'd given up, the next the light came back on. She reached up, wincing with the pain, making one last stretch to save her life. With Meg now taking her own weight, I was able to get more traction, pulling her up by her clothing, first back onto the turret, then over it again, onto the top of the tower. She was safe. I'd managed to pull her to safety. We rested against the wall, catching our breath, aware of the helicopter overhead monitoring it all.

Then, above the sound of the blades, the first clang of the cathedral bells. It was seven o' clock.

'Oh fuck ... Jem!'

CHAPTER EIGHTEEN

What happened afterwards was a blur of questions, flashing blue lights and people in uniforms. For someone who was used to talking to the police as a journalist, I realised that I didn't have a clue what it was like to be the one being questioned.

The minute that Sally's gun was out of the picture, the police had started to make their way up the final sets of stairs, having been given the go-ahead by the helicopter crew. But it was too late for Jem. There was so much mechanical equipment around the bells that they were still assessing the risks when the first click of the wheel mechanism came. That vital delay meant that he was still straddled across the floor with his head through the wheel when everything started moving to make the bell chimes sound out across the city.

As the first chime announced the start of a brand new day, the heavy bell swung on its wheel, ripping off Jem's head as it made its first rotation. It was a horrible way to die.

I was sad about Jem's death, of course I was, but most of all I was mourning the loss of friendship and regretting how much faith I'd put in him. It was a terrible end to a miserable story. I often wondered what must have been going through Sally's head in that moment when she decided to jump: hatred for Jem, contempt for Meg, disgust at me, fear for the future of the children and what the police might do. She'd taken things so far by that stage, perhaps it was difficult for her to find a way back.

Jem and Sally's kids were found at home – not in a hotel as she'd claimed – safe and asleep on the sofa. Sally had left them watching videos, and they were well supplied with sweets and goodies. The beat officer said they looked beautiful when they entered the house. A huddle of children, dressed in pyjamas, curled up like a basket of kittens, oblivious to their father's violent death and their mother's tragic suicide. Perhaps the worst legacy from the entire sad affair is that the kids were immediately placed into the care system, separated and without the day-to-day love of their parents. However big a piece of shit Jem was, I know he loved his kids.

Piece by piece, the truth came out. There was a full investigation, of course, long and detailed interviews and a blow-by-blow account of everything that had gone on over that weekend.

I was immediately separated from Meg. She was being treated as a possible suspect, and I was in need of medical attention. It looked worse than it was. I won't pretend that an air pistol pellet doesn't hurt, but it's hardly Rambo. It tore into the flesh above my eye, there was some concern about damage to my vision and the degree to which it had entered my skull, but it turned out to be a lot of blood about nothing.

I was soon back on my feet, bandaged and covered in plasters, anxious to speak to Meg again. But Meg didn't want to speak to me. She co-operated with the police inquiry, staying at a local hotel. She wasn't placed under arrest. I didn't return to the house either, other than to pick up some things. I learnt that there are actually people who make a business out of cleaning up crime scenes. Once the forensics guys were done with the house, the cleaning team moved in. I told them to remove everything with blood on it, however little it was. I didn't want any trace left of what had gone on there. I couldn't see me or Meg moving back.

When I returned to fetch my clothes, what was left of the furniture had been deposited on the bare floors, most of the carpet and underlay was gone. It was the same for the spare room and bedroom too. They'd done a good job, but I'd never be able to go into that house again without picturing a dead Tony Miller in the bed and Jason Davies' body bleeding behind the settee.

Martin told me that he was seeing Meg, as a friend and as a counsellor. I apologised to Martin, I felt that I owed him that much. I admitted that I'd thought he fancied my wife and that I'd underrated his abilities. I had been wrong about that. He'd shown himself to be reliable and trustworthy at a time when those qualities were in short supply. I still gave him some hassle about that Brompton bike, though. It was like having to assemble a Rubik's Cube before I could actually get anywhere.

Meg was working through what had happened. She didn't want to see me. Martin couldn't tell me everything, he was bound by the client and counsellor thing. It was like having to speak through an intermediary. He made sure that Meg could go to the house to fetch some things without the risk of running into me. He accompanied her. He wouldn't tell me which hotel she was staying in. He warned me that she'd be drawing down some savings from our account. Only half, not the full amount.

It was at that stage that I began to see the writing on the wall. Martin wouldn't be drawn on the dates for the baby and couldn't even confirm if it was mine.

'It's for Meg to decide what she shares with you,' he'd told me. 'I'm not trying to cut you out here, Pete, but I think she just needs some time.'

At least he was calling me Pete.

My impulse was to try to find her, to apologise and ask what was going on. But in a rare moment of temperance and good judgment, I held back. I didn't even know if she was fully up to speed with Ellie's part in all this, I wasn't going to push it. I wasn't sure if I could tell her the truth. If she decided to come back to me, giving her all the details about Ellie might be the final nail in the coffin. I kept away from her, frustrated by the lack of information, but thinking it wiser to wait.

It seemed to be an open-and-shut case as far as the police were concerned. It was good to know how the pieces slotted together.

I was right about Meg, she'd decided to come over to the hotel and surprise me on my birthday. It was a lovely thought, it would have been just what we needed. Right time, totally unexpected, a brilliant way to celebrate my fortieth birthday and move on. The pregnancy announcement would have topped it all off. If I hadn't been such a dickhead, we probably would have picked up from there. Things would have returned to normal.

I struggled over what to tell the police about Ellie. In the end, I told the truth. I asked the police if they'd have to tell Meg. They'd have to corroborate events, they said. Who knew what that meant? One of the cops, off the record, told me that they wouldn't drop me in it for the sake of it. Neither of us were suspects, they just needed to be clear about the timeline.

It turned out that Tony Miller had been following Ellie again, though he'd done a much better job of it since being frightened off by her brothers. Without Tony there to question, much of what happened would remain conjecture. It looked as if he'd followed her over to Newcastle and watched her return with me from the pub. CCTV showed that he'd actually entered the pub at one point, but Ellie had been too busy with me to notice. Fergus Ogilvy, the boring engineer, had let him into the OverNight Inn. Tony had been watching us as we walked along the corridor, he must have seen us through the glass windows in the fire doors. I didn't even know he was there.

The investigations team reckoned that he'd been going to follow us, or confront us, then discovered that the room next door was open, a place to hide and wait. Maybe he wanted to catch Ellie on her own. What happened in that room would remain a bit of a mystery, it was only when Meg came along that there was any clarity.

Jenny came clean too, or at least partially. She didn't say that she was meeting Jackson for sex, but she did admit that staff sometimes went for a nap in the empty rooms, especially when on late shifts. It was a good lie, it explained what Jackson was doing, and it kept her out of it.

Meg had come down the corridor to see me, but of course she went to the wrong room, Jenny had given her the number of the room next door. That's how she met Tony Miller – the rest played out in the Facebook Live video. That piece of evidence was eventually retrieved from Meg's account, the police had to file special documentation to request it off the servers from Facebook in the USA.

Meg would have filled in the gaps about why Tony decided to do a runner to our house. Apparently, he panicked when the fire alarm went off. He was waiting for Ellie to emerge from my room so he could try to intercept her. He'd realised what was going on in the room next door and decided to take Meg as a hostage when the alarm went off, a bargaining chip with Ellie. He punched her in the face when he saw that she'd recorded him killing Jackson. He'd thrown Meg's phone out of the window when they were driving back from Newcastle. The recording didn't get deleted until much later on – it had taken quite a while for the penny to drop with Tony. Even then, according to the police, he'd had to get Meg to delete the video via our home laptop, he was only clued up on the basics of social media.

Who knows what he was thinking of, but there it was. It was Ellie and me who pissed him off, Meg was just a timely arrival for him in his twisted fantasy.

It turned out that Sally had killed Tony. She'd had a row with Jem on the Friday afternoon before we all began to head off for Newcastle. It's why Jem was late. He'd been waiting along our road to see Meg. Who knows why? To confess his love? To admit what he'd done? We'd never know – with Sally and Jem dead, we just had Meg's word to figure out what had gone on.

Sally had followed Jem to our house that day. She'd seen Jem go in. He'd tried to encourage Meg into having sex with him – it was Meg who'd given him that scratch. That time he hadn't forced himself on her, it sounded like he'd genuinely fallen for her. He'd waited for me to leave for Newcastle, then he'd gone to my house to seduce my wife. An evil predator.

Meg had left some time afterwards. She knew she was pregnant and decided that it was time we sorted ourselves out. Only it didn't quite work out like that. Because of me. Me and Ellie.

Sally had been waiting in our house when Meg came back with Tony. After seeing what Jem had done the day before, she'd finally worked herself up enough to confront Meg. She must have got in with our emergency key, the one we keep in one of those false stones by the front door. It was hardly Fort Knox.

She was convinced that Meg and Jem were having an affair. According to Meg, she hadn't been expecting Tony. She slit his neck when he went to go for a pee in our en-suite. She was waiting in our bedroom, she'd been inspecting the sheets for signs of sexual activity.

Sally saw Jason coming too. She'd whacked him with our baseball bat. I kept one tucked inside the front door, just in case. We'd found it washed up by the sea on a holiday in Fife a few years previously. You always see people in the States fighting off intruders with a baseball bat. When we found that one on the beach, we took it home with us. I left it by the door, gathering dust, there if I ever needed it. I never needed it, but it served Sally well that night.

Jason was well built. She hit him hard over the head as he walked through the sitting room and finished him off by slitting his throat.

Meg didn't see any of this, she'd been secured with the parcel tape in the spare room. It was the same parcel tape that Sally used to restrain Ellie and Martin later in Martin's office.

Sally had wanted to have it out with Meg and Jem when Ellie drew up in her car. It was terrible timing. Sally had been spooked by Jason, she didn't know who he was or if the authorities had been alerted already. She'd become increasingly volatile according to Meg and Ellie. She sought sanctuary in Martin's office, and that's where I'd blundered in.

Sally had been contacting Martin constantly over the weekend, veering it seemed between taking his advice and getting revenge on Jem. She'd demanded he meet her at the offices at some unearthly hour on the Saturday night. He'd walked straight into a Quentin Tarantino movie.

She'd gone crazy when Jem joined them, cursing and accusing Meg and him of all sorts. She took them to the cathedral, where she and Jem were married. She was going to kill them both there. It was only when I popped up that it delayed things for a short time, she wanted to question me, find out what I knew about Jem.

There were a lot of gaps which the police would never fill in, not with so many of the key people dead. That was the best timeline of events that I could get out of the police. But the evidence seemed to fit the crime, the inquests were held and the bodies finally released for burial. It was only then that I learnt that things were not quite what they'd seemed.

It seemed to take forever for the bodies to be released, but it was a little over three weeks in the end. Time dragged. I was waiting for information, hoping that Meg would get in touch, and being fed occasional scraps by Martin.

I'd taken some time off work, I was too much on my own really, but I'm not sure that I could have stayed focused in the office. All the day-to-day shit seemed so insignificant after what had happened. I moved into a static caravan at a fading seaside resort a few miles away from the city. I didn't have to commit to a contract, but paid a month at a time. Perfect for me.

My car had been written off. I'd completely crunched the front of it, the insurance company just sent me a cheque. I bought a banger from a local garage to keep me mobile, something small and cheap.

I was anxious to find out how things had worked out in Newcastle, so I messaged Jenny via Erazerr: *Can I come over to catch up? When are you on shift?*

Hey Pete, great to hear from you. Where have you been? Come over Wednesday lunchtime. Let's have lunch in the bar.

We fixed the date and I made sure I was there in plenty of time.

It was a weird experience making the drive over to Newcastle. I saw the spot where I'd come off the road. You wouldn't have known it, there were just some muddy tyre tracks where I assume the tow truck had been. There was more undergrowth than I remembered too.

It was so good to see Jenny, I'm not sure why. Maybe it helped to close the circle. I was concerned about her too. I gave her a hug when she joined me at the table. It seemed the right thing to do, bearing in mind what we'd been through.

'So, did Bob find out your secret in the end?' I asked quietly, not wanting any of the other staff to hear what we were talking about.

'Only sort of,' she replied. 'Derek's a good guy you know, he knew what was going on, he helped me to cover. We just said we used empty rooms like a den. Bob was really cross, but he's not taking any action. I think he got a hard time from the police about the CCTV at the entrance. That's fixed now, by the way.'

She smiled when she said that. It looked like she was doing okay.

'How about Jackson?'

'I went to his funeral last week. It wasn't serious between us, you know. We weren't boyfriend and girlfriend, anything like that. It was only a bit of fun. Of course I'm upset about what happened but I'm pleased that it's over now. It was my first funeral,' Jenny continued. 'Very sad, but you know, I'll get over it. I just feel sorry for Jackson. He was a good guy, he didn't deserve that.'

'He was a good kid,' I replied, thinking back to the video that Meg had filmed. 'He tried to protect you, Jenny. I don't know if you know that. He did his best to keep you safe from Tony Miller. You could have done worse.'

She nodded and looked down. She was resilient. It had just been a casual fling, a way to liven up the long, dull nights at the OverNight Inn. She was more shocked by the violence of what had happened than she was upset at his loss. She'd get over Jackson soon enough.

'What about you, Jenny, what's your plan? Will you keep working here?'

'Bob's paying us extra to stay. He's terrified that the stigma of having a murder here will scare off customers. It's done the opposite. People are coming to see where it happened. I'll take the money while it's on offer, then find something else when it all calms down. It always suited me this job, it meant I could get my studying done. It's not the same now.'

It was nice to see Jenny, she was a good kid, like Jackson. I was pleased to hear that things were working out for her. I paid for the meal and walked with her towards the hotel entrance.

'Do you mind if we keep in touch?' she asked. 'Now it's

all over. Not with Erazerr. Via Facebook. Would that be okay?'

'Yeah, of course it would, Jenny. Send me a connection request, I'd love to stay in touch. It's been good meeting you.'

I gave her a hug, she was slight and slender, not the kind of figure I was used to holding. I gave her a smile, and we parted.

I had some catching up to do with Ellie and Alex too.

Ellie and I also met up over lunch, a couple of days after I'd seen Jenny. We'd Skyped in between times, but I was keen to see her in person.

'Hey, that looks sore,' she said, examining my eye wound and my nose.

'It is,' I replied, unsure if I should greet her with a hug. She put me out of my misery and wrapped her arms around me. We stood like that for longer than a normal greeting. We'd been through a lot that night. We'd started something terrible when we slept together.

'How's Dave?' I asked, deciding to go for a new subject first.

'Finally got the message,' she smiled. 'I should have done it ages ago. I know what happened was really shit, Pete, but some good came out of it. Tony Miller is gone. I'll never see him again, I only feel relief. I think Dave's just pleased he didn't get involved. I told you he's a squirmy little toad. I should have ditched him ages ago. I'm sorry, Pete, but this worked out okay for me. How are things with Meg?'

I sighed.

'Not so good, I don't know what's happening. I'm dealing with her through Martin at the moment. She must know what we did. We haven't talked about it, but she has to know. The baby changes everything too. I don't even know if it's Jem's. I don't know how pregnant she is ...'

Ellie squeezed my hand. I know it had only been a one-night stand, but I didn't sleep with just any woman, there has to be a connection for me. I'd like to think that's what separates me from someone like Jem. He didn't care, for him it was all about the power and the sex, but for me it's always been more about the person.

'What will you do now?' she asked, searching my face to figure out how I was really feeling.

'Who knows? It depends on Meg. We won't go back to the house, that's for sure. Neither of us wants it, she's moved out and so have I. If we stay together, I guess we'll rent for a while, sell the house, start afresh.'

'Will you stay at work?'

'I don't know, Ellie. I honestly don't know. I need to see how it goes with Meg. I just can't say at the moment.'

She looked at me again, she was deciding whether to say something.

'Look, Pete, if things don't work out, maybe you and me can see each other again. You need to make it work with Meg, I know you do. But if it doesn't work out ... well, I like you – a lot. I enjoyed our time together. You're a nice guy.'

I squeezed her hand.

'Thanks, Ellie. I can't think of a nicer person to be with if my marriage doesn't work out. I've got to tell you though, if Meg and I can't make it work, I might be up for a job move. There are too many memories in that office. I think it could be time to think about moving on.'

I saw the disappointment in her face, but I owed it to Meg to work on our marriage first. Ellie and I exchanged contact information and parted once again. It had been good to see her, to talk things through.

I spoke to Alex at the earliest opportunity after I'd been discharged from the hospital and given the police a full rundown on what had happened. I had a lot to thank Alex for. She had alerted the two bobbies in the house to what was going on. They'd been shocked to find a TV celebrity on my PC screen when they went upstairs. She'd filled them in on what we knew about the situation, convinced them to tread carefully, persuaded them that I was one of the good guys. She also gave them information about Jason Davies, explained why he was there, who he was.

Of course she felt guilty about Jason. She felt responsible. But what could any of us have done? We did what we could, it was a difficult situation. It was because of Alex that the helicopter had been on standby when Ellie had made her call to the police. They'd also got police marksmen ready – Ellie had just managed to provide the final location.

I confided everything to Alex, why wouldn't I? She'd once held the same position in my life as Meg, she was important to me. She knew who I was, I didn't have to explain myself.

We agreed to meet up. I said I'd see her in London once everything had calmed down again. After the funerals. It would be good to see her. If Meg and I got back together, I'd tell her the truth, let her know how Alex and I had almost started a family. It would be difficult, but it might help Meg understand.

It felt as if I'd met up with everybody who was involved in those events except the one person I was desperate to see. I needed to see Meg. I had to know what was happening. I didn't see her again until the day of the funerals.

It was chucking it down with rain on the day they buried Sally and Jem. They decided to bury them together. Not on top of each other, but next to each other in the graveyard. I didn't envy their ageing parents that decision. In the end, though, they made the decision for the kids. They were far too young to understand what had happened. It was just their mum and dad. It was the saddest thing about that funeral, seeing the kids.

I wasn't sure whether to attend or not. There was so much anger over Jem, what he'd done and how he'd behaved. I'd resolved to contact Anna again, I felt so guilty about how she'd been let down.

The ceremony was the usual religious bollocks. The vicar steered clear of anything controversial, focusing on the family that Jem and Sally had made together. It turned out that Sally had a history of mental illness. She'd tried to take her life before, many years ago, before the kids came along. Maybe that's why Jem felt trapped, who knows?

I was so angry with Jem. I felt completely betrayed. This man who'd been my friend. He'd raped my wife. He'd drugged her and had sex with her when she was incapable of giving her consent.

The police found an entire online history of drug orders. He'd been at it for years. A supplier from the USA. He didn't use the drugs every time, many times the sex was consensual. But if things weren't going his way, he'd spike their drinks and have sex with the girls anyway.

My friend was a monster. How did I not notice that? I'd been completely deluded. And Meg had paid the price. I could only feel sorry for Sally, he'd pushed her over the edge and destroyed their beautiful family. Those poor children, what life did they have ahead of them now?

As the relatives and few friends who could force themselves to attend filed out of the cemetery, I stayed behind, thinking, trying to make sense of what had happened. I was drenched, in spite of my umbrella, there's only so dry you can stay on a wet day like that.

I thought that I was alone. I caught a movement out of the corner of my eye. It was still giving me trouble after the gunshot wound, and I thought I was mistaken at first. It was Meg. She walked over to me, her face partially concealed by her own umbrella.

'I wanted to make sure the bastard was in the ground,' she began. She'd been crying, I could see that her eyes were red. I reached out to touch her, but she flinched.

'I'm sorry, Pete, I can't. I'm just so ... I just feel so angry. How could you do that?'

I hung my head. There were no excuses. I had no explanation. I could only hope for her forgiveness now.

'What do you want to do?' I asked, not sure if I was ready to hear the answer.

'I can't stay here, Pete. There are too many memories. I can't bear to think about what he did to me. I can't even remember, that's the worst thing. I thought it was my fault, I thought I'd done something wrong. I thought I'd encouraged him in some way.'

Again, I went to reach out to her. She brushed my hand away.

'No, Pete. I'm going away. I've requested a transfer at work. It should come through quickly enough, nobody wants to be a probation officer anyway.'

'What about the baby?'

She looked at me. I'm sure that there was still some love in there – somewhere – but she'd made up her mind. She hadn't come to the cemetery to discuss things, she was there to tell me what was happening.

'I can't face the tests just yet. It's too much. I can't end the pregnancy, not after what we've been through. I'll have the baby, then work it out.'

'And me? What about you and me, Meg?'

'I'm sorry, Pete. I can't forgive you for what you did. I heard you in your room. I was sitting there, terrified for my life, and all I could hear was you having sex with that woman. I don't blame her, I bet you didn't even tell her about us. But how can we move forward, Pete? You screwed everything up.'

I knew she was right. It was my fault. The blame rested with me. She'd needed my support and my loyalty and I'd been a complete tosser.

I didn't argue with her, I would have to accept her decision and move on. There was nowhere for me to come back from, any reconciliation had to begin with Meg.

'Can we stay in touch?' I asked. 'Will you let me know that you're okay?'

'Maybe soon,' she replied, 'but not now. Martin will tell you what's going on.'

'Okay,' I said. 'I'll speak to Martin.'

I sensed that there was something else she wanted to say. You don't spend that many years with somebody without being able to read their body language.

'What is it, Meg? What do you want to tell me?'

She burst into tears as if she'd been holding something back for a long time.

'I have to tell someone, Pete. I know you hate me right now, but you're the only person I can trust ...'

'What is it, Meg? You can tell me. You know you can trust me.'

'I didn't tell the police the truth, Pete. It's why I had to come here today, to apologise to Sally.'

I looked at her. I couldn't imagine that there was anything else left to say, things couldn't possibly get any worse.

'It was me who killed Tony Miller, Pete. I killed the bastard. He went to the toilet, he hadn't secured me properly and I stabbed him. I didn't know what else to do. He'd put his hand down my pants, felt my tits, I didn't know what he was going to do. I just kept stabbing him. He'd put the knife down while he was peeing.'

Jesus, how much worse could things get?

'Who killed Jason, was that you too?'

'That was Sally. It was that bastard Tony Miller that I killed. I hadn't got a clue who that Jason guy was. He just walked in on us while we were arguing about Jem. She whacked him with that bloody baseball bat of yours then slit his throat.'

'What did the police say? Do they suspect anything?'

'They think Sally killed Tony Miller. There's nobody to say otherwise. Sally arrived after I'd killed Tony, I lied about that, I said she was in the house earlier. When she picked up the knife, I knew I'd be in the clear. It's our knife anyway, our prints would have been all over it. And she made me help her move the bodies, we were both covered in blood, you saw us.'

'What about Jem? Whose idea was that?'

'She was mad, Pete. She went crazy when she saw the bodies in the house. She had that bloody gun too. She was waving it around like a mad woman. She kept accusing me of sleeping with Jem, like we were having an affair. She forced me to tie Jem up like that.'

I had no words. I just looked at her. We'd left that family without a mother. Sally had taken the blame for everything.

'I don't know what to say, Meg ...'

'You don't need to say anything, Pete. It won't come back to haunt me, it's all done and dusted as far as the police are concerned. Nobody can contradict me, they're all dead. But I'm so sorry about Sally, she didn't deserve that.'

'What if Sally had put the gun down? What if she hadn't jumped?'

'It was my word against hers. And besides, it would have been self-defence. When he touched me like that ... I couldn't help myself. I'm not proud of what I did, Pete, but I didn't feel I had a choice. I had to tell someone, though. I had to let you know. You won't say anything, will you? I know I can trust you.'

I wouldn't say anything. Who was I to blame her for what she'd done? She hadn't made Sally jump off the roof of the cathedral. And, if truth be told, Jem got what he deserved. I hadn't made any effort to help him. I could have done, but I chose to help Meg instead. It was horrible, but then how many lives had he wrecked?

'I'll keep quiet, Meg, don't worry. We've all had enough now. This needs to end. I'm sorry I did what I did. I love you, Meg, I have since the minute we met. I'm just sorry. For everything.'

'I love you too, Pete, but I have to do this. We've hurt each other too much. I can't be with you right now.'

She squeezed my arm and turned to walk away.

'Bye Pete.'

'Goodbye Meg.'

As she walked by the open graves, she turned and looked sadly at Sally's.

'I'm sorry Sally, I'm so sorry.'

She then turned to the hole in the ground where Jem

lay. She spat into his grave. 'Fuck you, Jem, you ruined everything!'

She didn't look back. She just kept walking. I watched her walk out of the cemetery, using the exit at the furthest end.

That was the last I heard of her. Until I received a post-card one year later ...

The Murder Place is available now. Start reading the second part of the Don't Tell Meg trilogy today!

Find out more about Paul J. Teague's thrillers at http://paulteague.co.uk

ALSO BY PAUL J. TEAGUE

Don't Tell Meg Trilogy

Book 1 - Don't Tell Meg

Book 2 - The Murder Place

Book 3 - The Forgotten Children

Standalone Thrillers

Dead of Night

Burden of Guilt

One Fatal Error

Who To Trust

Writing sci-fi as Paul Teague

Sci-Fi Starter Book - Phase 6

The Secret Bunker Trilogy

Book 1 - Darkness Falls

Books 2 - The Four Quadrants

Books 3 - Regeneration

The Grid Trilogy

Book 1 - Fall of Justice

Book 2 - Quest for Vengeance

Book 3 - Catharsis

ABOUT THE AUTHOR

Hi, I'm Paul Teague, the author of the Don't Tell Meg trilogy as well as several other standalone psychological thrillers such as Burden of Guilt, Dead of Night and One Fatal Error.

I'm a former broadcaster and journalist with the BBC, but I have also worked as a primary school teacher, a disc jockey, a shopkeeper, a waiter and a sales rep.

I've read thrillers all my life, starting with Enid Blyton's Famous Five series, then graduating to James Hadley Chase, Harlan Coben, Linwood Barclay and Mark Edwards.

If you love those authors then you'll like my thrillers too.

Let's get connected!
https://paulteague.co.uk
paul@paulteague.com

Made in the USA
Middletown, DE
10 February 2019